Splintered Ice

Splintered Ice

Stuart G. Yates

Also by Stuart G. Yates

- Unflinching
- In The Blood
- To Die In Glory
- A Reckoning
- Blood Rise
- Varangian
- Varangian 2 (King of the Norse)
- Burnt Offerings
- Whipped Up
- The Sandman Cometh
- Roadkill
- Tears in the Fabric of Time
- Lament for Darley Dene

For those who matter, have always mattered, and always will. This is for you, for you know the truth... and the truth is not so very different from this.

1

Cold, like bitter iced fingers ran along his spine.

The nightmare was real. Terrifyingly real. He didn't wake up from it until the world he knew appeared no longer recognisable, but one turned upside down.

Jed knew he should respond more positively, allowing some of the sun's warmth to percolate inside him and rise to the surface. This required effort, but somehow he never quite managed it, often forcing himself to smile regardless of the weight that hung like a yoke around him. Others turned away, avoiding his stare; no one ever stopped him to say 'hello' or ask how he was. Not that he cared. It was something he had come to terms with, accepted. His days were all like this one, inside and out. Heavy, black clouds, threatening to break but never doing so, bearing down on him, cloaking him in depression. And this particular day, as he came around the corner, the wind pinching at his face, he saw the people and groaned.

He usually reacted this way and shunned company. Ever since Mum had left.

He remembered the day as clear as those rare ones when the sun broke through. He'd come home from school, not feeling too well. The usual routine meant he stayed for school dinners, not that he ate very much of them. Slop, that's all it was. Slop followed by cake smothered in pink custard. Craig Watson, big fat cheesy face beaming like a buffoon, brainless, piling up his plate by taking everyone else's. God, he could put that stuff away! That particular day Jed had stood up to him, sick of his antics, sick of him. "Give us your dinner," grumbled Watson, voice like a constipated buffalo – which he must have been, given the amount of slop he shovelled into his ever-open gob. The others pressed against the dinner table, obediently did his bidding, staring down at the meagre scraps Watson had allowed them to keep, with all the grace of a nightclub bouncer. "No," said Jed. They'd all blinked at that, especially Miles, Jed's friend. Reaching over, he touched Jed's arm, trying to calm him. But Jed fumed inside, too far gone to notice, the limit reached. Watson looked as though he'd been yanked back by a winch, his whole body becoming stiff, head jerking, mouth dropping open. Sixteen years of age, grossly over-weight, Watson was a formidable bully. Despite being almost two years younger than Jed, he looked considerably older. Feared throughout the school. Nobody said 'no' to Craig Watson. But Jed had. And the whole world waited to see what would happen next.

Jed shoved back his chair, the bottom of the legs scraping across the bare floor, and he climbed to his feet.

"*Pick it up!*" Roared Mr Malone from the far end of the hall. Mr Malone used to be a professional rugby player, about a thousand years ago. But he looked more like a football now, the glory days long gone, as wide as he was tall, puffed up and red-faced, as if he were going to burst at any minute. But Jed liked him, thought him decent, in a gruff sort of way. Malone didn't take much messing from the kids, but very rarely paid any attention to what they got up to. A dinner monitor, not a teacher, just a poor old pensioner trying to earn a few extra bob to pay for his cats' upkeep. Apparently, so Jed heard, Malone owned lots of cats. But no one else. No wife, no family. Just the cats. And this job. Jed liked him and felt sorry for him and he thought, with no evidence to support his view, that Mr Malone liked him too. But it didn't look that way at that moment as Jed stood there, simmering quietly. "I've told you a thousand times," screeched Malone over the collective buzz of the dining hall, "not to scrape those things across the floor – to pick the damn things up! And what are you doing standing up anyway?"

"Don't feel well," said Jed, as quick as a flash. He glanced down at Watson, who glared at him. No longer the buffalo, he was now the predator, eyes narrowed into slits.

"I'm going to get you, Meres."

"In your dreams, Watson."

"Yeah, well it'll be your worst *nightmare* when I've finished with you."

"Jed, just leave it, yeah?" Miles said. Always the protector.

Jed smirked. He didn't feel particularly brave, more that he had woken up. The night before he'd heard his parents arguing. They always argued, so nothing unusual in that, but this sounded different. On another level. Dad had stomped out of the house, slamming the door behind him, and he *never* did that. Mum had stayed in the living room, television on low, and from his room Jed could hear the sobs. He listened to her padding across the hall, picking up the 'phone. She talked rapidly, in a whisper. He knew he shouldn't, and he felt guilty doing so, but he crept over to his door, pressed his ear against the crack, and listened. He couldn't make out most of what she said, but there were lots of, '*It's not going to be easy...as long as we've got one another... you've been so good...I know, I know, but...all right...please, just a little while longer...*'. What did it all mean? Something stirred inside him, a sudden lurching in the pit of his stomach. Ominous, like a premonition of something...something massive. So he'd gone back to his bed and slumped down, looking at the ceiling, feeling like everything had begun to close in. Stifling him. Nothing could change the fact Mum and Dad had drifted...anything they had long gone. Mum and Dad. For how much longer could he put those two words together and conjure up any meaning? Did anything have any meaning if they weren't going to be a family anymore? Because he suspected this was going to happen. The end. And it churned him up inside, making him angry, tying his stomach in knots and he rolled over, brought his knees up to his chest, and gnawed at his lips. Why? That was the question that burned – why?

So school and that day with Watson, they were like *nothing*. Little bits of trivia that had come along to test him. And he had decided to take the test full on, meet it, steel against steel. "You can try, Watson. But I tell you this," Jed leaned forward, grinning, "by the time you've filled your guts up with all *this*," he waved his hand over the other dinner plates, "you'll be so full of shit you won't be able to move…and I'll kick your fat, stinking head in." And with that, to the disbelief of everyone, Jed took up his plate of sponge and pink custard, and ladled it onto Watson's stack of beef-stew-slop.

The table gave a collective gasp, all of them stunned, especially Watson, who sat there, gaping in disbelief. Jed span on his heels and marched out. Malone followed and Jed pulled up, looking at him. The man's eyes had something like respect twinkling within them and Jed gave him a little nod, "I'm going to go home, Mr Malone. Sleep it off."

But when he got home, the house greeted him still and silent. Jed stood in the hallway for a moment, sensing something, something which didn't feel quite right. More than the usual atmosphere of nobody being home. *Empty.* Cold, unfriendly, any homeliness stripped away, like wallpaper replaced by something flat and lifeless. And charmless. No soul. Just a building, a house, not a home.

Moving quickly, anxious now, he went into the kitchen, the usual hub of the house. Everything looked tidy, almost too tidy, he thought. He ran a finger across the tabletop. Clean. He pressed the finger to his nose, breathed in the disinfectant. Like a hospital. Clinical. Now, into the living room. All the clutter gone, magazines and books neatly stacked, coffee-mugs and plates put away. It reminded him of one of those show-homes Mum and Dad used to drag him round to some years before. Very nice, but not real. A place in which you walked around on pins, afraid that you might spill something, or misplace a cushion and undo the careful fabric of the sanitised furnishing.

Jed ran up the stairs, taking them two at a time, and burst into his parents' bedroom, ripping open the doors to his Mum's wardrobe. He stopped, hardly able to breathe. No clothes. Drawers, the same. Make-up, perfumes, hair dryer, straighteners, the everyday necessities of the modern woman, all gone. Decks swept clean.

Dropping down on the corner of the bed, he sat there for a long time, just staring into space, not daring to admit what he knew to be true. She'd left. Gone. That phone call, that had to be the key. But to whom had she been speaking, he had no idea. Jed racked his brains, thinking of her old friends. Men. He dismissed each and everyone. When he looked up and caught his reflection in the full-length mirror on the wall opposite, he saw staring back at him a young man, vulnerable all of a sudden. He didn't like what he saw and he straightened up, the anger rising. He knew he would find out who had stolen her. And when he did…

No… no, he had to think about this. Be realistic. If she had left, then life had suddenly become bleaker. All at once, he felt trapped, useless, unable to do anything. For all his bravado, how could he find out who the man was? Life wasn't a movie. He had to get real, accept it, try and live through it. And prepare himself for what Dad would do. He glanced at his wristwatch. Dad would be home in a little under four hours. Jed groaned at the prospect of his dad's reaction.

The hours dragged by. Jed spent most of the time sat in the lounge gazing at the clock as the hands crawled slowly around.

Then the sound of the key. Dad had come home, at his usual time. He'd gone upstairs without a word, as usual. Jed waited, staring at his hands. He could hear the stomping of feet, imagining his dad sitting down, pulling off his boots, taking off his shirt, getting ready for a shower. Then the opening of the wardrobe and the stunned silence. Jed put his face in his hands. Hell had come to visit.

Dad had come down, heavy footed, and when Jed saw his face a surge of real fear raced through him. He'd never seen his dad's face so dark, so filled with barely contained fury. "I've got some bad news," Dad began, voice low, unsteady, close to breaking.

"I think I know, Dad," Jed mumbled.

For a moment, it looked as if Dad would explode. He wrestled with himself, face twisting into a horrible scowl. "Well, you knew a damn sight more than I bloody did!" He went out, slamming the door behind him.

After a moment, spent trying to quieten his booming heart, Jed gathered up what little courage he had, and went out to find his dad in the kitchen. "What are you going to do?"

Dad busied himself at the sink, washing a plate. A clean plate, taken down from the rack. Jed realized that his dad was in shock, doing things mechanically, without thinking. Jed wanted to reach over and put his arm around him. His dad, strong, dependable, just an ordinary bloke really. But his dad nevertheless. And special for that. But Jed couldn't. There had always been a barrier between them, a reluctance to show affection. It was just the way they were, and the habits of half a lifetime could not be broken, even when tragedy had struck.

"I'm going to have my tea," Dad said and that was the end of the conversation.

They hardly said a word all night and later, as he lay in his bed staring up at the ceiling, Jed could hear his dad in the next room, crying. It had to be the most awful sound he had ever heard. It grew so bad that he turned over, pulling his pillow over his head to muffle the noise. But it didn't work. He could still hear that mournful sound and it stayed with him all through the night.

The next day his dad did not go to work. Jed couldn't remember a time when his dad had taken a day off from his job. Jed sat in the kitchen, playing with his breakfast, thinking back to when he had been a little boy. He longed for those wonderful days when he'd help Dad get the bike out of the shed, that big heavy, green policeman's bike, and run down with him, pretending to push him along the road until he couldn't do it any longer, all the breath gone out of him. And he'd stand there, waving his arm so hard he thought it would fall off. Dad, turning the corner, raising his arm in response. Just the once. Jed let the spoon clatter against the still full bowl of cereal, put his fist in his mouth and tried to keep the tears at bay. He'd been young then, maybe seven. They were close in those days, him and his dad, before the clouds gathered and changed Jed into an unfeeling, uncaring, super-cool teenager who didn't give a moment's thought to anyone else. Not ever. Until now.

Mum leaving had rekindled all of his old feelings. He wished he were seven again. He wished the past would return and life would be good again. Warm and safe and together.

His stomach lurched once more and he pushed the untouched breakfast cereal away. School beckoned. And Craig Watson.

As soon as Jed walked through the school gates, he saw Watson standing there, a few of his cronies gathered around, faces split wide grins, anxious for the fun to begin. Watson gave them a knowing glance then stepped in front of Jed. "Lunch time, Meres. Up at the park. We'll finish this."

But Jed wasn't going to wait until lunchtime. Not that lunch time, not any lunch. He'd had enough and he knew of only one way to silence the big fat drip. Jed simply moved up close to the big slob and, without a word, butted him full in the face, his forehead connecting with Watson's nose like a hammer against a piece of wood. Jed felt the crack before he heard it, not that he could have heard much anyway with Watson screaming like a stuck pig. The big bully fell to the ground, a great lump of lard, floundering, hands pressed against his face, the blood spurting through his fingers.

Someone grabbed Jed by the shoulder and hauled him away. No one moved, no one spoke. Jed looked at them as someone frog-marched him into the main school building and he felt a little stirring of happiness inside. No one could find any words, all of them shocked, and he liked that. He'd shut the whole lot up.

Jed stood before the Headteacher. Mr Phillips, as hard as they came, leaned back in his seat, chewing furiously at his bottom lip. Reminded Jed of an old World War Two fighter pilot, great handle-bar moustache, very 'far-back' voice, but he had the build of an all-in-wrestler. Everyone feared Phillips, but not Jed. Not now. He knew he'd changed, from the moment he'd opened his eyes that morning. Something had happened. A new resolve to confront, everyone and everything. Past caring, he didn't flinch, even when the cane cracked against his backside. He didn't feel it, not the first one, not the sixth. Standing up, all he wanted was to go home, close his bedroom door and forget about the world and everything in it. Just spend the time with his dad. His dear, old dad, whom he'd left that morning sitting at the kitchen table, face in his hands, crying like a little boy.

"You're a bloody disgrace, Meres!"

He fastened his gaze on Phillips and nodded his head. "Yes sir. Sorry sir."

"Don't say sorry to me! God help you if Watson decides to press charges, you could end up in court."

"He won't do that sir."

"You – *who the hell do you think you are, Meres! God Almighty?*"

Phillips trembled, close to losing control. It was only Mr Henderson's presence, standing there in the corner as a witness, which prevented the Head from launching an attack of his own on Jed. Jed could see it, the Headteacher gripping the side of his desk, knuckles white, face red. Close to losing it. Henderson led Jed promptly out of the office and pointed him in the direction of the main school gates.

"You'll be hearing from us," said Henderson. "You're suspended. Your father will receive the official letter in the morning." And that was that. Jed made his way to the gate and glanced sideways as his old friend came up to him.

Miles, a worried look on his face, said, "Jed...are you going to be all right?"

"I'll be fine. Don't worry."

"But I *am* worrying! What's happening to you? What you did to Watson...what's going on?"

"Nothing, mate." A part of Jed wanted to tell him everything, but he just couldn't. Miles would never understand. And besides, right now Jed had no need of friends, had no need of anyone, except perhaps Dad. "I'll see you around."

He walked home in a daze, not thinking about anything, the sensations across his backside warming him, a reminder of what had happened. But that was all. When Jed got home, he could see Dad still sat in the kitchen, staring blankly at the walls. He barely glanced up as Jed came up to him. Without a word, Jed went to his room and showered. He needed to get the smell of school out of his skin, wash away the grime of a life he didn't want any more, not at that moment.

That evening, the police called round. Jed had a lump in his throat as soon as he opened the door and saw the uniformed constable standing there. His heartbeat thumped so madly he felt light-headed, sweat breaking out on his forehead. The policeman frowned, obviously noticing Jed's discomfort, but Jed needn't have worried. They hadn't come for him. Watson wasn't going to say anything to anyone. '*Fell down the steps on the way home, Mum.*' That's what he'd say, or something similar. The unspoken rule governed. Simple. It was just the way things were, the rule of the street, how it would always be. The unwritten code of honour. You never grassed-up your mates… even those who smashed your face in. No, the police called round because Dad had asked them to find Mum. "It's all right, Jed." Dad stood next to him in the hallway, beckoning the policeman to come inside. "I called them this afternoon." He'd done that whilst Jed was out at school, flooring Watson and shutting the big oaf up for the rest of his natural. They'd found her.

"She's in a caravan, Mr Meres."

"*A caravan?* Where?"

"I can't really tell you that, sir. Sorry."

"What the hell do you mean you can't tell me? She's my wife, for God's sake!"

"I know that, sir. I spoke to her, asked her if she was coming home."

"*And?*"

The policeman looked from Dad to Jed and back again. "Sorry, sir. She said 'no'."

"Was she all right?"

Both the policeman and Dad turned to Jed as he asked the question. Dad looked horror-struck, as if accusing his son of taking sides. Perhaps he was, or playing the diplomat, Jed didn't know which, and he didn't really care either way. Didn't Dad realize that she was Jed's mum, that he had feelings for her? Anger might have consumed Dad, even hatred, but Jed just wanted to understand it all. He still cared.

"She seemed fine."

After the policeman left, Dad shuffled back to the kitchen, like a little old man. The years had suddenly multiplied across his whole body, crushing him, laying waste his spirit. Jed followed him, thinking the cold surroundings sharpened his Dad's senses, made him realize that none of it was a dream. It might have been that, or it might have been that he wanted to be alone. Jed didn't know and he didn't have the strength, or the courage to ask.

With nothing coming from Dad, Jed went to his room and tried to sleep. That night was the worst of his life, thinking of his mum in some tiny, cramped caravan, stirring soup on a *Calor Gas* stove. She'd given up the family home for *that*? It didn't make sense, none of it.

Sleep came in short batches every night for the next two weeks, punctuated with visions of his mum, his dad. He found some photographs of them both. He hadn't been looking; maybe his dad had left them out. They were on the coffee-table in the lounge, just tossed there. Some snaps of them both on a weekend at Conway. Only last year. Dad looking happy, a bit like a little boy; big cheesy grin. Unaware. Blissfully ignorant. Mum her usual glamorous self, even on a windy day in North Wales. Jed kept looking at his dad. Clad in a long raincoat, trying to protect himself from the biting wind, but failing miserably. He didn't look like his dad at all, really, not how he thought of him. With a sudden jolt of realisation, Jed could see how much his dad had aged. Funny how he'd never noticed before, but then, when you're with someone every day of your life, do you actually see such things? The photograph made him see again, with fresh eyes, and he was shocked at how old Dad seemed; how everyone else must see him. An old man, fragile, well into the autumn of his years.

Jed had cried. For the first time since Mum had left, clutching the photographs tightly in his hands, he let it gush out of him, not caring. It didn't make him feel any better, but it made him feel a little less guilty. Just a little.

And now, here he was, walking into town on that Saturday. The first time he'd been out of the house since school suspended him for three days. The rest of the time he'd taken as sick. He couldn't face any of it. Watson didn't bother him, but Phillips did. The man had appeared physically shocked by the assault and Jed knew he would never stop mentioning it, would forever confront Jed in the corridors, berating him for 'bringing the school down.' Questions would follow, and not just from school. Everyone. No doubt they all knew, the neighbours; being a small town, gossip soon got round. It would be best to steer well clear, so he kept his head down low, sat in his room, listening to music, reading, trying to rid his mind of the conflicting emotions invading his thoughts. He adopted a scorched-earth policy, retreating, finding solace in novels, the books he'd bought but never read. Now he consumed them voraciously and he believed he had made it through. Jed didn't want to knock anyone else out, and now he felt calmer, more in control. At last his confidence returned and he felt able to step outside again.

But as he'd come round the corner and strolled along the road he could see the little gaggle of people and he groaned inside. Most of them simply brushed by, but there were some who stopped and stared. And then Mrs Roberts stepped up. Jed knew the moment he long dreaded had now arrived. All of his calmness, his quiet mind, pulled away, to reveal him again for who he really was – a frightened, confused teenager with no mum and a shattered, broken dad. Before he could say anything, Mrs Roberts turned on him, like a terrier, the accusations flying. God, how he hated it all.

2

Fractured thoughts lay strewn across his subconscious as Mrs Roberts questioned him, relentlessly. This was not what he wanted. He would have liked to have spent an hour or so in *Bookland*, browsing through the books, finding comfort in the thought of going home and sitting next to a roaring fire, curled up and cosy with a good book. *Hard Times* perhaps, which seemed to fit the bill and reflected his own dark mood. But she wouldn't let that happen, not Mrs Roberts, not now. She wanted to know everything and she had him, a fish on her line, and slowly drew him in towards the landing net. "I never suspected anything, well not at first you understand, but then she was always off out, wasn't she? I mean, she only learned to drive two years ago, makes you think that doesn't it, her having the freedom to go where she pleased. All falls into place when you think about it, not that I ever did of course because, like I said, I never suspected. Not at the time, you understand. Not at the time. Well, you wouldn't…" And so it went on, a tirade of meaningless sentences, all jumbled up and delivered at a machine-gun rate. Jed stopped listening after a few seconds, drawn more to the stumps of her blackened, bombed-out teeth than to the words that fell out of her wide mouth, spattering him like tiny nails or pins. Anything metallic really. Anything that hurt.

He'd never really liked Mrs Roberts. Neither had Dad. She used to call him *Mr Meres*, as if the use of his Christian name was anathema to her. Always called mum Doris though. Doris. God, Jed hated that name. Mum wasn't a Doris, anymore than he was a Sebastian. But that's what he was, Sebastian Jethroe Meres. Who in their right mind would call their child that? Thank goodness some enlightened soul nicknamed him 'Jed' when he was barely six months old. The name had stuck and that was what he had become. But Dad had remained *Mr Meres* and Mum Doris. Even though a horrible name that didn't suit her at all, she would forever be known as Doris.

"Of course, I've always seen Doris as one of my closest friends and I'm actually quite hurt, you know, by all of this."

"*What?*" The last sentence had brought him out of his daydreaming. *She* felt hurt? "Why do you feel hurt, Mrs Roberts? None of this has got anything to do with you."

"Well of course it has – she's my friend. That's what I mean when I say I'm hurt; because she should have told me, let me into her confidence." What, so the whole flaming world could know about it? Jed didn't say anymore, just nodded his head, shrugged, then exhaled. "So you'll let me know as soon as you hear anything?" Jed nodded again. "That's a promise now, isn't it?"

"Of course, Mrs Roberts. Goodbye, Mrs Roberts."

He moved away just as she prepared to launch herself into another soliloquy and he took some small delight in registering her obvious displeasure at him not wanting to listen to her anymore.

He couldn't shake the fact that her words had had an effect upon him. That mention of his mum deciding to take up driving lessons, to have passed her test, then spending more and more time going out in the little car she had bought herself. At the time he had thought of it as quite exciting. The family had never owned a car before. They could look forward to Sunday afternoon drives out into the country now, picnics and visits to interesting places, no longer having to rely on the vagaries of the local transport system. But as the weeks went by none of it had happened. Every weekend Jed would feel the build up of expectation, and every weekend he would be disappointed. Mum always seemed to be going somewhere else. Nipping out to the shops, taking her friends to *the tombola*...it all made sense now. Mum was having an affair.

Strange how things that are happening right under your nose go unnoticed, he mused. It never entered Jed's head to consider his mum could be seeing another man. Mums don't do that sort of thing; they stay at home and cook dinners and wash school uniforms. They don't carry on behind your dad's back. That sort of stuff was for television dramas and cheap, unbelievable romance novels. Never in real life, never in the safe and secure bosom of the home.

He crossed over the road and wandered down towards the park. The shops soon petered out and he took some time to lean over the railings and stare at the cricket pitch. The season would be starting soon. It seemed too cold to be standing around in white trousers and shirt, waiting for something to happen. But spring was almost here, despite the fact that a tingle of frost nipped at his cheeks. New beginnings. For his mum too, by all accounts.

The park was empty, apart from a few birds scampering across the footpath looking for titbits. They didn't even bother to move as he sauntered past. He wished he'd brought a thicker coat, the blue sky having lured him into a false sense of security. Down here, away from the press of houses and shops, it had grown bitter and he hunched his shoulders up, pulling his thin denim jacket closer, trying to rustle up some protection from the cold. He gripped the collar with his right hand, pinching the two sides together, head down, watching his feet as he followed the sloping pathway which led to the lake.

He looked up to catch sight of a lone fisherman on the far side of the lake, cocooned in a one-piece rain-suit. Green and hideous. He stirred at Jed's approach, the grip on the fishing rod barely shifting at all. Jed slowed, eying him with an intense curiosity. Why would anyone be fishing on such a day as this? The man – for it was a man, despite a great wide hood concealing his face – had broken a hole in the thin ice covering the lake's surface and through it had expertly dropped his line into the depths. Jed recalled someone telling him carp and roach were in there, but he wasn't sure. He'd only dabbled in angling himself, catching the bus down to the Shropshire Union canal twice in his entire life. He'd enjoyed it, sitting there on the bank, gazing out across the dappled water. But that was at least two years ago. Now, looking at the angler, he felt that he'd like to have a go again, but not today. Today was far too cold. Shaking his head slightly, Jed turned to continue his way around the lake, away from the man.

A loud cry pulled him up short – the cry of victory. Jed turned, half smiling, to see the man getting to his feet, the line taut, rod bending alarmingly. One hell of a fish must be on the end of it, Jed thought and watched, an eager witness to the battle to come.

But then something terrible happened, something Jed would never have believed possible. The man slipped, the weight of the fish pulling him towards the water's edge. He could have stopped himself, of course, but he must have lost his footing on the ice that lay black and shiny on the little path. His next cry was not one of triumph, but one of utter horror. The fish darted viciously to the side, taking the man by surprise and, desperate to find some sense of grip, feet doing a little dance, he slipped and fell. Rooted to the spot through disbelief, Jed wanted to shout out, tell him to let go; he could have let go of the rod; he *should* have let go, but he didn't. Perhaps it was expensive, his best one, his trusty weapon of war. Whatever the reason, the man clung on and pitched forward towards the surface of the lake.

Everything went into slow motion from that point.

The thin ice cracked and splintered as the man hit it, face down, with a tremendous slap, like that of a flat hand smacking down upon a tabletop. For one ghastly moment, the man lay there, spread-eagled, floating, not moving.

Knowing he had to do something, Jed forced himself to move and took a few tentative steps forward. Fearful that any sudden movement might break the fragile ice completely, he took his time, and watched the ice slowly begin to give way, cracks like spokes from a wheel, spreading out in all directions. An awful groan like a loud, bored yawn, then the ice shattered completely and the man plunged into the depths.

All at once, the water boiled as the man fought frantically, arms and legs flapping, panic setting in as the he desperately tried to keep himself afloat. Jed believed the lake to be bottomless and as he stepped closer, mouth hanging open, he felt sure it must be true. The angler floundered, pulled relentlessly under, the cold water dragging him down, freezing his limbs, escape impossible.

Debating only briefly whether he should to the man's aid, he waded into the icy, murky water, gasping as the cold hit him, snatching his breath away. But he was surprised to find that his feet could touch the bottom.

But of the man, there was no sign. With water at such a low temperature, he could be dead within seconds. Stooping down, Jed used his arms to dredge around, trying to find the body. But he had completely disappeared, the water thick and impenetrable with dirt and weed. So much weed. How could anyone fish in this? So black, so cold. There was nothing else for it, so he took a breath and plunged his face down into the blackness.

A pair of stark white hands erupted from the water and grabbed him, pulling him under. Jed, embroiled in a flurry of seething, writhing tentacles, gripping him around the neck with a strength that was frightening, did his best to pull away, but those arms, they were like steal, fingers digging into his flesh. Struggling, he fought back, lungs screaming, heartbeat pounding in his temples, eyes bulging. Pushing down on a clump of large rocks, he hauled himself upwards with all his strength, every sinew straining, and freed himself from the freezing water. Spluttering and coughing, gulping in the air, he clutched at the hands still clawing at his throat and dragged himself backwards, bringing the angler with him.

Reaching the bank, Jed fell, the sheer momentum ripping away the man's hands, and Jed lay there, stunned and breathless, looking up at the gloriously blue sky, thanking God he was free. Senses blurred, except for the pain where fingernails had raked through skin, he sat up and tenderly felt his throat. The cuts, probably deep ones at that, stung like hell where the water had hit them. But that was as nothing compared to the intense cold spreading through him, biting deep, solidifying his arms and legs.

Looking down he saw the lower part of his legs, still in the water. He saw them, but he couldn't feel them. And next to him, breathing hard like a floundering fish out of water, lay the man, eyes wide, water drooling from his blue-lipped mouth. Veins bulged from his skin, mapping out a fine irregular needlework pattern across his face. But he lived. Despite the cold, Jed experienced almost euphoric relief. Both of them were alive.

3

Someone must have found them. It might have been five minutes, it might have been five hours, Jed had no way of telling, but when he finally woke up he lay in a warm, bright hospital ward with his dad sitting beside him.

"Oh thank God," blurted Dad as soon as Jed's eyes fluttered open. A nurse came running to the bedside, face full of concern, her features softening as she smiled. She took Jed's temperature, checked his chart, then felt his pulse, and all the while Jed watched her, mesmerised. What had happened? How did he get here? "He's going to be all right," the nurse said to nobody in particular, then bent over the bed, bringing her face very close to Jed's. "You're going to be all right."

Later, after drinking lots of tea and explaining to his dad what had happened, Jed slid out of bed and padded down the ward to where the other person lay; the angler, the one he'd saved. The nurse told him where he could be found.

Jed stood at the foot of the bed and stared at him. With the bed-clothes tucked under his chin, he looked as in a funeral parlour, laid out, awaiting his burial. But he wasn't dead, his breathing deep and regular. As Jed stared, he took in the features of a young man, a few years older than he was. Thin face, sunken cheeks, wide forehead and straight, light brown hair, cut very short, like an inmate of a prison camp.

Or a concentration camp.

Yes, that was it. The more Jed stared the more he believed this person had spent time in some dreadful place, starved to become stick-thin. But more than that. Even though he slept, Jed could see the deep lines of worry and fatigue etched into the sallow, parchment like skin. His pulse throbbed in his temple and his Adam's apple, very pointed and prominent, bobbed rhythmically in time with the throb. Jed so engrossed by its movement, didn't notice that the man was awake until he spoke. "It's you."

Jed blinked, startled, and looked into huge, saucer-like eyes of the most perfect black. He stepped closer, feeling drawn towards those eyes, unable to resist, not even wanting to. The man reached out his hand and took Jed's own, the softness of the grip so unlike the vice that had almost killed him in the lake. "Thank you."

Jed sat down on the little stool beside the bed, with the man continuing to hold his hand and Jed not wanting to pull away. He swallowed hard. "Are you okay?"

The angler nodded, a thin smile spreading over his face. "I am now," he said.

Jed returned the smile, pretending he understood. But he didn't; he didn't understand any of it. He looked down at the man's hand, bony fingers, veins so blue and thick, railway lines under his flesh. He needed a good meal, a hot bath, a roof over his head. Who was he?

"My name is Jonathan," the man said softly. His other hand covered Jed's, and he patted it. "Jonathan Kepowski. I am Polish, at least my father was. My mother…" he shrugged and smiled, "Who knows. She left us when I was very young. We came to England back in sixty-two. I was ten years old. In all that time, I've never seen you."

Jed frowned. He heard the man's words, but they meant little to him, except to confuse him still further. Twenty years of age, looking like someone who was sixty? A Polish refugee, who fished in a frozen lake and tried to kill the person who was saving him…His hands felt soft. Not an angler's hands. Not a worker's hands.

"I see you two are getting on fine." It was the nurse, the same one who had come to check on Jed. She was pretty, as Jed realised as soon as she'd bent over him. Her face. Smooth, defined, beautiful. She smiled when she glanced down and saw Jonathan's hands holding Jed's, a smile that grew wider. "I'll get you boys some tea, shall?"

"That would be very nice, nurse Willis," said Jonathan, reading the name badge on the young nurse's lapel. "And then, I want you to come and sit here with me and tell me all about yourself."

Jed gaped at him, then looked at the nurse, half expecting her to brush away the invitation for the inappropriate suggestion it was. "Yes," she said, "that would be lovely," and off she went, a skip in her step, Jed following her with his eyes, astonished at her response.

"Very pretty," said Jonathan, at last releasing Jed's hands and sitting up in bed.

His pyjama top was only loosely buttoned and Jed could see the ghastly hue of the man's skin, the collar bones protruding, the puce coloured nipples. It seemed to confirm all of Jed's suspicions that this was a man close to starvation.

"You mustn't worry about me," Jonathan said, "a hot cup of tea and a few hours spent with the lovely nurse Willis, and I will be fine."

Jed didn't know what to say. This man had the air of someone so much older, blessed with a supreme air of confidence that simply didn't fit with his wraith like physique. Jed sat for a long time just staring at the sickly pallor of the man's flesh.

"When we get out of here," Jonathan said suddenly, "we will get to know one another better. I am going to show my gratitude to you, Jethroe. I am going to let the world know about the service that you have done for me."

Jed held up his hand, a little embarrassed, then stopped. He felt a chill running down his spine, a knot developing in his stomach. He'd called him *Jethroe*. No one ever called him that. At school, some of the teachers called him Sebastian, or Seb, but never Jethroe. Jed. Always Jed. But that was when they knew his name. He hadn't had chance to tell Jonathan his name. And even if he had... *Jethroe?*

Nurse Willis returned, with a tray bearing two cups of steaming tea. Jed reached out and took his, and she sat on the edge of the bed and passed Jonathan's over to him. Smiling, the nurse held Jed's gaze. "I think you should go back to your bed now, there's a good boy."

Jed stopped in the act of raising the cup to his lips and peered over the rim at Jonathan who winked, then nodded. "We'll talk again tomorrow."

Getting to his feet, Jed slowly made his way back to his part of the ward, pausing after a few steps to look back to see the nurse pulling the curtains around the bed, creating a little private area for them both. Jed waited, and soon he realized just exactly what Jonathan had meant by Nurse Willis telling him all about herself as the sound of her moans filtered from behind the curtains.

* * *

Jed tried to sleep, but couldn't. The muffled cries from Jonathan's screened off bed drifted across to him, sending his mind into a whirlwind of desire. He pressed the pillow around his head, to block out her moans, but that didn't prevent the images looming up inside his head. He knew what they were doing and it took all of his self control not to each to his own enflamed passion. At one point, he threw himself over onto his stomach, pressing his hardness into the mattress beneath him. It helped, but only slightly. And then, so much later, as she shuffled down the ward, Jed watched her out of half-closed eyes, tucking her blouse into her skirt, readjusting her uniform, trying to press out the creases. But she wasn't doing anything about the grin on her face, or the flush of her cheeks. Then again, she probably didn't want to.

Dad came with a change of clothes and Jed slowly got himself dressed. He didn't see Nurse Willis again; she had presumably gone off duty, and had been replaced by a much older, much more serious lady who patrolled the ward with a sever looking face. Coming away from Jonathan's bed, she looked furious, muttering something caustic under her breath. Jed could guess why she was so upset, and went to go and talk to Jonathan about it. He was surprised, and a little disappointed to find his bed empty. Already discharged, Jonathan had left without saying a word.

"Perhaps he felt a bit embarrassed," said Jed's dad.

"Embarrassed? Why would he feel embarrassed?"

"I don't know...people do, in extraordinary circumstances."

"But I saved his life, Dad."

"Yeah, I know...and I need to talk to you about that."

During the taxi ride home, Dad told Jed all about the newspaper and local television interest. Apparently, they'd tried to go to the hospital, to interview Jed about what had happened, but the hospital had refused, concerned that Jed might be concussed, or even poisoned.

"Poisoned?" Jed looked worried.

"It was only a precaution – you'd swallowed quite a bit of that water, and it's filthy by all accounts. But not to worry, all the tests came out negative."

"And so...the newspapers? They really want to interview me?"

"Yeah. You're quite a hero, Jed."

Quite a hero indeed, as he discovered the following day when he went back to school. Mr Phillips was waiting for him at the school gate, a wide grin on his face, handlebar moustache well waxed. He clamped his arm around Jed's shoulders and gave him a fatherly hug. "Welcome back, Jed, how are you feeling?"

Shocked at the Head's total turnaround, Jed became instantly suspicious. These feelings grew as two more people loomed up behind Phillips, big grins on their faces, camera shutters blinking. Representative of the press and suddenly it all fell into place. Jed could see the front page now, Phillips and Jed together, smiling happily as if they were the closest of buddies. Total crap.

In the Head's office, there were more photographs and an interview. *Did you know the person, what made you dive down into the water, didn't the thought of being drowned ever cross your mind, have you ever done anything like this before, would you do it again, what's it like knowing you've saved someone's life?*

There followed a special assembly. Jed gaped when he saw his dad sitting there, proud as punch, and next to him some large guy with no hair, black suit, chain around his neck. The Mayor? More photographers, and a television crew, jostled for position, calling out to him to smile, wave, shake the Head's hand. Jed blinked repeatedly as the flashguns went off, and then cringed with embarrassment as the entire school stood up to cheer and applaud. He shuffled around awkwardly on the stage. He wasn't anybody special, never ever thought he would be, happy being just an ordinary, everyday sort of person. He had few ambitions, in fact he rarely thought about what he wanted to do with his life. It was effort enough just getting through the day, one at a time. All of this attention, it was beyond anything he had ever sought. It was beyond painful – death by slow torture.

"Sometimes we go through life, living from day to day, never thinking that anything out of the ordinary or unexpected is ever likely to happen to us, to make us change our minds about who we are and what our place in the world is." Phillips was enjoying himself, all of the cameras turned on him. He'd laboured long and hard over the words he now recounted from his script, that was for sure. Every so often he would cast a glance towards Jed, giving him a little nod, before twiddling at the sides of his moustache and diving once more into his speech, "I've been a teacher for over thirty years now and I've seen many things, believe you me. I've had to deal with some difficult pupils, solving problems to do with relationships, misunderstandings…unpleasantness…" A broader smile in Jed's direction. Jed squirmed. "But sometimes an incident comes along that reminds me why I do this job. An act of kindness, a moment of thoughtfulness that reaffirms my faith in human nature. What Jed did, saving that young man's life, was beyond selflessness, it was sheer, unbridled bravery and it is an honour to stand here this morning and salute one of this school's most unassuming and yet most talented students – Jed Meres!" Phillips stepped back from the rostrum, a dramatic sweep of his hand towards Jed, inviting him to come forward as the assembled throng rose as one, the applause booming out, school-mates cheering, whooping. The staff all stood up, cameras flashed, Dad put his face in his hands and cried, the Mayor in his black suit smiled so broadly it looked like he'd split his face in two. And Jed sat there, wondering what to do next. As the noise in the hall reached fever pitch, Phillips came over and gently pulled Jed to his feet, steering him towards the rostrum. Jed's ultimate fears were about to be faced – he had to make a speech, in front of his peers. He felt his stomach turn to mush, his knees buckle, and he wanted to run and hide somewhere very, very far away. But he couldn't, there was nowhere to go, so he did the only thing practical at that moment: he fainted.

4

Coming down the stairs the following morning, Jed managed a groan
for a 'good morning', then slumped down in a chair next to his dad,
who put a cup of tea down in front of him. Jed looked at it, wondering
whether he should drink it or pour it over his head. "God, Dad, I am
such an idiot."

"Don't beat yourself up," dad was buttering some toast. "Everyone
understands, Jed. You've been through quite a lot, and then that thing
at school...I should have warned you. Sorry." He smiled, a guilty look
on his face, and gently slid the toast over to his son. "I spoke to Mr
Phillips and he said not to come in until Monday. He's been very kind,
very understanding."

Jed didn't answer, choosing to nibble at the corner of the slice of
toast instead. There was only one reason why Phillips was *very kind,
very understanding* and that was so he'd look good in the papers. Jed
knew it, and he guessed that his dad knew it too. But he didn't push
anything, content to just sit and feel awful. The embarrassment of it
gnawed away at him, the pictures coming into his head constantly.
How would he ever be able to show his face in public again? He could
already hear the taunts in the school playground. No doubt he'd have
to butt Watson again and, like a great big circle, it would all come
round once more and he'd be the villain again, like always. He groaned.

"The mayor said that when you're feeling up to it, he'd like to honour you at the Town Hall. Just you and me, a few invited guests..."

Dad looked away for a moment, his voice suddenly cracking.

Jed frowned, "Dad? What's up?"

"Nothing. I just thought your mother might have called, that's all."

He got up and went to the sink, his back towards his son. Jed chewed at his bottom lips. His mum, what would she make of all this. If he was honest, she hadn't really come into his thoughts at all over the last few days but now, after what his dad had said, it was curious that she hadn't phoned, or sent a letter. Anything at all, just to show she cared.

But, perhaps she didn't. If she did, she would never have left.

* * *

Jed wandered through the streets of Liscard, head down, shuffling self-consciously, half-expecting people to suddenly jump out and grab him, shaking him, congratulating him at one moment for being a hero, the next berating him for being such a wimp. To faint at an assembly especially arranged just for him – the shame of it.

But nobody did jump out at him. No one gave him any attention at all; the shop assistant in *Bookland* never recognised him at the best of times, despite him going in there at least twice a week. In a peculiar sort of way, Jed felt a little deflated by this lack of attention. Although he dreaded the idea of people shouting out at him in the street, the fact that not a single person gave him so much as a second glance galled him a little. Strange thing fame, and so fickle.

There *was* somebody, however. As Jed came out of the shop, clutching a copy of Sven Hassel's 'March Battalion', he caught a movement out of the corner of his eye and looked up to see Matthew standing there, looking slightly self-conscious. Jed froze, eyes smarting.

"Shit. Matthew."

Matthew. Jed hadn't seen him for well over five years. He wouldn't even know if he was still alive had it not been for the traditional Christmas and birthday cards. Always the same message, *All my best.* It never wavered, never changed. And now here he was, standing there, looking at him with those piercing blue eyes of his. "Hello kidder."

Wincing, Jed felt a mixture of shock and anger coursing through him. Five years, with not a single phone call. Some brother he was.

"Let's go and get a coffee."

So they did, in the coffee shop next door to *Bookland*. Matthew gently laid down the two cups of *espresso* then grinned, sitting down with a heavy sigh. "I saw you on the tele last night," he grinned even more broadly, "made me feel quite proud."

"Really? Why's that then?"

"Don't be like that, Jed. I'm your brother, I've got a right to feel proud of you."

"Who says?"

Matthew drew in a deep breath and shifted uncomfortably in his seat. "Look, I know I should have got in touch sooner, what with Mum and everything…but, you know…"

"Yeah. You've been busy." Jed wanted his words to sound sharp, and they did and he was pleased to see the pain running across Matthew's face. "So how did you find out?"

"About Mum?" Jed nodded, his eyes firmly locked on his brother's. Matthew shrugged, "She wrote to me."

"*Wrote* to you? What did she say?"

"Just that she was leaving your dad – and you. And would I try and explain things to you, when I got the chance."

"Like now?"

"Like now."

"So go on then, explain it to me."

"Jed, I know you're angry but—"

"No you don't – you don't know anything about how I feel, or what's been happening. All you think about is yourself, that's all you've ever thought about." Jed breathed hard, struggling to keep control.

"No it isn't, Jed. You don't understand. You think you do, but you don't."

"Well you explain it to me then. You try and make me understand, because you know what? *I don't*. All I know is that I've got to get up every morning and see my dad's face, watch him falling apart inch by inch. Do you know what that feels like, have you got a single clue? But, you know what, none of this is about me, not really. I've got my life ahead of me – but my dad…he thought his whole future was mapped out for him, living it out with Mum, growing old together…" He had to look away, his own words biting deep, bringing tears to his eyes. A silence settled between them and when Jed recovered, he looked at his brother again. "So, you tell me what I don't understand."

"It's happened before."

Jed took a moment to register what Matthew had said. He blinked, shaking his head slightly. "What do you mean, *it's happened before?*"

"Mum. When I was a kid. She ran off with some other bloke, leaving me and *my* dad to get through it, together."

The enormity of Matthew's words struck like dead weights slamming into Jed's chest. He felt crushed, unable to comprehend the meaning of what Matthew said. "But…but Dad…he never said – never said *anything!*"

"He probably didn't know. When he met Mum, her and my dad were divorced. I was living with Nan, my dad down south, trying to pick up the pieces of a life smashed because Mum had decided to have it off with someone else."

Stunned, Jed didn't know what to say. What could he say? His brother had lived with these truths for years, and had never spoken about any of it. That was a huge burden to carry around. And now, here he sat, off-loading it all, in one great lump. Jed felt overwhelmed.

"I'm sorry, Jed. I should have got in touch as soon as I found out, but I didn't know how to, or what to say. I wasn't sure how your dad would react to me turning up on the doorstep. I thought about writing, but…Anyway, then you were on the news and I thought it was best for me to just come on over. I waited for you, outside your house. I followed you up here. You still like your books. How many have you got now, a thousand?" He laughed. "You know, I've only ever read two books in my life. The first one—"

"Fuck off, Matthew – I'm not interested in anything about you, all right? Just tell me what you know, and then piss off back to your life."

For a moment Jed thought he'd gone too far. A look came over Matthew's face, dark, menacing. But the moment passed, and his brother went over to the counter, got himself another coffee, then came back with a heavy tread, no doubt dreading what he had to say next. He took a sip of coffee and stared at Jed for a few moments. "All right. Here it is. The man Mum's run off with, the guy she's been seeing behind your dad's back – he's the same one she ran off with when I was little. The same one that broke my dad's heart has now broken your dad's heart. Mum's in love with him, and she always has been. That's why I know *exactly* what you're going through, because it's all happened before. All of it – the letters, the empty house, Dad crying in the night. The only difference is, I was so much younger. And Nan, of course. Thank God for Nan. She looked after me whilst Dad…well, he went to pieces. Tried to find her, couldn't. Started drinking, got into fights, got arrested, spent a few months inside. When he came out, he went down to London. Not a word to me. Not for two years. Two bloody years…" He ran a hand through his hair, staring at the table top, gathering his thoughts, regaining some composure. "I hated him for that. He just abandoned me, left me with Nan."

"And Mum?"

"She came back… eventually. Her and Nan, they *talked.*" A tiny snigger. "God, did they talk. Anyway, the upshot of it all was that Mum and me dad would get a divorce. In those days, that was pretty scandalous, you know. Mum had to go away, leave this bloke she'd met. I remember the shouting, the pleading, but Nan, Nan was a stalwart, hard as nails. She told Mum there was no choice, could never be a choice. So, Mum left and Nan looked after me. Raised me. I was six years old."

"Mat…I had no idea – I'm sorry."

He shrugged, "It's not your fault, Jed. None of it. When Mum came back, she got a job with the Civil Service. Things got a bit calmer, a bit easier. The years went by and slowly things got better. As they do. I was about twelve when she met your dad. A year later, they were married, and then you came along." He drained his coffee cup. "And now, here we all are, nearly sixteen years later, and it's all happening again."

"But…Mat, are you sure it's the same bloke?"

"I'm sure, Jed. I've seen them."

They strolled down to the lake and sat on a bench. Matthew had come prepared and threw a few scraps of stale bread into the water for the ducks. The brothers watched the birds without speaking, the silence heavy between them. Jed's emotions were running wild, all at once confused, angry and sad, but most of all, betrayed. His mother had been seeing this man for years and years, living a sort of double-life. Everything was clear now. Not only the business with the car, but other things. The way the telephone would ring, just twice, almost every night at about the same time. Dad complained to the Post Office about it, but they couldn't explain it. Mum had said she'd been to see them and they'd told her it was a nightly check on the line, making sure the connections were working properly. Nobody questioned this explanation, there being no reason to. Dad, happy in his ignorance, accepted the lie. Jed didn't even think about it. But of course, now it was all clear. It was him, ringing Mum to tell her he was thinking of her. Just two rings. Made her feel happy.

It all made Jed feel sick.

He should have noticed that something was wrong, he should have been able to protect his dad, save him from all of this…this *hell*.

"I used to blame myself," said Matthew suddenly, sensing Jed's thoughts, perhaps. "At night, lying in bed, I could hear my dad crying and I'd say to myself, *why is this happening, where has my mummy gone…*I didn't understand it, none of it. Six years old, Jed. At school I started getting into trouble. I remember I kicked Miss Stretch, right in the shin. God, that was good – got me into loads of trouble, though. Then I started wetting the bed and dad – well, never mind about any of that. It all happened a long, long time ago. And, I guess because you're older, you'll be able to handle it better."

"Where have you been, Mat? Why didn't you ever get in touch? All those years, nothing but cards. No phone calls, no visits. Why?"

Matthew sat back, stretching out his long legs before him. "I was inside, Jed. Did an off-license. Me and two other blokes. I got sent down for seven years. Served four."

"*What?*"

He nodded, "Yeah…stupid." He winked, "Should have done a sub-post office instead."

"Don't joke."

"I'm not – that bloody off-license had about thirty quid in the till, but, because Harry had a shotgun – well, all water under the bridge now, eh?"

"I don't…" Jed put his face in his hands and sobbed. Matthew gently put a hand on his shoulder and waited until the tears had subsided. It took quite a while.

"This is where it all happened then? Your daring rescue?"

"Yeah. He was just over there, fishing. Slipped on some ice and went straight under."

"Who was he?"

"No idea. Never saw him before. Really weird looking guy, dead thin. Like a ghoul."

"A *ghoul*? What the hell does one of them look like?"

"You know, really pale and thin. Almost like a skeleton. Flesh just hanging off his bones. Horrible, really. Anyway, I got talking to him in the hospital and he was really nice – but then he just left, and I've not seen him since."

"Were you expecting to?"

"Dunno. I suppose. I feel a bit, you know, let down. Then all this television malarkey, and the newspapers – and that damned assembly at school." Jed had told his brother what had happened, how he'd fainted at the crucial moment. Matthew didn't say anything, just nodded grimly, as if he knew all too well the pressure Jed had been under. "I don't suppose I'll see him again."

"You never know. Do you want to?"

"I guess – just to make sure he's okay."

"He didn't make any plans, then? To meet up with you, I mean?"

Jed frowned. "You seem really interested in this guy, Matthew. Do you know him?"

"Know him? How could I possibly know him?"

"I don't know, just a hunch."

"A hunch? That's what policemen have, Jed."

"You'd know about that."

"Eh?" For a moment, Matthew seemed tense, sitting up slightly, looking awkward.

"You being inside, having lots of dealings with them."

Matthew smiled, a little too widely, almost as if he were relieved. But relieved about what? Had Jed's words touched a nerve, and if so, why?

Matthew patted Jed's knee. "Well, maybe after he reads your story in the papers, he'll get in touch." Matthew clapped his hands together and rubbed them vigorously. "I'm off now, Jed. I'll give you a ring in the next few days. Maybe we can, you know, go for a drink or something…"

"I'm not old enough, Mat. Not for a pub."

"Yeah, but you look it though. You haven't half grown. What are you, six foot?"

"Six-one. Gets me into trouble sometimes."

"Yeah, but you can handle yourself, right?"

"I guess." Images of Watson crumpling to the ground, nose bleeding like a tap. Yes, he could handle himself. Perhaps a bit too well.

Matthew took his hand and shook it, the grip firm and dry. "You take care, yeah?" Then he was gone, arms swinging, marching off without a backward glance.

Jed watched him, wanting to run after him, ask all the questions running round in his head. Especially the name, the name of the man who had stolen Mum. Nothing else mattered, except for that. He wanted that name, he wanted to find him.

He let out a long, controlled sigh. The time would come. All he had to do was wait.

5

September, 1947, cold, but bright. The morning air bit sharp as she stood on the doorstep, dressing gown pulled close. She leaned against the door well and watched her husband stomping off down the street. He paused at the corner, looking back, raising a hand in a solemn goodbye. She smiled, gave a little nod, and then he was gone and the loneliness closed in upon her like a prison door.

In the tiny living room, Matthew sat amongst a mess of strewn building blocks. He barely looked up when his mother came in and flopped down on the settee next to him. A little while later she got up and went into the kitchen to make herself a cup of tea.

Trudy was there, sitting in her basket, her little tail wagging, big eyes all expectant. "Later," was all her mistress said, filling the kettle then settling it on the gas ring. She swilled out the teapot, shovelled in two heaped teaspoons of *Mantunna Tea* and leant back against the sink to watch the kettle come to the boil. Just another long, long day, stretching out forever. That's all she had waiting for her, once again – the same routine, unchanging, every single day of her life.

She jumped when the doorbell rang, and a little thrill ran through her. Anything to break the monotony.

It was the postman. He made a double take as she pulled open the door and she wondered for a moment why he was standing there, eyes on stalks. Then she gave a little embarrassed giggle, and pulled her dressing gown closer, covering up her breasts. He was bright red and she leant against the door well, looking him straight in the eyes. "Can I help you?"

The postman kept his eyes averted, not daring to match her stare as he fumbled in his bag and brought out a small parcel. He handed it over and she took it from him, her fingers brushing against his for a moment. He looked up and this time there was the flicker of a smile.

From inside the house, Matthew gave a cry of triumph, followed by the sound of crashing bricks. She glanced down the hallway and sighed. "Ah well, back to my extraordinary life." She looked at the postman again and shrugged, subconsciously gathering her dressing gown even more tightly about herself, then slowly closed the door.

"I did it," shouted Matthew as his mum came back in. He beamed. "I made the biggest tower ever."

"Well, you'll have to rebuild it now, so I can see."

Enthused, Matthew quickly took to gathering the bricks together once more. Sighing, she took the parcel into the kitchen just as the kettle began to whistle.

Pouring the boiling water into the pot, she sat down and fingered the parcel, a deep frown crossing her face. She never got anything through the post. Frank, her husband, received everything, including the bills, but this one had her name written across the front: *Mrs Mary Cowper.* There was something vaguely familiar about the handwriting. Very even and very neat, all of it in upper case, great care taken to form each letter. Yet, the formation of the 'a' reminded her of something…

Teasing open the wrapping, curiosity and excitement gathered. But as she pulled away the brown paper, her heart stilled and the frown on her face grew deeper.

There was nothing inside except for some folded up tissue paper. No note, nothing. She sat back, arms crossed, and stared at the torn open package before her and wondered what on earth was going on.

The doorbell broke through her thoughts and she slowly got up and padded to the door. Who could it be this time?

She pulled open the door and gaped.

It was Frank.

Before she could say anything he was on her, like some wild cat, right hand gripping her around the bottom jaw, forcing her lips together, hurting her. As she tried to tear herself away, his left hand came across, slapping her with brute force, knocking her off her feet. She fell against the far wall, her head making a sharp crack as it hit the plaster. She slumped down, blood coming from her mouth and he straddled her, features contorted with rage, fists bunched. "I saw you, you bloody bitch! I knew this was going on, I just knew it."

"Frank, for God's sake—"

He drew back his fist, "Bloody bitch – I knew it, I just knew it!"

Matthew came out of the living room in time to see his daddy punching his mummy square in the face.

They'd met during the War. He was a friend of her cousin's. Frank Cowper. Nice enough, lovely smile. He had a bit of reputation, but she didn't mind that. In fact, she found it all rather exciting. He was wiry, broad shouldered, had the look of a troublemaker about him. Rumour had it that he fancied himself as a street fighter and was always getting into scraps. But she didn't mind that either. In a funny sort of way, it made her feel safe. He was in a 'reserved occupation', a dockworker down in Birkenhead. That pleased her, because if anything did come of them walking out together, then she wouldn't have to worry about him going off to Africa or somewhere and getting himself killed. Ida's boyfriend, Terence, he'd been shipped off abroad, to fight the Italians. Two weeks he'd been gone, then his mother called her round. They'd received a telegram, from the government. Killed-in-action it said. Ida had been inconsolable for ages, only emerging from her house after a month or so. Terence, gone. Mary never ever wanted to go through anything like that.

When Frank had called, together with his friend Stanley, he was driving an old Ford. Its headlamps were fitted with black card, a rectangular shape cut out of it, to make the beam a mere slit so that the German bombers couldn't see it in the blackout. That meant they would have to drive slowly. But not on the way. On the way, Frank drove at breakneck speed and Mary and Ida, in the back seat, squealed with delight. It was exciting driving in a car, something neither she nor Ida had ever done before. A boyfriend with a car. The stuff of dreams. The two girls grinned at each other. Nineteen years of age and the whole world ahead of them.

New Brighton Tower ballroom was full to bursting that night and the band was particularly good. They danced and chatted and laughed more than any other time she could remember. Frank was so funny, always cracking jokes, and he had a particularly clever way of rolling his cigarettes with one hand. He said he'd learned it from watching cowboy films down at the Court Cinema but she didn't care. It was wonderful and so was he.

When the air raid started, no one took a blind bit of notice. No one ever did. The music continued, pausing only briefly for the manager to make the announcement that he could take no responsibility for any injuries caused if people decided to remain in the ballroom during the raid. Everyone just jeered and whistled, the music started up again, and the dancing continued.

About five minutes into the raid, the landmine struck. Its impact shook the whole building like a toy, as if it were the epicentre of an earthquake. The entire stage upon which the band sat collapsed, sending up a great cloud of dust and debris. The lights went out and there was pandemonium as people ran around in every direction, screaming and shouting in a wild stampede. The manager tried to calm everyone, shouting out to them not to push, but the microphones weren't working, his voice drowned in the chaos. Ignoring the pleas for calm, everyone made a mad scramble to get to the exits.

Frank took charge, grabbing Mary around the waist, and he pushed his way through the mad crowd towards the exit sign. The emergency generator had kicked in and a soft red glow above the doors directed them towards the outside. Mary wasn't so sure if that was the best place to be right at that moment. As they neared the door, the sound of falling bombs drew closer. It was a heavy raid, perhaps the heaviest yet.

The press of screaming people at the door was frightening. Frank elbowed one man in the jaw, knocking him down, and kicked another one out of the way. It was madness, everyone battling each other, legs and arms flailing about, kicking, pushing, gouging, a mad, uncontrolled rugby scrum, nobody giving a damn about anyone else. Except Frank, of course. He held Mary close and he wasn't letting go.

At last, they burst into the night and he pulled her round and hugged her hard. The night sky was lit up with the glow of a thousand incendiary bombs, spotlights arcing through the blackness, the drone of the bombers high above them and everywhere the screams of people as they floundered about. Some fell to the ground, sobbing uncontrollably, others wandered around as if drunk. Mary glanced back towards the ballroom and felt sick. It appeared as if made of paper, scrunched up into a tight ball, twisting and buckling as the flames lapped through broken and distorted masonry. The landmine must have been huge and the tower had taken the brunt of the explosion. Then Frank was pulling her away, heading towards the car, and he bundled her inside.

"What about Ida?" she screamed.

Frank looked at her, debating whether he should go back or not. He bit his lip, looking at the people spewing out from the exit doors. In the distance, the heavy crump of bombs exploding in the night, incendiaries bursting into flames, a curious smell filling the air. A scene from a nightmare, dazed, confused figures moving like gyrating ghosts, blurred and indistinct in the night, briefly illuminated every now and then by a flash from exploding bombs. Faces unrecognisable in the gloom. He shook his head, "I'll never find her."

"Frank, *please* – we can't just leave her!"

His shoulders sagged and he gave her a wink, a brief nod, and then was gone, plunging into the crowd, his wide shoulders making him stand out for a moment before he disappeared, swallowed up by the night and the surging mob.

She staggered over to a little grassy hillock and sat there for a moment, wondering what she could do. Weeping women and crying men whirled past, drunk with fear, some mumbling, deep in shock, others calling out the names of friends and loved ones. Another terrific blast close by spurred her into running into the car park and the few vehicles waiting there. Breathing a sigh of relief, she found Frank's Ford with little difficulty and tried the door. It creaked open and, in the comforting, darkened interior, cocooned against the bleating madness of those outside, she put her face in her hands and cried.

The War, once so distant, *phoney* as some had called it, had suddenly become so immediate. There had been raids before, but nothing like this. She pulled back her head and, through her tears, peered at the night sky, lit up by a hundred orange-red fires. New Brighton stood opposite Liverpool, the prime target for the bombers. Everyone had made jokes about it all at first, laughing it off, making insults about Hitler and his goose-stepping storm-troopers, but no one would be joking and laughing anymore. This was all too real. How many more nights would there be like this one, she wondered, before Churchill finally came to terms with the Germans? The whole of Europe lay under the jackboot and soon Britain would be too. She imagined a troop of German soldiers marching along the Prom, hard chiselled faces, the new masters, and he shivered at the thought.

Pressing a screwed-up piece of tissue against her mouth, she watched people stumbling about, wide eyed and terrified. The car rocked as another blast erupted nearby and she pressed herself down into the seat, curling her body up into a ball, the tissue crammed tight in her mouth to muffle her cries. This was the night from hell, the night she'd always dreaded and always hoped would never come.

She cried out as the door tore open, but then Frank's reassuring voice made her relax, telling her it was all right, and she felt such relief she almost swooned. Ida, crying uncontrollably, she fell into the back seat, and Stan was there, blood running from his scalp in little rivulets to drip off the end of his jaw. He looked hideous in the gloom, but they were alive and they were safe and Mary held them both.

Soon Frank took the car down onto the prom and carefully guided it up Victoria Street. The blackout was in full force, but the incendiaries gave off more light than any streetlamp. Far more than the useless headlamps anyway, the meagre drizzle of light as good as useless. Frank had his face pressed up against the windscreen, jaw set, concentrating with every fibre of his body as he slowly guided the little car up the street. He didn't see the crater until it was too late, the car tipping downwards sharply, all of them shooting forward, Frank's head hitting the windscreen, cracking the glass.

Mary was always grateful that it didn't shatter. To think what a mess it would have made of Frank's face – a thought too dreadful upon which to dwell. He was lucky, they were all lucky. But it was impossible to get the car out of that hole and they had to clamber out and abandon it there, with the bombs still coming down and the Ak-Ak guns popping off, making more noise than the Germans ever could. Keeping their heads down they ran through the streets, darting from shop doorway to shop doorway until an ARP warden roared at them to '*get under cover!*' The closest place was the Victoria Hotel, and the warden marched them inside and directed them towards the basement. He was far from happy and took Frank's name and address. To everyone's relief, the details he gave were false and nothing more ever came of their traumatic escapades of that dreadful night.

They'd often laugh about that night, but it was more from relief than any feelings of enjoyment. The night had brought them all closer together, in more ways than one. He took her down a side alley next to her house, pushed her against the wall, his hands groping under her skirt, lifting her. She wanted to stop him, but the thrill of it, the awfulness of the night, the chaos, it all combined to bring such a longing that all her powers of resistance were lost. The feel of him, so hard inside her, forcing her to cry out, his body taut, strong. No sooner was he in her, than it was over and he stepped away, gasping, mumbling words of apology. Giving none of it any mind, she kissed his cheek and from then on, Mary and Frank saw one another regularly. There was no repetition of their brief, physical contact but a year later, they were married. Some people were full of trepidation, saying that it would never work. Frank was too unpredictable, had a short fuse, couldn't be trusted. But Mary never saw any of that. All she saw was a big strong man who had saved her life, and that of her friend. She'd never forget that.

But it was hard. Especially when he started hitting her.

He took to following her, every time she went out. And if he didn't follow her, even when she went to the baker's for some bread, which was only a few yards up the street, he'd want to know where she'd been. "For God's sake, Frank, I've been to the bloody baker's." Then he'd hit her, not because she swore at him, but because he knew the baker was a 'bit of a ladies' man' and he knew, for certain, that Mary fancied him. "Don't be so stupid," she'd say, and he'd hit her again. She very quickly learned that it was safer to keep quiet. That way he only ever hit her once.

Life took a very predictable course and Mary fell deeper and deeper into despair. She learned that it was best to stay indoors, only ever entraining her friends at home. But even that was fraught with danger. If Frank wasn't there, he wanted to know who'd been round for tea, and if it was Ida why wasn't there a lipstick stain on the cup? So he'd hit her again and he'd accuse her again and the whole, awful sequence would play itself out as it always did. He'd accuse her, she'd remain stoic, then the slap, sometimes the punch, and she'd fall down, and then he'd rip off her clothes and make violent love to her, ramming into her like a rutting ram, teeth clenched, face screwed up as if he were in pain. Then he'd let loose his orgasm with a loud cry and collapse on top of her, breathing hard, body bathed in sweat. When he finally rolled off her, he'd lie there, staring at the ceiling, telling her how much he loved her, how he never wanted her to leave, how he'd always look after her, protect her.

When she fell pregnant, he was ecstatic. She felt like a prisoner, condemned to a life behind bars.

Ida sat across the kitchen table, head propped up in one hand, staring at her friend with such a look of anguish that Mary felt she would have to ask her to leave it made her feel so uncomfortable. But Ida wasn't going anywhere. "Why the hell don't you leave him, May?" Ida's use of her nickname for Mary seemed so much poignant right at that moment – Ida was the only friend she had.

"And where am I supposed to go? With Matthew and all?"

"Anywhere. You've got to. His mum can take the boy."

"I couldn't do that; I couldn't just palm him off to that woman – she's almost as bad as Frank."

"She may be, but what choice have you got? Anyway, doesn't she ever speak to you about any of this? She must know what he's doing to you, for God's sake. Everyone else does."

"Do they?" Mary put her face in her hands, "Christ, I had no idea."

Ida reached over and took Mary's hand in hers. "You've got to do it, May. Before he kills you."

Mary looked up, wincing as she tried a smile. The bruise on her cheek was responding to the dabs of witch-hazel Ida had administered earlier when she'd called, taken one look, and cursed loudly. It still hurt like billy-o. "I'll think about it."

"Honestly?"

"Honestly."

She saw Ida out and stood there on the doorstep, breathing in the clear air. It cooled her cheek, made her feel a little better.

"Are you all right, Miss?"

She started, snapping herself out of her daydream. He was standing there, very young, very handsome, dressed in a grey pinstripe suit, holding a little suitcase by his side. She stared at him blankly and he stepped closer.

"You look a bit – Christ, what's happened to your face?"

Subconsciously, her hand reached for the bruise. She gazed at him, horrified. Then she shook herself and narrowed her eyes. Without a word, she whirled around and slammed the front door shut, pressing herself back against it, breathing hard. How dare he be so familiar, whoever the hell he was. Cheeky bugger. A travelling salesman probably. She smiled. He'd seemed kind, concerned. Perhaps she had been a little hasty, and rude, slamming the door the way she did. He had a little name badge on his lapel and she'd taken it in with a glance. Kind, but very young. And very, very handsome.

His name, she'd noticed, was David and she decided there and then to keep an eye out for him, offer him an apology. A cup of tea. A ready smile. Suddenly, the day felt a little brighter.

6

Dad looked like he was tearing himself up inside. All this talk about Mum, it must have got his emotions all jumbled up and his eyes were wet. Jed hadn't asked him to say anything, but when he'd come home from seeing Matthew, it all sort of spilled out, uncontrolled and he didn't think he should stop the revelations in mid-flow. So, he just let his dad talk. And he'd spoken all about how mum had been treated in the War, how Matthew's father had beaten her, regarded her more like a possession, jealous and controlling. Dad didn't stop for a second, almost as if he needed to talk, to rid himself of the memories, bare his soul. Jed had known nothing about any of it, why should he? It had all happened long before he'd been born.

"We met years later," Dad continued, his eyes still clouded with that distant look, as if he were seeking out the years, the past, disentangling them from the chaos of the present. "Your mum took Aunty Ida's advice, left them all to it. I don't suppose Matthew ever really forgave Mum for that. You can't blame him, I don't suppose." He sniffed, ran a hand across his nose. "She went up to the Lakes. She had family there, near Kirkby Lonsdale. They ran a little hotel and she got a job as a chambermaid. Not much of a job really, but better than nothing. Especially in the circumstances. Not that anyone asked, not that anyone cared. She was just another young woman, trying to make ends meet in those after-War years. Everything was all so tight in those days, what with the rationing."

"What happened to Mat?"

"His Nan looked after him, Frank's mother. She brought him up well, by all accounts." He shrugged, perhaps not really believing his own words. Jed knew more about it than his dad probably gave him credit for. Matthew had told him about the armed raid, but Jed decided not to reveal the details, allowing Dad to continue, cleanse his soul. "She was working there when I met her. I'd just come out of the army. The War was long over, but I'd stayed on, doing some reconstruction work over in Germany. When I came back I was lucky enough to get a little job doing some painting and decorating in the town. I'd gone back, to see my mum, but she wasn't well. Things had changed a lot since I was overseas. And I hadn't kept in touch…" His voice trailed away and he suddenly looked old as he sat there, hand clawing at his scalp, suffering with the memories. Not bad memories. Dad tortured himself, looking back at a time when he was hopeful and full of joy in sharing happiness with someone, someone he cared for. Mum. Now, everything was so much darker, so much more morose. Jed stood up to go but Dad reached out a hand and clutched at his son's forearm. "Jed – I need you to understand…"

"Dad…don't…" Jed pulled in a deep breath. He felt unsteady on his feet as if he didn't have the strength to support his own weight. These revelations, first from Matthew and now from Dad… He didn't need to understand, not yet anyway. That time would come. For now, all he wanted to do was go into his room and read something, anything, to lose himself in another world.

Dad looked grim. "I need to do this." He pulled himself up straight, eyes clearing, and released Jed's arm. "We got on really well, your mum and me; we had so much in common, you see. My dad's family had come from Wallasey. Martins Lane. Not so very far from her own mother's. It was a wonder we hadn't bumped into one another before. We'd sit for ages and just talk about the town, New Brighton, the prom, the ferry. It turned out that we'd even been to the Tower ballroom at the same time, but not on the night of the raid. Nineteen forty, I think.

I was visiting some family, to say goodbye, just in case. My call-up papers had come and I was off.

"Well, one thing led to another, as they always do." He turned to look out of the window. "I didn't know anything about her past. She told a few little scraps, but not a lot. And I never asked, never really thought it was important. I noticed she was very edgy at first, never liked being alone with me in those early days. I just thought she was shy, you know, not used to men..." He gave a little snigger, "A right bloody fool, wasn't I?"

"No Dad. You weren't – and you're not." Jed sat down again, shoulders heavy, dejected.

"You think not? Wish I shared your conviction, Jed. I truly do." He rubbed his forehead. "We got married up there. Lovely little do it was, very quiet. Then we had our honeymoon in Switzerland. Nineteen fifty-two. That was a happy time. Not a care in the world...And it stayed like that, the two of us just content with each other. I didn't know anything about what Matthew told you, not about the other bloke. The one she'd met when she'd been with Frank. I don't even know his name, not even now." He turned around again and looked at Jed and his eyes streamed uncontrollably. A little boy lost. "I don't know what I'm supposed to do, Jed. Do I try and find her? What do you think?"

What *did* he think? What was he supposed to think? His mother had run off with another man, left them both to get through the fallout. Shouldn't they just shoulder the burden together, get through it as best they could? He shook his head, not able to offer up any advice. "I don't know, Dad...I suppose she'll be in touch."

"When she wants something. That'll be the only reason. I thought I knew her, Jed. The woman I'd fell in love with, married..." He put the heels of his palms into each eye, squeezing away the tears.

"Whatever happened to Frank, Dad? I've never met him."

"No, and you're not likely to." Suddenly angry, Jed's dad stood up, tucking in his shirt, rearranging himself, "I've got to go over to your gran's now. It's time to bite the bullet."

"What, you haven't told her yet?"

He shook his head, just the once. "Didn't think I could. But, I can't put it off any longer." Standing next to him, Jed was a good four inches taller than his dad and, this close, he must have been quite intimidating. "My little lad," Dad laughed, clamping a hand on Jed's shoulder, despite the height difference. "You're going to be all right, yeah?"

"When will you tell me about Frank, and what happened?"

His dad pressed his lips together, breathing out a long sigh. "Soon." Then he brushed past to put on his coat. The weather had turned ghastly and rain threatened. Jed remembered what had happened to his granddad, his dad's father. In bed with pneumonia, a proud and stoic man, he had insisted on getting up for work. The rain teamed down, pinging off the road and pavements like tiny ball bearings. Dad had found him at the top of the road, clinging onto a wall, a horrible shade of green. He was dead two days later.

"You be careful, Dad."

"Don't worry about me, son. "

"But I do, Dad. I don't want you doing anything stupid. You're all I've got."

A smile. "You are too, Jed. But, as long as we've got each other, eh?"

For a moment, Jed thought they might have to hug one another. Showing emotions, baring his soul was not something which came easy to him. So he held back and Dad gave a nod and nothing more, and then left, buttoning his coat up to his throat. Jed stood, staring at the front door, wishing, not for the first time, that he was that little boy again and he was going to help his dad ride his bicycle along the road to work.

7

It was all over the local news the following day. "At least it keeps you out of the public eye," said Dad laconically. Jed ignored him, keeping his attention on the television screen. A young nurse, found brutally murdered in Earlston Park, behind the library. She had been sexually assaulted before being strangled, then her body lashed to one end of the sea-saw. Jed felt something like a vice squeezing his heart. Dad leaned over the chair Jed occupied and let out his breath slowly. His voice sounded full of shock when he spoke. "Who the hell would do that?"

Jed looked up, his eyes wide, terror rippling through him. He swallowed hard, struggling to control his voice. "Dad...I know her."

The police detective, a man by the name of Sullivan, took up most of the armchair on which he sat.

He held a small, black notebook open in front of him, and a stubby pencil hidden amongst his fat fingers. He was peering at his notes in some sort of confusion, frowning. "All right," he wheezed, "going back over what you said, the only time you ever saw her was at the hospital...is that about right?"

"Yes." Jed sighed, irritated. Two minutes before he was about to pick up the telephone and call the police, the knock had come at the door and Sullivan stood there. He had with him two uniformed constables, both of whom stayed outside in the little Panda car.

"And you say that this fellow you rescued from the lake," he thumbed back a few pages, "Jonathan Kepowski…you say he got friendly with Nurse Willis?"

"Yes."

Sullivan nodded, tapping his bottom teeth with the end of the pencil. "You see, that's the bit that I don't quite understand."

"I don't see what the problem is," said Jed, unable to hide his impatience, "he had her in the ward, under the sheets, if you know what I mean."

"Mmm…Yes, I do know what you mean, but hardly likely is it?"

"Pardon me?"

"Having it off with a girl he'd only just met. Do you ever go to The Grand?"

"The Grand? What, the nightclub?"

"The very same."

"No. I don't think I've ever been."

"He's only just eighteen," put in Dad, who had been sitting next to Jed on the sofa, listening to the exchange with growing unease. "Hardly likely to be going out to nightclubs, is he?"

"You'd be surprised, sir. Believe you me…" Another smile, then another look at his notes. "So, you've never been to The Grand?"

"No. I told you – Dad's told you."

Sullivan shook his head slowly as he shifted uncomfortably in the chair, reaching into his trouser pocket and bringing out a small, white business card. He held out his hand with the card. "Is that your signature and photograph?"

Both father and son craned forward. Suddenly, it was as if the walls were pressing in from every side. The heat rose up from Jed's collar and he could feel the sweat on his face. Dad gave a little yelp of surprise. On the card, a membership card for The Grand Nightclub, as clear as day, a photograph of Jed smiled out to the whole world.

Sullivan sat quietly for a moment, allowing the enormity of the revelation to sink home. "So – let's try again. When was the last time you went to The Grand?"

Jed's mouth opened and closed a few times, but it was if the words were stuck in his throat. His heart pounded in his ears, causing Sullivan's voice to sound from a hundred miles away. And Dad's, like he was calling him from inside a tunnel. A tunnel which was very dark and very scary.

"*Jed*, for God's sake, son, answer the bloody question!"

Jed blinked, looking at the membership card still in his hand. He was trying to say something, trying to tell them both that this was all some horrible mistake, a coincidence. Someone with a face impossibly like his own, with his name, was a member of The Grand. That was the explanation, that was the truth.

"You see," Sullivan spread out his hands, "the problem I've got, is that Ellen Willis was found tied up to that sea-saw, in some horribly bizarre sort of way, having just spent a night in The Grand nightclub. And I've got about six, maybe more witnesses who swear blind that you were with her most of the evening." Jed looked at him, a nervous tic beginning to play at the corner of his eye. He wanted to rub it, but he felt he shouldn't. Would that affirm his guilt? "They recognised you, from the tele. Seeing that you're so famous, having rescued that..." Sullivan looked down at his notes, "that Jonathan Kepowski. Is that why nurse Willis was so desperate to be seen with you? And is that why you were so happy to be with her; after all, she was quite attractive by all accounts. So, no more messing about, eh? You left the club with her, at what time would that be, approximately?"

"Just hold on," Jed stood up, suddenly feeling angry, all of his previous unease and uncertainty replaced by a new assertiveness. His dad was about to speak, but Jed silenced him with a firm outstretched hand, "No. I'm not having this. I never met with Nurse Willis, that night or any other. I've never been to The Grand and I haven't got a clue what this is," he hurled the membership card towards the policeman, who merely followed it with his eyes as it floated down to the carpet. "Now, if you have nothing else to say, Mr Sullivan, I'd like you to leave."

But Sullivan didn't flinch. He sat back, beaming, seemingly impressed by the outburst. "I wasn't expecting something like that from someone as young as you, Jed. I can call you Jed, can't I?"

"*Mister* Meres, if it's all the same."

Sullivan shrugged. "Very well. I hadn't banked on how much you've grown up in the past few days and weeks. No doubt because of the way your life has been ripped wide open, any shreds of immaturity and boyishness all thrown to the wind, eh? Here you are, a confident and determined young man, forceful, a little arrogant and very angry." He paused, letting his words sink home. "Do you know someone called Craig Watson, Mr Meres?"

Blinking, Jed didn't know what to say for a moment. The question took him by surprise. "What? Craig Watson…of course I do. What's he got to do with any of this?"

"He's signed a statement, you see. Apparently you threatened him, didn't you, Mr Meres? In fact, you did more than that, didn't you? You assaulted him."

"Now hang on, you've got this all—"

"What, Mr Meres? All wrong, is that what you're going to tell me? Do you *deny* head-butting Craig Watson, Mr Meres?"

"No, of course I don't but…" Jed looked desperately towards his dad. "Dad – you know what happened."

Sullivan didn't wait for any interjection. "We all know what happened, Mr Meres. You were suspended from school, and then you rescue Mr Kepowski and you become a hero. Fortunate that, wasn't it? Timely."

"Where is all this going, Mr Sullivan?" Dad's voice was unsteady. He wasn't enjoying the exchange.

"I'll tell you. Sit down, Mr Meres." Jed did, without argument. "What your dad doesn't know is that you went to visit Craig Watson, threatened him, told him that if…" he looked down at his notes, running his forefinger under the words as he read them, "Yes, you told him, '*if you ever say anything more about my mum, I'll kill you. You and anyone else.*' Sounds fairly frightening, doesn't it Mr Meres. So what was it Nurse Willis said that triggered you into an act of unparalleled violence towards her? Did she dare to ask you an uncomfortable question, regarding your mother? Questioning her fidelity, her faithfulness?"

Dad tried to react, but it all happened so quickly. The red mist came down over Jed and he simply snapped. Dad managed to get some sort of a grip on his son's arm, but it was to no avail as Jed launched himself at the policeman. From somewhere, Sullivan managed to cry out. Even before Jed's fingers locked around Sullivan's throat, the two uniformed police officers were already coming through the door, pushing Dad aside. He sat on the floor, watching the ensuing melee with growing horror. Punches were thrown and bones broken. Reporting later, in the local press, the police officers said that they had never confronted such controlled aggression. It was like coming against a trained expert in unarmed combat, they said. It was only when one officer managed to crack Jed across the carotid artery with his truncheon that it ended and Jed's dad, aghast at what he had seen, let the tears tumble unbridled down his face.

8

Remanded in custody. Youth offender. The words fell off Sullivan's tongue like treacle. He was enjoying himself, but then he probably had good cause. Jed had hit him hard in the mouth, chipped one of his teeth, causing his lip to swell like a small balloon, making speech difficult. He still managed a contented smile however. "You can go and visit him at Risley," said Sullivan, squeezed in behind his desk, with Jed's shell-shocked dad opposite. "Perhaps you can convince him to start telling the truth, Mr Meres – the whole truth."

"I believe he's already done that."

"Well, I don't, and witnesses seem to confirm it. So, do him a favour – convince him."

The journey to Risley was long. Meres left home at around eight o'clock to get to the remand centre for his arranged visit. By the time he got there, some three and a half hours later, he was tired and irritable. The prison guard at the gate appeared surly, looking down his nose at Meres as he scanned the visiting order a little too diligently, keeping Meres out in the cold longer than was necessary before letting him in.

It was an oppressive and dark place, a smell like wet nappies permeating from every crack in the dilapidated walls, Meres feeling dirty almost as soon as he stepped into the visitors' waiting room. Packed with others, silent and grim, all wrapped in the same depressed mood, nobody making eye contact. Every few minutes or so a huge guard emerged and shouted out some name. People sauntered up to him, bowed heads, heavy hearts and waited. Meres wished for the ground to swallow him up whole.

"Mr Meres, isn't it?"

He looked up, startled that someone could speak in such a place. When he saw who it was, his mouth went slack. "Mrs Randall? What..."

She smiled, showing her full set of perfect teeth. She slid up next to him. "Brian, my eldest. Got himself into some bother. Nothing much, but you know how it is..."

Meres didn't. He knew only in passing. He knew she lived around the corner in Pelham Road, that her daughter had run off with the milkman and her son, Brian, was constantly in trouble with the authorities. Neighbours blamed it all on the fact he didn't have a dad, that she didn't have the time to look after him properly. Occasionally he would see her in the shops and offer up a smile, rarely reciprocated. Since doing all his own shopping, these encounters became more common and they'd often exchange a small nod of recognition in the butcher's, or the greengrocer's. A striking woman, very slim, with shoulder length hair cut pageboy style, legs bronzed. And here she was, so close, he could breathe in her perfume.

"So...any reason?"

He realized she'd been talking to him and he hadn't even noticed. He blushed, embarrassed. "Sorry, I was miles away..."

"That's all right," she placed her hand gently on his knee. He didn't pull away, and she didn't move her hand. "I heard a little bit about it. They tend to go off the rails when unfortunate things happen..." She noted his blank look. "Your wife...must have been a shock?"

The fact that it was a question, not a statement, should have angered him a little. But her hand was on his knee and his pulse rate was soaring. He didn't want to shatter the moment. "Yes – oh yes, but Jed, you know...always has had a bit of a temper."

"Temper? You mean – my God, you're not saying he actually *did it*, are you?"

Her hand suddenly snapped back, and she gaped at him, appalled. He realized with a jolt that they were at cross-purposes. He thought she'd been asking about the assault on the police, not the murder of the poor Willis girl. He gushed, "Oh dear God, no – no, I didn't mean…No, no, I thought you were talking about what happened with the police." She shook her head slightly. "Sorry. No, I know he didn't do it. Not that girl. Not that."

She sat staring, measuring him, then she smiled, her face lighting up, the horror all gone. Meres felt himself relax. She gestured towards the order in his hand. "What time have you got for your visit?"

"It says twelve noon, but it's already half-past."

"They always run late. I've got a quarter-past. Why don't we meet up for a coffee afterwards? You can wait for me outside if you like, then I'll drive you back."

"Drive? Oh God, that would be wonderful. It took me over three hours to get here by public transport."

The hand descended on his knee again, "Well, you won't have to worry about that again…not for a while anyway."

Jed looked far worse than Meres expected. Sunken eyes and hollow cheeks, the shock well settled in. The police were quick to act and he was up before the magistrate the very next morning. Remanded without bail. Meres thought Jed would faint, standing there in the dock. He didn't and now here they were, father and son, on opposite sides of the grill.

Perfunctory questions came. Did he want anything, was he eating, what were the other prisoners like, sorry, of course, they're not prisoners, not prisoners until they've *gone up in the blue*, but you've got to keep believing, don't let them wear you down, keep your nose clean…

"What the hell do you know about it, Dad?"

"Not much."

"Well then…Just see that solicitor, get things moving. I've got exams to revise for."

"Exams? Jed—"

"What? Do you think I'm going to throw everything away just because I chinned a bloody twat of a copper? Or maybe you think I can't do it anymore, the studying, now that Mum isn't here to encourage me, make me do my homework, brush my teeth, change my underwear?"

"Jed…" Meres squirmed in his seat, looking around at the guard who stood silent and stoic in the corner, blank stare, not a care for anyone or anything. "Jed, I didn't mean, you know—"

"No. You didn't mean to think that this is all going to stand against me. That my life has been pissed up the wall? Is that it?"

"Why the hell are you so angry at me? I haven't got anything to do with all of this – it's not my fault."

"Isn't it? Is that what you think? Is that what runs through your head every night when you're lying there, crying over Mum? You honestly think it's not your fault, none of it?"

Meres stared at his son in astonishment. He'd never heard Jed sound so bitter, so full of venom. Of course it wasn't his fault, how could it be? He'd done the best he could for his wife and family, sacrificed everything, worked all the hours God had sent to try and make ends meet, keep a roof over their heads. What more could he have done, what more was there? His voice was very small, like a child's when he asked, "And what part of it is my fault, Jed? You tell me that."

"Dad," Jed leaned forward, his face up against the mesh, his teeth clenched, "she went off with another bloke – the same bloke who ruined Matthew's dad's life. And, for all I know, for the same reasons."

"You bloody little shit!" Meres leapt off his chair, the fury boiling up, uncontrolled, fingers clawing at the mesh. He had no thoughts, just blind anger, the desire to rip off Jed's head. Then, the guard appeared, grappling with him, pulling him back. And Meres, the mist fading, could see Jed, sitting there, that same look of defiance on his face. And something more, something which made Mere's blood boil once more. His son's eyes said it all. Accusing.

"You look awful."

Meres forced a slight smile as Mrs Randall stepped out into the blustery afternoon. It was threatening rain and she'd pulled her coat tightly to her, exaggerating the slimness of her waist. It cheered him to see such a lovely looking woman, and it cheered him even more when, as they crossed the road to her car, she slipped her arm through his.

"How was he?"

"Jed? Oh, you know…" he shrugged, not really wanting to relive the horrific moments that had just passed. Instead, he clambered in next to her and waited until she turned the ignition. Soon, he watched the world go by as she drove the car through the streets towards Liverpool. "Kids, eh?"

She gave a little laugh. "It must be hard for you, everything happening so quickly the way it has. And for Jed, too. I'm sure it will all turn out for the best – in the end."

"You think so? I'm not so sure." It started to rain and he saw people scurrying into shop doorways and breathed a sigh of relief he didn't have to suffer getting soaked. He turned to her, "Thank you so much for this, Mrs … I've just realized – I don't know your first name."

"Hannah."

He laughed, "Please to meet you, Hannah."

"Me too, Mr Meres."

"It's Lawrence. But everyone calls me Larry."

"Then I shall too."

It was only a cup of coffee. At least that's what he kept telling himself. A nice house, well ordered, scrupulously clean. She sat on the sofa, legs crossed. With her raincoat off, her blouse was straining at its buttons and his eyes settled on the swell of her breasts. How long had it been since he had slept with a woman, felt her skin beneath his fingers, the smooth undulations of her body? He hadn't shared anything physical with his wife for…he took a moment to count the months – no, the years. Four years to be exact. Rhyl caravan park on a wet August Bank Holiday weekend. Jed was with his gran and they were alone. They planned it that way in an attempt to rekindle the flame that had died. He'd done his best, had risen to the occasion and gone through the required routine before entering her, then thirty seconds later pulled away, spent and feeling cheap. She'd sighed, loudly. No words, just a look. God how that look withered him, "Is that it then?" And it was – he didn't have to say. She'd gone out that night, to the Park Social Club. He never asked her why she came back so late. He didn't need to.

If anyone had known the story, some might have asked why he stayed. And his answer would have come back automatically – because he loved her, and Jed, of course. Larry Meres knew he could not live his life without Jed.

But Jed was older now, almost a man, arrested for assaulting police officers, risking everything by being sent to a young offender's hostel. Borstal, some still called it. Larry shuddered at the thought.

"You don't say much," Hannah patted the cushion next to her, inviting him to join her. He did so, a little awkwardly. "You look so sad. Is it Jed, or is it your wife?" A look of alarm swept across Larry's features. "I don't mind if it is, honestly I don't."

Then, unexpectedly, she was turning his face towards hers and she was kissing him, softly at first, but then, when he responded, with more urgency. He surrendered to the rush of desire, the softness of her lips, the stirring in his loins. He cared for nothing else other than to consume her. They fell to the floor, hands everywhere, her body soft and firm, legs slim and well muscled. She smelt of musk and cucumber, a heady mix, strong and clean. Her nuzzled into her throat, tasting the flesh, revelling in it.

She pushed him over and he didn't resist. As her fingers tore at his belt and trousers, sudden, stupid thoughts loomed large in his head. What if he couldn't manage it, what if it all ended the same way as it did with Mary; the disappointment, the shame? But then, she delved beneath his pants, took him between her fingers, and all thoughts of inadequacy disappeared. She lowered her lips and ran her tongue over his blood-engorged flesh and he arched his back, moaning. "It's all right," she said softly, almost as if she were giving him her permission to let go. She sat back, slipping off her clothes and as he gazed, breathless at her slender body, she pulled away his trousers and took complete control.

"Oh Hannah," his voice croaked, thick with desire, throat constricted, head swimming. No resistance, no thoughts of betrayal, it was all too wonderful and something he never wanted to end.

9

They'd become friendly, a natural development in the confines of the remand centre. Jed knew Brian Randall by reputation, that he was on the fringes of some of the more undesirable elements in town. Now, brought together through circumstance, they met on a daily basis, gaining strength from knowing one another; a friendly face in a sea of resentment and, quite often, anger.

It was during a tea break late one afternoon, after both their respective parents had visited, that they first exchanged some friendly banter.

"Embarrassing when they come in like that," said Brian, staring down into a plastic cup of tea, "All blubbering and asking if everything's going to be all right."

"I don't think my dad expects me to be in here long."

"Well, maybe he's right – it might not even get to trial."

"You don't think so?"

"Coppers will probably want to do some sort of deal, they always do."

"I'm not so sure...they don't like being punched by a schoolboy."

Brian sniggered. "Wish I'd seen it."

"Wish I'd never done it – stupid it was."

"Nah. You've made your mark here, Jed. People respect you for it. How many of 'em have come up to you and spoken to you?"

"The other lads you mean?" Brian nodded. "None."

"There you are then – you have a reputation. Respect. It'll work wonders for you, if you do get sent down. But, like I said, I don't think it'll come to that."

"And what about you? What'll happen to you?"

"Who knows? I'll probably get probation, or a suspended. Either way, I won't be going down. My brief is pretty good. Look," he checked around the large social room, just in case anyone was close by. A small man, perhaps just peaking five foot, shuffled by. Brian gave him a furious glare and the little man quickly changed direction. "I can give you my brief's address if you like, you know, for the future. Just in case."

"Bri, I don't intend to make a habit out of this. Thanks anyway."

"You never know."

"No, you don't. It's not something I'm planning on doing again."

"You don't know what deal the coppers will ask you to make. They're clever, you know. Especially that Sullivan guy. Nasty piece of work he is, but he's got it all in there," he tapped his head meaningfully.

"You know him?"

"Course I know him! Everyone who's been in a few scrapes knows Inspector Sullivan. He got friendly with my mam not so long ago…"

Jed raised his brows in surprise. "What? You mean…?"

Brian nodded. "I blew a head gasket, I can tell yeh. Imagine, me mam and a copper, getting it together." He shivered, drained his tea and looked very sick. "Made me skin creep."

"God. Are they still together?"

"No way – I soon made it clear I wasn't having him in the house. So, anyway, you think about that solicitor. Name of Perryman. Clyde Perryman. Good he is."

"Thanks. I'll remember it."

Three days later two prison wardens came to visit Jed whilst he lay stretched out on his bunk, trying to catch up with some reading. The remand centre library wasn't the finest in the world, but he had been able to find a dog-eared copy of *Jude the Obscure*. He peered over the top of the book as the men came in.

"Get your things, Meres. You're going home."

* * *

It was all true, despite Jed's disbelief. Apparently, the police had withdrawn the charges. Jed, suspicious, especially after what Brian had said about deals, tried not to reveal his thoughts. He quickly got changed, packed away his things, then marched down to the main reception area. After he'd signed the release for his more personal items, he gave the guard behind the counter a hard stare. The guard grinned. "See you soon," he growled.

"I don't think so," returned Jed and held the man's gaze. Then the other two were pushing him out of the entrance into the grey afternoon. Jed turned to look at the guards, and then breathed a deep lungful of air as the door firmly closed with a bang. Freedom. Nothing had ever tasted quite so good.

Sullivan sat waiting for him in an unmarked car across the street. He wound down the window as Jed walked by. "You wanna lift, or are you thinking of walking all the way back to Wallasey?"

Without a word, Jed eased himself into the passenger seat, throwing his holdall into the back. Sullivan shook his head slightly as he eased the car into the traffic. "A 'thank you' wouldn't go amiss."

Jed looked at the policeman as if he had grown another head. "Thank who? *You*? Don't make me laugh. The only reason you've done this is to get something from me."

"That's a bit cynical, Jed. Been talking to someone, learning the ropes?"

"What if I have? It's the truth, isn't it?"

"If you say so." Sullivan reached over to the glove compartment and released the catch. The lid fell down sharply, cracking against Jed's knees. Fumbling around inside, Sullivan brought out a flimsy looking black and white photograph. "Do you know him?"

Jed took the picture and peered at the face. There was something vaguely familiar about the closely cropped hair, the flat nose, the hard, square chin. "I'm not sure...who is he?"

"His name is Peter Davey." Sullivan pulled the car up to a junction and looked at Jed for a long time. "He's Nurse Willis's boyfriend." Jed stared right back at the policeman. "Or should I say, *was*. He was found last night, in Central Park, his skull smashed to pieces."

* * *

Larry Meres lay on his bed, staring up at the ceiling, the memories burning through his mind. After they made love on the living room floor, she stood up and walked to the door, her lithe body olive coloured, without a blemish. She smiled and motioned for him to follow. Upstairs, in her bed, she caressed him and stroked him until he was ready again, and their love making the second time was much slower and more sensual. They lay together afterwards for a long time, without words. Now, alone, recalling the wonder of what happened, he didn't feel the slightest pang of guilt. His marriage had been a sham for too many years and although he had always held out hope that Mary would come back to him, he knew deep down she never would. Not in the truest sense. And now, returning to the arms of her lover the way she had, Larry at last accepted his marriage was truly over. Hannah Randall, and how she had made him feel, confirmed it.

He rolled over, the image of Hannah's face, her slim, taut body, always there. A constant reminder of how wonderful life could be at times. The unlooked-for always the sweetest.

His heart filled with electricity, a vibrant buzz running through his limbs, exhilarating him, making him feel like a teenager again. Such emotions remained dormant for so long. So many times he wondered if he would live out the rest of his life without ever again experiencing the touch of a woman. Now that it had happened, and so unexpectedly, he felt as if his life had taken a new turn. Buoyed up with so much energy and excitement, he couldn't stop grinning.

He forced himself to think sensibly, and not get too carried away. It had been wonderful, of course, but perhaps that's all it was, a moment of lust, need. Hannah hadn't said very much afterwards. She seemed unemotional, offering him a simple kiss of the cheek as they parted at the front door. He didn't wonder about it then, but he did now. Did she regret what had happened, he asked himself, having lost all sense of sensibility? A moment's madness, now forgotten? He hoped not. He longed to see her again, even though only three days had passed since they rolled around on her bed. He had phoned her the following morning, but received no answer. He wasn't brave enough to go to her house, but now felt he should. He hadn't seen her in the street or in the shops. The thought crossed his mind that she had gone away. Given the pressure she was under, with Brian locked away, this wouldn't surprise him. What did surprise him, however, was her lack of contact. Not surprise, perhaps. Concern. Having met such a woman and spent such an unforgettable few hours with her, the last thing he wanted, or needed, was for it to have been nothing more than a 'one-night stand'. Apart from the purely physical, they actually had a great deal in common. A platform from which to build, for them to become close, perhaps 'an item'. He hadn't dared hope for anything like that at the time, or voiced his feelings. It was only in the subsequent days, thinking about her constantly, reliving the tenderness, the caress of her hands, the smell of her flesh that he began to formulate little scenarios for the future. Visits to restaurants, theatres, perhaps a holiday…just the two of them…

He shook his head, angry at himself for being so whimsical. This was the stuff of schoolboy adolescence. He had to be realistic, snap himself out of this fluffy fantasy he had busied himself with creating. He got up and went downstairs to make himself a cup of tea. Daydreaming was not really for someone of his age, certainly not for someone in his situation. "Let's just take it one step at a time," he muttered to himself out loud. "One step at a time."

It was cold in the little kitchen and he rubbed his hands together. It didn't help. And he knew why. The Arctic atmosphere had little to do with the weather. The house was empty without Jed. Without Mary.

Mary. The thought of her made him crease up in a surge of guilt. He flopped down on a chair and put his face in his hands. He hated all of this, hated his lack of strength, his weakness of character. Most men would be lapping it up, boasting to their mates, not giving a moment's thought to what it all meant. But he wasn't like that, never had been. Was he being a fool to himself, he pondered. Why had Hannah come on to him so strongly? He was no great shakes to look at, a middle-aged man past his best, with little to offer. A woman like that…she could have anyone.

Later on, to keep himself busy, he went out shopping. It was early afternoon and the local supermarket was not busy. Larry wandered down the aisles, picking out the few bits and pieces he needed. Life without Jed was very inexpensive he had found. Not a comforting thought. Life without Jed.

At the checkout, he paid for the items and stepped outside, the carrier bags heavy in his hands. He looked to the sky and groaned. Rain threatened so he hurried across the road and was about to turn into St Albans Road when he stopped abruptly. Coming out of the travel agents on the corner, was Hannah Randall. She saw him and her face went white.

Larry forced a smile. "Hello. How are you?"

She looked around, panic crossing her features, then she recovered herself a little, returning his smile. "Larry, so lovely to see you. I'm fine. Fine. Been shopping?"

It was idle chit-chat, which coming from her, seemed forced and false, as if she were speaking to him out of nothing more than politeness. It made him feel uneasy; positively gloomy. He sucked in a breath. "Why haven't you answered your phone? I've been calling you every day. Is there something wrong?"

She noticed the change in his look and grew serious, "Larry." A pause, but only briefly, a chance to lessen the blow, "I don't think we should have a relationship. It was lovely, but – I'm sorry, but…" Her voice trailed away.

He stood there, rooted to the spot, not really believing what he was hearing. *Relationship?* What did she mean by that? They'd spent a few glorious hours together, time he believed was mutually pleasurable. Afterward, he hadn't said anything to her, nothing that would lead her to believe that he wanted anything more from her, despite what he hoped. When they'd left, with that kiss on his cheek, he hadn't declared his undying love for her, never even asked if he could see her again. *A relationship?*

She reached over and gently touched his arm. "You're a sweet man, Larry. I'm sorry."

Then she kissed him, again on the cheek. He could smell her, just fleetingly, musk and cucumber. Strong and fresh. There came a surge of desire, lancing through his loins. The thought of her, the feel of her…He bit his lip, wanting to shout out, '*Why? What have I done to you, what have I said? What haven't I said? Hannah, please, for pity's sake…*' But he didn't. Instead he just smiled, deprecating, not revealing the depth of his own despair, "Yes. You're probably right." And then he watched her as she drifted away into the distance and out of his life.

Or so he thought.

It struck Larry, almost as soon as he pushed the front door open. A strangeness, something out of place. Different than before he left. He stopped, key still in the lock, body coiled like a spring, waiting. Then he heard it, the faint sound of someone lifting themselves from the front room armchair and his heartbeat began to race. Before he could fully comprehend what was happening, Jed came out into the hall, a great grin on his face. "Hello, Dad."

Dropping the carrier bags, Larry ran into his son's arms, embracing him. It was a rare show of affection but Larry was beyond caring. All of his pent-up emotions broiled up to the surface and he held, clamping his arms around Jed in a steel-like grip.

He stepped back, eyes were wet, smiling. "Why didn't you ring to let me know?"

"I didn't know myself until this morning. The police dropped the charges."

Larry nodded, without fully understanding. The joy of Jed's return was all that mattered. The explanations and machinations could come later. His son was home. Everything else was small by comparison. Even Hannah Randall.

10

They walked together to school, Jed dragging his feet, not wanting to go. Larry, also reluctant, knew how difficult it was going to be, especially when school friends caught sight of him. Already he could hear the playground taunts.

Mr Phillips took some persuading. He sat, silent and moody, arms folded, leaning back in his chair, his gaze unflinching as Larry set out all the reasons why Jed should be given another chance to stay on at school, get his head down, study hard and pass his GCEs.

"I'm not sure if I want him here at school, Mr Meres." Phillips cast his dark eyes over Larry and Jed. "I have the reputation of the school to think about, and the safety of the other students. Besides, I doubt if he can pass any of his exams, not now."

"But you can't *legally* prevent him from coming back to school, can you Mr Phillips?"

"I can do what I like, Mr Meres. If I don't think it would be advantageous to have Jed back in my school, then that is the decision I will make. This is nothing personal. I like Jed, he used to be a good student. In fact, I can't remember a single instance of ever having to speak to him about any misdemeanour whatsoever, not until that business with the Watson boy." He blew out his cheeks. "His gallantry aside, what happened with those police officers…"

"All charges have been dropped."

"Yes, I realise that, but—"

"Well then…"

Phillips gnawed at the inside of his cheek. "If you can prove to me that the opposite is the case, that he can somehow transform himself into a model student…" he shrugged, "then, I shall base my decision on that, and nothing else."

"Then let me make that promise to you now, Mr Phillips." Larry glanced over at Jed. "It's been a difficult few days and none of it was of his making. All he needs is this one chance."

"Guarantees, Mr Meres? Can you offer any of those?"

"Mr Phillips, he's not a monster. He's just confused."

"*Dad…*"

"No, Jed. I'm sorry, but all of this is because of what's happened." He turned to Phillips, his face hard and flat. He didn't want sympathy, he simply wanted some understanding of the plight that Jed had been going through. "My wife had left me, Mr Phillips. It's hit both of us quite hard."

Phillips tugged at his moustache, thinking. "I didn't know – I'm sorry. Was it something which had been brewing for a while, or…?"

"She left me for another man." Larry leaned forward. "You can appreciate how difficult things have been."

"Yes. Yes, I can. Well," Phillips flipped open Jed's file and quickly scanned down the first few pieces of tightly written paper, "Given the circumstances…"

They wandered back home in silence. It was quite a walk, all the way along Poulton Road, but at least it was a pleasant enough day. The rain had kept off and as they turned into the main gates of Central Park even the foundations of where the *pre-fabs* had stood seemed somehow brighter and more cheerful.

"I remember when they were still being lived in," said Jed. "Funny how things stick in your mind."

Both of them stood for a moment, just staring at the sad, lonely rectangles of broken concrete. The only remaining memory of the homes that had stood there, hastily erected after the War, to help provide homes for those whose own houses had been bombed. "Someone should clear it all away."

"Then there won't be anything." Jed looked at his dad. "I think memories are important, even the tiny ones."

"What does that mean?"

"I don't know. You must have memories, of when you were younger. Before you met Mum."

"Of course. But, I rarely look back – not if I can help it. What's done is done." Larry thought of Hannah and knew his words were hollow. He often reflected on all the things that might have been. Should he tell Jed about what happened with Hannah Russell, would he understand, or would it ignite another eruption of violence?

"I sometimes think all the best things in my life have already been," Jed said.

"But that's a silly thing to say – you've got your whole life ahead of you."

"Have I?"

"Of course you have. If anyone, it should be me saying that."

"But you never know, do you. I mean, you could meet someone else…"

Larry's eyes widened. Did Jed suspect?

"That's if you wanted to. You loved Mum, didn't you?"

A tiny pause but enough, perhaps, to plant a seed. "Yes."

Jed's eyes remained flat and unfathomable. He started walking again, with Dad a little way behind. "What Phillips said, accepting you back in to school, that was decent of him." Jed nodded, but didn't speak. "You've been given a chance, Jed. Don't throw it away."

"I won't."

They drew level with the bowling greens, where a group of elderly men were chatting to each other, inspecting the grass.

From out of the small, ramshackle clubhouse, another figure appeared, wiping his hands on an old rag. He looked up and stopped. So did father and son.

It was Matthew.

A short word to the men and then he was striding forward, grinning. "This is a surprise. What are you doing here?"

"We're not here to see you, Mat," said Larry agitated. Jed remained silent. "Just a coincidence, that's all."

"Well…now that you're here. I've been meaning to talk to you, Larry. About things."

Larry glanced across to Jed. "Do you want to hear this, whatever it is?"

"It's really for Jed's benefit," interjected Matthew.

"Is it really?"

The brothers both winced at the sarcastic tone. "I want to hear it," said Jed.

Meres grunted and they all walked over to a nearby bench and sat down.

An awkward fell over them, no one really knowing how to start.

"We haven't spoken for years," said Matthew.

Meres shrugged. "If you need to talk to Jed, then talk."

"All right." Matthew leaned forward, elbows on knees, hands clamped together. "Why did the police let you go?"

Unexpected, the question jerked both Larry and Jed bolt upright.

Jed coughed and took a breath. "Sullivan met me outside, told me what route to go down if anyone asked why I was out. '*Just tell anyone who asks that we didn't feel that the case was strong enough.*' That's how he started. '*That you had been unreasonably provoked. They may not buy that, but at least it's not so unbelievable as to be questioned too deeply.*'"

A quizzical look crossed Mat's face. Jed shrugged. "I'm not going to argue, am I? I'm free."

Larry snorted, "Didn't want to make themselves out to be fools, more like. Three of them, tackled by a schoolboy…" He sniggered again. "Can you imagine the headlines?"

"So, no deal then?" Mat's voice sounded hard, unconvinced.

Perhaps Mat wasn't going to let it go. "Not as such."

"What does that mean?"

"It means I'm not going to tell you." Jed looked his half-brother square in the face. "At the end of the day, it hasn't anything to do with you, has it?"

Mat rubbed his chin, glanced down to his shoes and did a little dance with them, appearing uncomfortable. "I talked to Jed about what happened with Mum, Larry. The last time she walked out, when she dumped me."

The change of subject caught both Larry and Jed unawares. They exchanged a quick glance. "I'm not sure whether I should thank you or not, Matthew. Most of the story is still a mystery to me." Larry's breathing grew laboured. "I don't know if I *ever* want to hear it. Not now. And how can it help, digging it all up again? Is that what you want to talk to us about, Mat? How your mother destroyed your dad's heart?"

"Not exactly – not that part anyway. More an attempt to explain things, give some meaning to why it's all happened again."

Larry stiffened. "You *knew* about what she was planning on doing?"

A terrible silence hung in the air, pressing down over all of them. Larry's eyes bored into Mat, whose face drained of colour. "No, of course I didn't. But I wasn't surprised. I just thought that if both of you knew what had happened, the reasons for it, it might make things easier. That's all."

"And how do you know?" Jed's voice was low, quiet, the voice of someone trying desperately to come to terms with betrayal, and failing miserably.

"Because my dad told me."

11

Over the course of the next twelve months, give or take, Mary would see him and they would talk. Gradually their friendship blossomed and she found herself looking forward to catching sight of his cheery face. He was kind and thoughtful, always had something good to say; usually about her. This cheered her no end and was almost enough to get her through the day. Almost. Her husband often came home in a black mood. Sometimes Frank would accuse her of being with someone else and she grew terrified someone had dropped a hint to him, or he'd noticed her cheery mood. Was he spying on her, the way he had with the postman?

He continued hitting her. An innocent glance, a disparaging word would send him into a rage. If she went to the local shop to buy a loaf of bread, he would follow her. And if he saw her talking to the man behind the counter, he would fly at her, accusations screaming out of his mouth. She denied all of it, but he'd retort, 'But I saw you, with my own eyes!' and a beating would follow. Home gradually became more of a prison as Mary chose to stay indoors rather than run the risk of another slap or punch.

One morning, she got up the courage to tell David how low she was. As an apprentice draughtsman, he had day-release at the local metropolitan college. Wednesday afternoons he finished early. Wednesday was always supposed to be Mary and Ida's day, when they would take the bus over to Birkenhead market and shop for bargains.

But this particular day, Ida was unwell. "There'll always be next week," said Ida, looking and sounding dreadful when Mary had gone round to visit her old friend. "And, besides, it will give you some time to think about things."

"Think about things."

"Yes, about you and Frank. It can't go on, May. He's going to hurt you badly one of these days. Whilst Matthew is at his gran's, you try and sort things out. I'll support you however I can, but in the end it's up to you."

Of course, she knew the sense of Ida's words. No one was going to do it for her. Only she could make the decision to pack her suitcase and walk out. But to walk out on Matthew? How could she do that, how would she ever be able to live with herself?

The solution was simple – she could take Matthew with her. But where? To live in a lodging house? She shuddered at the thought of it.

David found her in the corner shop. She turned and almost cried out when she saw his smiling face, beaming away at her. Her stomach did a little somersault when he spoke, "Hello Mary. You're looking lovely, as always."

She was wearing an old, faded *pinny* with a printed floral design that did nothing for her except exaggerate the fact that she was a hard-working, very unhappy housewife. She knew he was talking nonsense, but it felt nice nevertheless.

Mr Emery behind the counter clicked his tongue and handed over Mary's bag of shopping. "Not off to Town today then, May?"

Mr Emery was probably the closest thing she had to a father, and she had no intention of lying. "No. Ida's sick. A lazy day at home for me today."

"Well, you'd better go straight there, then. Hadn't you?"

Those last few words, heavy with insinuation, caused the heat to rise to her cheeks. Brushing away a lock of hair from her forehead, she gave David her best effort at looking demure, and floated out, heart thumping.

She hadn't reached as far as the street corner before he came running up next to her, and took the carrier bag from her hand. She gasped, startled by his sudden appearance. "What are you doing?" she asked, letting her fingers slip from the handle of the bag.

"Just helping. You look tired. Doing too much, I shouldn't wonder."

They usually spoke for around two or three minutes. Just idle chit-chat about this-and-that. He made her laugh. He was young, only seventeen, but he seemed so much older. He had a confidence about him, an assuredness that belied his years. And now, here she was, a grown woman, her heart fluttering at his attentions.

"Where's the little one?"

"Matthew? Oh, he's at his gran's. I usually go to Birkenhead today, but…" She shrugged, smiled.

"Yes. You said. Your friend's ill. So, you'll be all alone. Doesn't seem fair somehow, does it."

"Fair?" she laughed, awkwardly, no humour. "Since when has life been fair?"

"Look, why don't we catch the number eleven down to Vale Park, go and have a bite to eat at the teahouse?"

She gawped at him. Had she heard him correctly?

It was his turn to laugh, "It was only a suggestion – you'd think I'd asked you to run away with me."

"You may as well have – if Frank ever found out—"

"Well, he's not going to. Look," he linked arms with her and steered her towards the front door. "Why don't you go and put some powder on, or whatever it is you ladies do, and I'll go and get change. I'll see you back here in fifteen minutes, just in time to get that bus."

Before she could raise an objection, he was gone, handing back the bag then breaking into a brisk jog across the road to his aunt's house, where he was staying. She stood there, speechless, heart pounding. It was some time before she recovered her wits sufficiently enough to go back inside and put on that powder.

Mary felt like a schoolgirl playing truant as they sat on the top deck of the bus. He lit up two cigarettes and past one over top her in his best Paul Henreid manner. If she was feeling like Bette Davis, she didn't say anything, but inside she was in turmoil. Here she was, sharing intimate moments with a young man with whom, up until then, she had innocently chatted with in the street. She would never have believed it possible that she would find herself in this situation. She looked out of the window and smiled, tummy doing tiny summersaults, thrilled, despite everything – her doubts, her worries about Frank. Glancing around, convinced that every second person glared at her with eyes burning with accusations, she slowly realized she didn't actually care what they thought. It was wonderful to be away from the house, away from the street, away from the smell and feel of Frank. To be alone with another man, my God, could she have ever hoped for such a thing again in her life? Trapped, saddled to the sink, life mapped out for her. Yes, she had plans for running away, but that's all they were ever going to be – dreams, fantasies, call it what you will, she knew in her heart of hearts that she would never do anything about any of it. This was her existence. Frank. Frank and his foul temper, his stinking armpits, that pigeon-chest that gleamed so white, like chicken skin, freshly plucked. What did she ever see in him a hundred years ago when they first met? Wasn't he kind and strong and brave then? Wasn't he just everything she had ever wanted in a partner? What had happened, where had that dashing hero gone? And would she want him back if he simply reappeared on her doorstep…the way David had? Young, fresh, so gentle, so kind…David…

Mary didn't pull away when they linked arms and walked along the prom towards Vale Park. So what if anybody recognised her, would they say anything? Frank didn't have many friends, and those he had would be at work. Everything was going to be all right, it was the perfect plan because it was all so spontaneous. And so wonderful.

As if to confirm her happy mood, the sun was out and the grass smelt fresh and clean, newly mown. Some older couples, sipping tea at the little cafe, huddled up in their overcoats despite the sunshine, were the only other people out and about. She turned to David and caught him smiling. She laughed and he said, "Do you think we'll be like that one day?"

She almost gasped, but did her best not to react. Was it meant, or simply an 'off the cuff' remark? She held onto his arm tighter still, "I hope not," she breathed and he pulled her closer, then paused to look at a large flower bed, planted out in the shape of a clock face, ready to burst into bloom.

"I reckon all couples say that, you know." He seemed far away for a moment, staring at the flowers that had not get sprung into life, just a few green stubs beginning their courageous struggle to meet the sun. "We spend our whole lives not wanting to grow old and then, suddenly, we are. Then all we do is look back, wishing we were young again."

"David," she said, aghast, "you mustn't talk like that – you're only young."

"Yes." But he remained distant, thinking of something, something dark, or so it seemed to her. Then, just as quickly, he brightened, and turned to her, holding her by the waist as he looked down into her wide eyes. "Let's go and get some tea and a slice of cake."

"Decadent," she said sweetly.

"Ooh yes, I do hope so!"

Laughing, they rushed to an empty table.

It was warm as they strolled towards Egremont Ferry. "I've had a lovely day," she said.

"Me too. What time does your husband get home from work?"

She stiffened a little, reality biting home. "Around six-ish. It depends. Sometimes later, never earlier. He works long hours."

"And what time do you pick the little one up?"

"Oh…Frank normally goes and gets him on Wednesdays. It's our little routine, you see. Wednesday is my day. Weekends are his. He's off out all day Saturday, down to the pub with his mates. Bookies, ciggies, lots of drinking. There's usually a match he goes to, either Liverpool, sometimes Tranmere. If there's no football, then it's rugby.

Summer is horse-racing and cricket. There's always somewhere he's off to. Then Sunday he's in bed."

"Bloody hell, doesn't leave you much time to yourself does it. One day a week. Doesn't seem fair, somehow."

"Since when has 'fair' ever been part of married life, David?"

"I thought it was supposed to a partnership, of equals?"

She laughed, "God, how idealistic is that."

"I suppose you're right, although I'm no expert."

"Would you like to be?"

"What?"

"Married?"

"*Married*? Good God, I – well, I don't know, to be honest. It's something I've never considered."

"Have you got a girlfriend?"

"No. Not really."

"*Not really*? That sounds intriguing."

He grinned. "Oh Mary, don't be coy – you know full well what I mean."

She didn't, she honestly didn't. She told him so and for the first time since she met him, he blushed. Then she knew, realizing what he meant, and she blushed too.

At her doorstep, she thanked him once again for such a wonderful day. He stood looking down at his shoes, kicking at an imaginary stone. "I had the best day of my life," he said very quietly.

She went up on her tiptoes and kissed him gently on the cheek. For a moment, they stared into one another's eyes. She wanted to kiss him properly, but if anyone saw... Instead she let her hand brush across the back of his, then she was gone, closing the door softly behind her.

Mary leaned back against the front door, breathing in the cold, empty atmosphere of her little house. How unfriendly it seemed now, and already she was dreading the moment when Frank's key would turn in the door. Closing her yes, she relived for a few precious moments the highlights of the day. The way they had laughed, his smile, the feel of his arm in hers. Seventeen. Good God, he was like a grown man he was so confident. It was all silly nonsense of course, thinking these thoughts. She was a married woman, trapped in an abusive relationship with nowhere to go. She had hopes, but that's all they were. And David wasn't going to change anything. He was just a wonderful diversion, an opportunity to forget the rigours of her life. That's all, nothing else.

She snapped open her eyes and strode towards the kitchen. It was time to get the tea ready.

The week crawled by. Every so often she would catch a glimpse of David. Sometimes he would see her, and throw her a smile, or a little wave. He seemed to be aware of just how precarious the situation was. Frank didn't say anything, so no one had revealed to him what had happened at Vale Park. Not that anything had, of course; it was all innocent. Just two friends enjoying one another's company. But Frank wouldn't see it that way of course.

Soon it was Wednesday again. David would be home early. It was something Mary had been mulling over ever since she'd closed the door on him seven days previously. Should she attempt to manufacture a 'chance' meeting in the hope that they could spend another day together? How could she succeed in finding an opportunity, a moment to catch him, to ask him – the thought made her heart go into overdrive. With every waking second, she could think of nothing else. In the evenings, sitting there listening to the radio, she felt sure Frank could hear her brain working through the various scenarios. But he remained indifferent, preferring to flick through the newspaper back pages before he would spring up and declare he was going to the Pool Inn for a 'quick pint'. She'd sigh with gratitude and relief when he closed the front door, his hobnailed boots clumping off down the street. Left alone, she'd sit back and close her eyes and let herself drift away, imagining all sorts of scenes with David, laughing and joking and sometimes kissing. It made her feel all warm and tingly inside.

And then, suddenly, it was Wednesday, the day when she was supposed to go shopping with Ida. But when Ida called round, Mary wasn't dressed, hair bedraggled, make-up not applied. "Oh Ida, I'm sorry…it's my turn to be ill."

"Oh God," Ida smiled and shook her head. "I hope you haven't got what I had. It took me days to get myself right. You take care, keep yourself warm. Do you need anything, from the chemist?"

"From the chemist?"

"Yes. Pills or something, make you feel better?"

"Oh – no, I'm fine. Thanks all the same. I'll call round when I'm feeling up to it."

"Frank's mother got Matthew?"

"Thank goodness."

"All right. Well, take it easy."

Mary stood in the doorway. As Ida closed the gate, he was there, just across the road, coming home from college. Ida might have noticed him, she might not, but David didn't look up, pretending to fix something on his jacket. Mary knew he was loitering, hopefully with intent. And when Ida had turned the corner, sure enough he came over, flashing that smile of his.

"No shopping again this week?"

"No, I…" she shrugged. "Another lovely day, isn't it."

"Yes. Vale Park again? Do you fancy it?"

She had to stop herself from shouting out and she took a breath, biting her lip, looking around, her best piece of acting since those dreadful school plays at Christmas time. She always played Mary, mother of God. Her name fitted, and her acting ability. Quiet and serene. Not like now. Not hardly. She brushed away her hair. "That would be…nice." Then she smiled, gushing now. "I'll put some powder on, should I?"

"I think that would be nice too."

The day was not like the previous week. There was a seriousness about him this time. As they sat in the cafe, at the same table, drinking from seemingly the same teacups, he was quiet, distant, the world's worries on his shoulders. She reached across and touched his arm. He didn't flinch but he looked sad.

"David…what's the matter?"

He shrugged. "Oh – you know, thinking."

"About what? Do tell me, you look so…*pained*."

"You could say that. I suppose I am…" he forced a smile, but it soon faded. "Mary…" his hand came down on hers, "I see you every day, watch you from my bedroom window. Did you know my room looked out over the street? No, how could you…Well, I sit there and I just watch your house, the lights going on and off, Frank going to the pub at the same time every night, and I wish…I wish I had the courage to come over and sit with you. Be with you. And then, during the day, before I go off to the office, I always glance over. Sometimes you're there and sometimes you smile. But more often you're not, and I'm depressed all through the day. Mary…" His hand squeezed hers, quite hard. But she didn't pull away. She was mesmerised by him, his words like the warm lapping waves of a faraway south-sea island. They were wonderful. "I don't know how to say this other than to just let it all just spill out…"

"Say what, David? Say what?"

"Don't you know? Haven't you guessed?" She shook her head, holding her breath. "I've…oh God…" He put his face in his other hand, ran his fingers through his hair. He looked as if he were in pain and sat there, breathing hard. "Christ – I never…" He looked up, stared deep into her eyes, unblinking, "Mary, I've fallen in love with you."

It took her a moment to register what he'd said. Suddenly those gently lapping waves came to a stop. "*What?*"

He nodded, just the once. "I love you."

Deciding not to take the bus, they walked home, both of them needing to. It was warm, the sky blue. It was as if the whole of nature had come out to cheer David's revelation. But Mary wasn't feeling quite so joyful. His words had left her in a spiral of confused thoughts and emotions. He loved her? Is that what he had said? It was nonsense, of course it was – he was so young, so innocent. Wasn't the truth really a lot more simple – that he was actually *infatuated with* her? Mary ground her teeth, not allowing herself to accept the truth of his words, because if she did then she would be lost. Vulnerable, lonely, full of desire. Her desire to be loved made her an easy target, a vessel waiting to be filled. God, what a mess.

Her head ran in a multitude of directions, all of them ending in confusion. He frightened her, or at least his words frightened her. The implication behind them. Flattering, but meaningless. There could never be anything between them, not like that…not *love*!

Suddenly, they stood outside her house. Hardly any words had crossed between them, but at the door, as he turned to go, she asked him in. He stood for a moment, his head down. She reached out, fingertips brushing his arm. "Just for a minute," she said quietly. "Please."

She held the door open for him, not knowing what might happen, but knowing the air needed to be cleared. David had to understand that life was hard, impossibly hard. Being friends, snatching a few secret moments, that was all well and good, but that was all it could ever be.

He squeezed past her and she felt his body, causing a thrill like an electric shock to run through her. They stood in the hallway, the only sound their breathing. Fast. David looked up and then she felt it all just peel away, all those layers of doubt, questions, confusion. Fear. She stepped forward, hands touching his chest. A tiny sigh and suddenly they kissed.

All the pent-up passion rushed out, the flood gates open at last, and neither seemed able to help themselves. His arms were strong and muscular, the flatness of his stomach, the tautness of his thighs. Youthful, tough and so desirable. Why had she resisted, why had she kept her feelings buried so deep?

They went upstairs and she fell onto the bed. He was kissing her more urgently now, across her throat, down to her breasts. She lay back, overwhelmed by it all, not thinking, just letting it happen. His hands plunged inside her blouse, fingers groping around, urgent, desperate to release her from her clothing and she helped him with her bra. How wanton she felt, how deliciously open. He kissed her on the mouth, his tongue exploring inside and then he sat back and pulled off his trousers and she saw him.

"Oh my God…" she gasped and closed her eyes as he fell onto her again, her skirt torn away, underwear now just a memory and she gasped again as he went into her and she was lost.

"You seem happy."

Mary looked back from the sink, frowning. "Just been a good day, that's all. You?"

Frank shrugged and sat down, sighing loudly. "Like any other. What's for tea?"

"Scouse. Your favourite."

"Christ, we haven't had that for ages. What's the occasion?"

She shrugged, went up to him and leaned over, kissing him gently on the lips. "Just thought you deserved it, that's all."

Frank looked up at her frowning. Mary just smiled and went back to the sink, singing softly as she did so. Life had suddenly become a lot more bearable.

But, as with everything in life, the bubble always bursts. And this particular one was destroyed in the most violent fashion. Neither of them knew about it of course, not until his key was in the door. Those dreadful few seconds of disbelief. The look that flashed between them. The terror.

It was a Friday. Mary had manipulated things so that Gran could take Matthew 'just for a couple of hours' whilst she caught up with some household things. And as it was Friday, David was home early. The house was theirs, and two hours was more than enough. By now they didn't need to rush, everything so gloriously slow, especially the feel of him. She glowed and purred. He was so gentle, so considerate of her needs, bringing her to the peak of satisfaction over and over. She wallowed in him, melded her limbs to his, wrapping herself in the sumptuousness of those moments.

And then Frank came home.

Why he came home at that moment she never discovered. Had someone said something? Perhaps it was his mother, suspicious, guessing that something wasn't quite right. But Mary had never given any reasons for such a reaction. She had been so careful. Frank, too, had never so much as given her a look. No, it must have been pure coincidence.

Whatever it was, David had barely pulled up the zip of his trousers when Frank came through the door. For a second, the world stood still. Mary sat on the edge of the bed, grappling with her bra. She pulled up the bed clothes instinctively, eyes wide and wild. Frank stood transfixed, not really understanding what he was seeing, not daring to believe any of it. Three people, caught in time, none of them knowing what to do or say.

From where she sat everything appeared in slow motion. Frank's reaction, when it came, like a bear awakening from hibernation, disturbed in its cave. He bellowed, rushing forward, his hands outstretched. He rugby tackled David around the waist and they both fell crashing against the dressing table, David crying out as the edge jarred into the small of his back, stunning him momentarily. Quickly recovering, he brought both his fists together in a heavy hammer-blow delivered to the back of Frank's neck. Frank grunted, fell forward onto his knees, his grip released. David swung his knee up hard under Frank's chin, lifting him into the air. As Frank fell backwards, David also fell, his hands holding onto his back, his face screwed up with pain.

Mary screamed. Frank, he was on his feet already, the blood dripping from his mouth, but his eyes filled with fire. Fists bunched, he charged again. But this time David was ready and, from his kneeling position, he launched himself into Frank's midriff and they both went down, fists flaying, a mad tangle of twisted limbs. Mary was out of the bed, screaming, pleading with them to stop as they rolled around the floor, first Frank on top, then David. She was beside herself, not knowing what to do, so she pulled at her hair and stood on the bed, the tears pouring down her face. Frank was like something possessed, screeching like a banshee, cursing and swearing repeatedly, trying to find the knockout blow. Mary had no doubts, having felt the force of Frank's fists on so many occasions, that he would prevail. David was too young, too inexperienced. His body was slim and lithe, where Frank's was larger, stronger. It was only going to be as matter of time. And then what would happen, with David laid out on the floor, what would Frank do then? To her? The thought terrified her.

A left jab as they got to their feet, a head knocked back, then a right cross, superbly delivered. Another left, hard into the midriff, followed by the same left cracking into the temple, and another right cross. It was almost like a boxing match. Well-placed blows, superbly timed, delivered with enormous power. The results of hours and hours in the gym, toning the body and the mind. Accuracy and finesses, over-coming uncontrolled aggression. That's what the trainer always said, '*Never lose your temper. Once you do that, you're dead. Keep focused, wait, and then, when the opening occurs, strike!*' And he did, the final left hook hitting the mass of nerves just below the ear and the lights went out.

Frank hit the floor like a sack of potatoes, crumpling into uncon-sciousness, his nose smacking against the carpet with a sickening snap, the blood leaking out instantly.

Mary stopped, hands against her mouth, hardly daring to believe what she witnessed. David stood there, bent double, breathing hard, one hand clamped against his back. He put his other hand out to steady himself, but he missed the side of the bed, lost balance and fell to his knees. Mary jumped over to him, holding him, pressing her face into his shoulder, sobbing uncontrollably.

It was over. All of it. Not just the fight, but the snatched afternoons, the visits to Vale Park, the wonderful moments in bed together. All of it, destroyed in a few short minutes. When Frank finally came round, what would he do, what would he say? And Matthew? What was to happen? Life had been ripped violently apart into shreds and there was no way it could ever be put back again. So she held onto him, not wanting him to go, not wanting it to end. Not yet, not just yet.

"Christ Mary..." He pushed himself away, wincing as he got to his feet. He looked down at Frank's inert body, pinched the bridge of his nose and took a deep, rattling breath. "Christ..."

She tenderly led him over to the bed. "Lie down, on your front."

He did so, happy to let her cool fingers examine the growing bruise across his back. "Don't move," she said and ran downstairs to the part of the kitchen where she kept the medicines. She came back up at a rush. Frank still lay there, but she couldn't give a damn about him. Sploshing witch hazel onto a piece of lint, she gently dabbed at David's rapidly expanding bruise. He gasped, arching his back as she applied the liquid. "Just lie there," she said, kissing his neck, "you'll be all right."

"Will I?"

"Of course you will. My God, David. I never believed I'd see anyone do that to Frank. How—"

"I box," he said simply. "I've been boxing since I was seven years of age."

"You *box*?" She almost laughed. She obviously knew there was something; he was superbly muscled, his body taut and lean. But his face, there wasn't a mark. None of those tell-tale signs, the flattened nose, the heavy, thick eyebrows. "I never realized."

"Charlie, my trainer, says I'm good. Taught me everything I know. He boxed for Scotland in the national championships, before the War. Tough as old boots he is. God, he's going to murder me when he hears about this."

"Murder...?" The word sent a shock wave through her body. Because that was something she knew Frank would be capable of when he finally came round. David rolled over, grinning up at her. His torso was heavy with perspiration and she ran her hands over his chest, feeling the hardened muscles there. "You were amazing." She looked back at her unconscious husband. "Is he going to be all right?"

"I hope so. Is he still breathing?"

"God, don't say that."

"Why? Isn't it what you want? To be free of him?"

"Yes, but not like *this*...God, what the hell are we going to do?"

"I don't know." He held her arms and slowly sat up, bending forward to kiss her. "One thing's for sure, you can't stay here. Get a bag, pack it with whatever you need, then you can come and stay with me until we figure out what we're going to do."

But doing that was going to be a long and fraught process, one which might never give them the ending they both yearned for. To be together.

12

On the same morning that Brian Randall received his package, brought to him by a sneering prison warder, Larry took Jed to one side and sat him down in the lounge, a cup of tea in front of him.

"That story Mat told us," Larry Meres said, shifting uncomfortably in his chair, "it got me to thinking."

"About what?"

"Stuff. Honesty. Being honest."

"I don't get you, Dad. What are you talking about? Don't you think Matthew was telling us the truth about what happened, is that it?"

"No, not him, Jed. Me. I want to be honest about *me.*"

"Now I'm really confused." Jed took a sip of his tea and made a face. "No sugar!"

"Sorry." It was a welcome pause and Larry went off into the kitchen to get some sugar. He leaned against the sink for a moment, wondering if he was about to do the right thing and sorted it out in his head how best to proceed. He felt like a blind man stumbling down a darkened tunnel, hopelessly lost.

"Dad?"

Larry jumped and turned around. He smiled, handed over the sugar bowl. "Sorry."

"What's wrong, Dad?" Jed heaped in three spoonfuls. "Has it got anything to do with me going back to school on Monday?"

"No." Larry sat down and gestured for his son to follow. "I just need you to sit there, listen for a moment and – and try not to judge me too harshly."

"Huh?"

"Look, this isn't easy, so I'll just come right out with it." He took a breath. "You know that woman who lives around the corner. Mrs Randall."

Jed frowned. "Yeah."

"She's – well, she's attractive, wouldn't you say?"

Jed sat back. "I've never really noticed."

"No? Well, trust me, she is. Very."

"I met her son. Brian. He was inside with me, in Risley."

"Ah, yes… of course. Well, it was whilst you were *inside* that it happened."

"What?"

Larry took in a deep breath, head down, staring at the tea, conscious of Jed's eyes boring into him. This was it, the moment. Time to bite the bullet. "I slept with her."

Brian Randall sat on the edge of his bunk, fingering the photographs in his hand. There was no note, just six photographs, very clear, well focused. They were of his mother and a man, a man he vaguely recognised, both of them locked together in various stages of undress. As he sat, he wondered why anyone would send them to him. She lived her own life, had admirers, but nobody serious, not since Sullivan. And the man in the photograph was not Detective Sullivan, that was for sure. He'd confronted her about the policeman, shocked and disgusted as he was. She didn't say much, offering up no reasons, no explanations. In the end, he put to the back of his mind. And now these. A series of lewd photographs of two middle-aged people having sex. He turned one of them over and thought for a moment. What was the point?

It was the third one that had the name written on it, in thick felt-tip: *MERES.*

Here was the reason.

Brian looked at the face of the man again, contorted as it was in ecstasy and recognised him. Jed Mere's father.

"I can understand why you're upset, and I'm sorry."

Jed Sat, unable to think straight, stunned by his dad's revelations. The past few days had flashed by in a sort of hazy, otherworldliness, difficult enough to understand let alone this. His anger boiled, at everyone. Matthew alone revealed the secrets of his family. So he sat and he looked but said not a word.

"At least say something."

Shrugging, Jed folded his arms, "I'm not upset, dad. Surprised, maybe even shocked, but not upset." Looking at his dad, the anger slipped away. Dad had lost everything and each unearthed piece of information about Mum forced him to revaluate his feelings for the woman he thought he knew "Are you going to see her again? I mean, is this the start of a new relationship?"

Larry let his head drop. "No, Jed. It was – it was nothing more than a brief and very stupid fling. It was over before it began."

"So why tell me? Why now?"

"After today, after what Matthew told us, I thought it for honesty and openness. About everything."

"Everything? I'm not sure if I want to know *everything*, dad."

"Everything to do with us, don't you think? Too many unspoken things have gone on, too much hiding in dark corners, frightened of the truth. I wanted you to know before you heard it from someone else. I didn't want you to be on the receiving end of someone's vicious attempt at hurting us. I think we've both been hurt enough."

Jed stood up, leaving his tea, went upstairs to his room and flopped down on his bed. Staring at the ceiling, he tried to keep his mind blank, letting the moments drift by, emptying his head.

From a hundred miles away or more, the telephone rang. He didn't stir. It was only when his dad called out who it was that Jed sat bolt upright in his bed, suddenly very alert.

It was Jon Kepowski.

13

They arranged to meet by the lake, where Jed had rescued Jon from the icy depths all that time ago. Coming round the corner, it seemed like a very different place, the frost having retreated, snowdrops sprouting. Elderly couples drifted by, mothers pushed prams. Spring was in the air, lightening everyone's mood.

All except for Jed.

"Jed!"

He looked up and saw Jon Kepowski, waving furiously. He appeared healthier, less gaunt. His eyes still burned with the same intensity Jed had first noticed in the hospital. Strangely hypnotic, those eyes drew him in, causing Jed's heart to beat faster, bringing such a rush of emotion he struggled to stop himself from flinging his arms around him.

But as they drew closer, Jed noticed the same ghastly grey pallor and suddenly he was in anguish.

"God, you look awful," Jed said without thinking.

"Thanks. You don't look so bad yourself."

"I'm sorry, I mean—"

Jon held up his hand, grinning broadly, his cheekbones prominent beneath the rice-paper skin, the teeth like piano keys, far too large for such a thin mouth. "How have you been?" He hugged Jed without preamble, sending a surge of warmth over him, causing his knees to weaken. Gripping his newfound friend's thin, yet well-muscled arms,

Jed beamed, realising nothing else mattered, except being close to his friend. Safe at last.

"I'm fine," Jed gasped.

Jon held him at arm's reach and looked him straight into the eyes. Jed felt as if he was being spun round in a wild, flamboyant dance, losing control, head whirling, becoming giddy, out of control. From somewhere a voice, calm and soothing, spoke to him, the words indistinct, yet wrapping him in a warm blanket of well-being. He never wanted this moment to end.

Slowly, he grew aware of Jon talking and everything was back as it was. "Come and sit down," said Jon. He took Jed by the elbow, he steered him towards a park bench. "Now, tell me all about this police nonsense."

Jed shook his head, still recovering from what had happened, breathless and confused. "Police nonsense?"

"They interviewed you."

"Ah, yes. It was nothing – I lost my temper, took a few swings—"

"No, I meant about this nurse girl. The one they found murdered behind the library. Do they think you did it?"

"God, I hope not."

"But they took you in for questioning?"

"Yeah, but they released me…although I'm still a suspect, apparently."

"I see. Then you hit a couple of policemen and found yourself in remand. Why did they let you go?"

This was like being back in the police interview room. Jed shifted uncomfortably, "They said…they said that there were mitigating circumstances – that because of what happened I wasn't responsible for my actions."

"With your mum leaving?"

"That's right." How did he know all this? Who had he been speaking to, and why all these questions. Jed felt a buzzing like a bee in his head. He pressed his knuckles against his temples, trying to ease the increasing pressure. "I don't feel too good."

"No, I know, but it's all right." He squeezed Jed's hand, just as he had in the hospital and Jed felt instantly relaxed. "So, they let you go. Just like that. You did a deal with them, is that it?"

Jed looked up, his eyes narrowing as the buzzing increased, "No – I told you – God, my head!"

A whooshing sound, like that of water bursting from a damn, replaced the bee. A massive rush of sound.

"Look at me, Jed."

Taking him by the jaw, Jon turned Jed's head towards him.

Those eyes, so beautiful, so kind, they swallowed Jed up and he didn't resist. He didn't want to. Drawn ever deeper, the whooshing diminished, and soothing relief washed over him, bringing such a sense of bliss Jed relaxed totally, sinking into a warm, luxurious bath of sheer ecstasy. His body grew limp and he hung there, supported in Jon's grip, surrendering to the gorgeousness swirling all around him.

"Tell me, Jed. Did you do a deal?"

"Yes." That single word floated from between his lips, unforced. The thrill of the confession made him want to cry, the release venting from him; to be in this person's control was so luxurious, so wonderful, almost like entering a state of grace.

"Tell me everything, Jed."

Jon's voice, so warm yet so powerful. A glorious voice, liquid velvet, like a song sung by an angel. A voice that he could listen to forever.

"Unburden yourself, let it go. Don't resist. Tell me."

Oh, but he wanted to. Electricity coursed through his stomach, loins enflamed with desire, and his erection grew uncontrolled. He would do anything Jon asked of him, anything at all. "I love you," he said, voice barely a whisper.

Jon smiled, stroking his cheek, "I know you do, and it's all right. Everything is going to be all right now. What did Sullivan want you to do?"

Without taking a breath, Jed let it gush out, "He wanted me to stay friendly with Brian Randall. To get close. *Closer*. Become part of his gang, his operation. He wanted me to find out details of meetings and transactions and then, when the big deal came in, he wanted me to tell him where it was all going to take place, and when."

"Drug deals? Is that what he wanted?"

"Yes. The names of the *big-boys*. He's not interested in Brian, he's just small-time. He wants the whole operation."

"And did he mention me in any of this?"

"You? No."

"Are you sure, Jed? You wouldn't lie to me, would you?"

"I'd never lie to you. I promise."

"Good boy."

Slowly, Jon let go of Jed's face and turned to stretch out his legs, facing the lake.

Jed stared into nothing, mind clouded by sleep. He felt groggy, head thick with cotton wool. Gradually, feeling returned to his limbs, senses normalised. A glow pulsed through him, exhilarating in its intensity, a breath-taking adrenalin rush as if he had experienced the most exciting fairground ride of his life. Head fizzing, he broke into unconstrained laughter. Jon laughed too and that seemed to make it even more special. Jed put his head on his friend's shoulder and closed his eyes as Jon's arm snaked around his shoulders. He was safe now and nothing else mattered. Jon was here.

Sunday, the sun full, bringing a sense of fulfilment, almost joy to Jed as he slipped out from under his bed sheets, went over to his window and looked out at the view. He wasn't sure why he felt so good, but he knew it had to do with more than just the sunshine, however welcome. He thought he might go for a walk, maybe catch a bus down to Parkgate. He used to do that when he was younger, with his parents. He always loved strolling down the old quayside, calling in to buy some freshly caught shrimps, followed by the marvellous homemade ice cream. Another existence, before his mother decided to shatter the lives of those around her. A wave of bitterness rolled over him but he fought against it, knowing dwelling on the past never did him any good. What was it Jon had said...

His eyes opened but he no longer focused on the view. All he was aware of was the massive gap in his memory. Not memories of long ago, of his parents, or of ice creams, but closer, more recent ones. It hit him like a blow – he couldn't recall a single word that had passed between him and Jon during their meeting, not one! How could that be possible? He ground his teeth, trying desperately to trawl up something – anything. He remembered the lake, greeting him, but then…nothing. A total blank. Did they even speak to one another? A vague image swam around, of walking home past the allotments, the smell of compost bringing him out of a sort of daze, but that was all. No recollection of any conversation. It was bizarre.

After a shower, this nagging worry over his lack of memory turned into a deep concern. How could he forget everything like that? He'd heard of mental blackouts, of people blocking out huge chunks from their lives due to some massive trauma, an incident so terrible that the brain refused to accept it. Was that what had happened to him? Was he suffering from delayed shock over his mother leaving, was that it? Flopping down on his bed, he slipped Ziggy *Stardust and the Spiders From Mars* onto the turntable and waited for the opening chords to take him to another, far better place. Rolling onto his back, he closed his eyes.

He sat up with a start, rubbing his eyes, the record long since finished playing. Something had woken him, something sinister, but he didn't know what. An image of Jon Kepowski's face loomed large in his mind, those eyes burning with a frightening intensity, like one of those voodoo witch doctors, tainted with insanity, capable of the most heinous acts. The image changed, Jon metamorphosing into a bright red-skinned genie, gyrating wildly, mouth wide open, rotting black stumps of teeth gnashing away, drooling lips, a rabid animal.

Crying out, Jed swung his legs over the edge of his bed and gaped towards his window, the world beyond the glass so calm, so reassuring. And as he stared, he realised why he couldn't remember.

Jon had hypnotised him.

14

As usual, Jed found Dad rooting around in the freezing confines of the garden shed, and placed a steaming hot cup of tea on the workbench. He smiled his thanks, wrapped his cold, red fingers around the cup and took a sip. Smacking his lips he said, "I've lost some tools, don't suppose you've moved anything, have you?"

"No." Jed rubbed his hands together, and shivered. "How can you stand it in here, Dad? It's freezing."

Larry shrugged, "Don't think about it. Anyway, thanks for the tea." He returned to pulling away planks of wood and old tarpaulins in his search.

Jed wandered back into the house, picking up his own tea from the kitchen table. He was about to go into the living room when the telephone rang. It was Jon.

"Jed, my good friend, how are you feeling?"

Unease settled over him, the question strange, baseless. "Fine. You?"

"Peachy. Listen, you fancy coming out for a drink tonight? I need to talk to you about something."

"A drink? I'm not really—" he stopped himself before saying something, which might invite derision. Jed was eighteen, so could legally enter any pub, but his discomfort over the previous day clung to him like a second skin. If Jon had hypnotised him, what was to stop him doing it again. "I'm sorry, Jon, but I'm not feeling too well and I'd—"

"You'd like to come," said Jon, voice as smooth as silk. So warm, so soft, a lovely, thick fleece wrapping around Jed's shoulders.

Jed drifted, lost in the wondrous, seductive, irresistible tones of his friend's voice. His throat thickened with desire and he breathed, "Of course I'd like to come. Anything for you. Anything at all. What time would you like me there?"

* * *

Dad grunted when Jed told him he was going out, but not where. '*Just out to see a friend,*' he'd said, '*I won't be long.*' Now he was lying to his dad, but somehow, he didn't care, his mind overcome with excitement at meeting his friend once again. Even as he stood outside the entrance to *The Clarion* public house some hours later, picturing Dad sitting in the lounge, all alone with nothing to do except stare at the television, he didn't care. Jon was inside. The world could fall apart around Jed's ears, but nothing would stop him from racing up to Jon Kapowski and bathe in his glory once again.

The public bar stank, as he expected it to. The faces of the few locals ensconced against the counter turned and glared at him, just like the worst scene in the worst type of Western. Avoiding them, Jed went towards the barman and was about to order himself a pint when a heavy hand came down on his shoulder. He turned round and breathed a huge sigh of relief.

"Thought you'd never get here," said Jon, beaming broadly. He clicked his fingers at the barman, who snarled at first, but was soon grinning as Jon leaned forward and said, loud enough for all to hear, "Two pints of larger please Jeff. On the slate." Jeff nodded and poured the drinks without a word. Jon gripped Jed's shoulder even tighter, "We'll go upstairs and have a game of pool. It starts getting busy in about half an hour, so we'll chat first before playing a game or two. You play pool, don't you?"

"A little."

"A little is all we need."

Jeff slammed the lagers down on the bar

The lagers came down with a slam and Jon immediately picked up his glass and downed it in one, smacking his lips when he'd finished. It all appeared a little too theatrical and Jed suspected this was the beginning of some sort of test.

Jon waited, not saying a word, his eyes looking to Jed's glass. Picking it up, Jed took a tentative sip. It tasted flat and not very good.

"Good, isn't it?" Jon winked and ordered another, then took Jed by the elbow and led him upstairs.

At the top of the stairs, the room opened up in a sort of L-shape, dominated by at least ten pool tables laid end-to-end. At the far end stood a small bar, closed for the moment, with a juke-box and a trio of one-armed bandits adjacent. A group of young toughs sat at a nearby table, sipping their drinks, but they were the only customers. The place was dark, dank and unfriendly. Jed hated it.

"The atmosphere heats up when people start arriving," explained Jon and sat down on a stool beside the first pool table. He slapped down a twenty pence piece, reserving their position for the first game. "Winner stays on," said Jon. "If you're good, you hardly have to spend a penny. Are you good, Jed?"

Jed caught the mocking tone, the single arched eyebrow, the expectant look. Jon's question appeared loaded with innuendo, but Jed kept his voice as neutral as he could, saying, "I'm okay, I guess."

"Well, we'll soon see, won't we?" Stretching out his legs, Jon's settled his unblinking gaze on his young companion. "Jed, I need to ask you something. It may seem strange, but…Well, it's just something I need you to do for me."

Intrigued, Jed sat forward, taking another sip from his pint, which was becoming more palatable. "Go on."

Jon's voice grew more hesitant, almost as if he were thinking things through as he spoke. "I understand how tough things are for you right now. The police, that trouble with your mum…and your exams will be here soon. May, isn't it?" Jed nodded. "I need to go to Scotland, Jed.

I have to go and talk to someone up there, and I was wondering…if you'd come with me."

Taken aback, Jed gave a snigger. This was not what he was expecting. "Scotland? Well, yes, sure, I'd love to but… But, when, Jon? Like you said, my exams…"

"I know, and I've thought about that, but you have exam leave, don't you? A few days between each one? You see, it'll only take three days, perhaps even two. We would only really have to stay over one night. It'll be a rush, but we could do it."

"I suppose…I'd have to look at my timetable, when I get it tomorrow." Another sip. Definitely tasting better now. "Why do you need me to go with you?"

Jon chuckled to himself, drank, then turned his face towards Jed, who gasped, those eyes so intense. "Protection."

"*Protection*? What does that mean? Protection from what?"

"Oh, you'll see…" Jon turned away to stare into the distance.

Studying him, Jed unconsciously rubbed his fingers over his throat, massaging away the lump developing there.

He became aware of others trickling into the room, exchanging greetings with the toughs at the far end. None so much as glanced towards Jon and Jed, until a large shape loomed close by and a voice, filled with menace, rumbled, "Well, well, if it isn't my old mate, Jed."

Sighing, Jed had no need to look up to know who the owner of the voice was, but he did so anyway. "Hello Watson."

Still sporting an impressive bruise across the bridge of his nose, Watson stood with arms folded, head tilted to one side, leering. Two others flanked him whom Jed didn't recognise but who were equally as large as Watson.

"A friend of yours?" Jon asked, touching Jed's arms lightly.

The atmosphere grew charged, a heavy threat hanging in the air. Jed sat back, trying to look relaxed. "Oh yeah, Watson and I go way back."

"Yeah," Watson's head bobbed forward a few times, his smile false. He touched the bruise and the smile faded. "We've got some unfinished business, Meres."

Jed smirked. "Thought you would have had enough of *lessons*, Watson. Didn't you learn anything from the last one?"

Watson bristled, conscious no doubt of his friends so close. "You were lucky – took me by surprise you did, you little shit."

"That's not what I heard."

Several sets of eyes turned towards Jon in astonishment. Watson's lips curled back over his teeth. "And who the fuck are you?"

"A friend."

"Oh. And what have you heard, *friend*?"

Everyone waited, including Jed, who longed to hear the answer also.

"I understand Jed here bounced you on your big, fat arse. And not before time either."

Watson gaped at Jon in horror, but before hell erupted, Jed leapt to his feet, forcing a smile. "Jon, please, just leave it. Watson, this is between you and me. Tomorrow, after school, we'll finish it."

Watson, still glaring at Jon, barely registered Jed's words. "Eh?" He turned his burning eyes Jed's way. "Yeah, all right, but you keep yourself nice and warm and cosy until then, eh Jed? Wouldn't want you getting a cold or something, keeping you off school."

"I'll be there, Watson. Don't worry."

"Oh, I won't be worrying, Jed. Not me. You see, it's you I'm really worried about, now that mummy's not there to tuck your shirt in."

Jed held his breath. "What did you say?"

It was as if the film had gone into freeze-frame. The audience agog, expectant, waiting to see what would happen next. Watson, who seemed oblivious to the affect his words were having, ploughed on. "Yeah. Heard she ran off with the milkman, or was it the postman?" He swung around to his mates, his chosen audience for the night. "Jeez, it could be both of them for all I know. For all *anyone* knows."

Jed hit him then. A short punch, delivered with tremendous power, striking Watson on the point of the chin. It was just like before, in the playground at school. Watson went down like a bag of spanners, except this time his head hit the edge of the pool table as he fell, making a sickening, dull thud. As he crumpled it became clear he wouldn't be getting up again for quite a while.

They stood there rock still, everyone shocked at the suddenness of it all. So quick, so utterly massive in its outcome.

Breathing hard, like a wild beast, snarling, fists clenching and un-clenching, Jed turned to Watson's two compatriots, coiling himself like a loaded spring, preparing to strike, "You want some."

"Fuck off!" said one of them. Jed didn't know which one, and he didn't really care. All of his anger and frustration, fears and upset boiled over in that single instant. He tore into them, fists lashing out, head thrusting forward. He caught the nearest one in the throat with the three fingers of his right hand, and the boy fell back, gagging, spluttering, as if in a drunken stupor. The second, so much bigger, and perhaps more experienced, brought his arms up to protect his face, a move which proved useless as Jed cracked him in the shin with the toe of his shoe. Yelping, the teenager pitched forward and Jed hit him in the side of the head with a swinging left hook, square on the temple, dropping him to his knees. He would have hit him again, but Jon was there, arms around him, hugging him in a bear-like grip, holding him back, yelling down his ear, "Leave it, Jed – *leave it!*"

Struggling like one possessed, Jed tried his best to tear himself from Jon's embrace, but failed whilst, at his feet, stunned, aware the fight was over, were Watson's two companions, their eyes wild, betraying their fear.

As for Watson, he remained flat out, his face a ghastly shade of grey.

"I'll kill him," cried Jed, desperate to get loose, unleash more pain, more violence. But Jon proved too strong and bundled him down the stairs before anything else could happen.

"What the hell's going on up there?"

The barman met them on the bottom step, eyes round with concern. Jon held up an appeasing hand, "Nothing, Jeff. Nothing at all. Just a little argument. It's all over now."

"I don't want no trouble with the police," growled Jeff. "Not after the last time."

"I told you, it's all sorted. "

Jon wrestled Jed out into the cool evening air and slammed him against the nearest wall, pinning him there, a hand on his throat, a physical demonstration of his control, his power. And Jed could feel his strength. He squirmed as Jon snarled. "What the hell was all that about?"

"You heard him – you heard what he said!"

"I heard him, yeah. But the other two? What are you trying to do, get yourself put down for murder? You could have killed that lad, Jed. Christ, when his head hit that table…I'm going back in, make sure he's all right. You go home. I'll ring you tomorrow. After school. Get those dates when you can manage to get away, and we'll arrange the trip to Scotland." He stepped back, letting out a long breath. "Just go home, Jed. Relax, try and forget what's happened. I'll ring you tomorrow. All right?"

Jed nodded meekly, the red veil slowly slipping away. "I'm sorry, Jon. It just…I don't know, I couldn't control myself. Sorry."

Jon smiled. "Don't worry. Everything's going to be okay."

But everything wasn't okay.

Jed got up the following morning, barely giving the previous night a thought. What had happened had happened, but at least there were going to be no repercussions. Not like the last time. As he went out the front door, he smiled as the bright sun hit him flat in the face. Spring was definitely in the air making returning to school bearable. Even when the patrol car slid up next to him, he didn't think anything was amiss, not even when the door opened and a uniformed policeman stepped out to bar Jed's way.

"Jed Meres?"

Jed pulled himself up and frowned. The man didn't look pleased. "Yes."

"Do you know a young person by the name of Craig Watson?"

He should have known. Watson, for all his bravado was nothing but a wimp. A lying, chicken-livered wimp. He'd grassed him up, betrayed the code. Jed's shoulders slumped. "Yeah, I k now him. What's he been saying about me?"

"*Saying*?" The man leaned forward, "He hasn't been saying anything. He's dead."

15

The two police detectives sat across the interview table from Jed, Sullivan, looking crumpled, and a fresh-faced ginger-haired detective sporting crisply ironed shirt, immaculately pressed jacket and sensible tie. He seemed keen, in direct contrast to Sullivan whose eyes smouldered under heavy, brooding brows.

"April 14, nineteen seventy-one, Detective Sergeant Thomas Sullivan and DC Nolan, Wallasey CID. It is..." Nolan pulled back his cuff and peered at his watch, "8.52 am. Interview with Jethroe Meres, known as Jed. Mr Meres has refused legal representation. Is that correct, Mr Meres?"

Jed nodded.

"You have to speak, Mr Meres. For the tape."

"For the tape?" Jed spat back, voice laced with sarcasm. He sat back, smirking. "That's right, I don't need legal representation – I haven't done anything."

"Hopefully that is what this interview will determine. Did you know Craig Watson?"

"You know very well I did."

"Could you just answer the questions, without all the elaborations, please, Mr Meres."

"It's Jed, and *yes*, I know Watson. We went to school together. Same class."

"*Went?*"

Sullivan had interjected, leaning forward, jaw set hard. Jed frowned, confused. "Sorry?"

"You said *went*."

"Well, he's dead – isn't he?"

Jed caught the glare from Sullivan before he turned to Nolan, who blew out his cheeks. Sullivan coughed and sat forward on his elbows, resting his chin on his fists. His eyes never left Jed's. "We know one another, don't we Jed? We've spoken before, about Nurse Willis. You remember that, don't you? What you said? I'm going to ask you some of the same questions, Jed, only this time I want you to be absolutely truthful in your replies. Do you understand that, Jed?"

"Of course I do, I'm not an idiot."

Nolan gave a tiny chuckle and Sullivan shot him a dangerous glance. "DC Nolan is now showing Mr Meres – Jed – some photographs."

The younger detective gave a start and hurriedly reached inside his jacket to produce a thin, manila envelope. He opened it, took out a series of black and white photographs and laid them down on the tabletop, one at a time. Jed looked at them. The first one was of the nurse, her face smiling out at the camera. Natural, like a holiday snap. It was a little out of focus and looked as if it had been blown-up, to concentrate on just her head and shoulders. The second was of a tough looking young man, unsmiling, eyes contemptuous. Not taken at any holiday, it seemed to Jed like one of those photographs he had seen on the television, taken on arrival at prison. Full face, then profile. It was Peter Davey, the nurse's boyfriend. The third was of Watson, a school photograph, big chubby face, dimpled chin and cheeks. He looked almost kind.

"I've seen these before," Jed offered, feeling bored. He tapped the one showing Peter Davey. "I don't know him, not personally. But you told me last time it was Nurse Willis's boyfriend. That's all I know about him."

"You threatened Craig Watson that you would kill him if he said anything more about your mother," continued Sullivan unabashed, "and last night, he did, didn't he?"

Jed's stomach lurched as the memories of the previous came rushing back to him. Suddenly, he felt ill. His face must have betrayed his feelings because Nolan sprang forward, eager to strike. "You attacked him, didn't you? Just like you did at school, only this time you went further, didn't you? This time you killed him, in a fit of rage."

"No, I—"

"You've got one hell of a temper, Jed, Sergeant Sullivan can vouch for that. Touchy about your mum, aren't you? Don't like anyone saying anything about her, do you? So, when Watson starts bad-mouthing her, you hit him. And then later, when he comes out of the pub, you follow him and you murder him, just like you did Nurse Willis. Just like you did Peter Davey."

Trapped, a rabbit in the spotlight, Jed snapped his face from one policeman to the other. "No, you're wrong."

"Wrong? I don't think so, do you Sergeant Sullivan?"

"No I don't. You murdered him, Jed. In cold blood."

"No, no, it's not like that," Jed blurted out. "All right, I argued with him in the pub, I hit him. Too right I did, he's a shit and he deserved it – but kill him? No, I couldn't – I *wouldn't* do that. I didn't go back to the pub; I didn't follow him. All of that, none of it ever happened."

"So what did happen, Jed?" Sullivan voice quiet this time, not angry like Nolan's. They had a deal, didn't they? An arrangement, an understanding? Sullivan knew the truth. And there was another connection.

It hit Jed right in the face, the full glare of the flood lights switching on, hurting his eyes. He saw it all so clear. Sullivan, Brian Randall and his mother Hannah – and his own dad. There was the link, the connection. Sullivan was working them all in some wildcat scheme, and now he wanted Jed out of the way. Jed shook his head, rubbing his fists into his eyes. "This is madness," he said quietly, voice barely above a whisper. "I went straight home; my dad will vouch for me."

"We've spoken to your dad," said Nolan, continuing to sneer. "Nice man, your dad. Cares. He said you got in around midnight."

Something gripped Jed, something cold and terrifyingly strong, squeezing him tight. Slowly he dragged his hands from his face and gaped at Nolan. "No," his voice tiny, very afraid. "No, that's not true. I got home no later than nine. I left the pub and went straight home. Dad was watching tele and I went to bed – Christ, I'm supposed to be at school today."

"You waited outside the pub and followed Watson. He went along the prom, past the *Floral Pavilion*. It was there you confronted him, hit him again, dragged him into the theatre gardens and there you bashed his head in with a hammer."

"Just like Peter Davey," said Sullivan. His voice sounded almost sad.

Jed's eyes darted from Nolan to Sullivan. His mouth now so dry he could hardly speak. He was behind the wheel of a runaway vehicle, no brakes, careering out of control. There was nothing he could do, nowhere to go, no one to help.

"You still sure you don't want legal representation?"

Jed put his face in his hands and tried to gather his wits, escape from the nightmare all around him. Why would Dad say he didn't come in until after midnight? Why tell a lie – for what reason?

He stopped. A horrible thought reared up inside.

What if it were true? There was the blackout he'd suffered over the meeting with Jon, and Jon was with him at *The Clarion*. What if he'd suffered another bout? Had he actually done these terrible things without realizing it? Could he truly be a schizophrenic, his mind detached from his actions?

Sullivan placed a plastic cup full of steaming tea in front of Jed, then sat down with a sigh. Nolan had gone off somewhere and the tape machine stood silent. "I can't protect you if you don't tell the truth."

Jed looked up. He felt exhausted. The questions had continued, on and on, without let up. Eventually he chose to clam up and that was when Sullivan had called for a break. *An opportunity*, he had said, *to get your brain in gear!*

"I didn't do it."

"I hope not. But it's not looking good. Both Davey and Watson murdered in almost identical manner, your alibi as weak as dishwater – you've got motive *and* opportunity, Jed."

"But we had a deal."

"That was before you started falling apart, Jed. I thought I could use you to help me find a way in..." He shook his head, his face looking sad. "I'm not sure it would work now."

"Why? Why wouldn't it work?" Jed threw out his hands, despair welling up inside. "You know I didn't do any of this, I'm just not *capable*. You're framing me, and I think I know why."

"You've been watching too much TV, Jed. We don't frame people, not in the real world. We don't have to. We deal with evidence, witnesses, *proof*."

"Are you sure about that, Sergeant?"

Sullivan cocked his head to one side, "What does that mean?"

"You know I know. That's what this is all about, isn't it? It has nothing to do with Watson or anyone else, because if it had you would have charged me by now."

"That could still happen. We're just waiting for the lab results. Once we match the blood on your jacket to that of Watson, you're going down, son. It's as simple as that."

Smiling, Jed shook his head. "Well, his blood will be on my jacket, won't it? I knocked him out, in the pub. You know that, so don't try and scare me into confessing something I didn't do. Like I said to your sidekick, I'm not an idiot."

"You're too damned cock-sure, that's for certain. No wonder you haven't got any friends."

"I've got friends, Sergeant Sullivan." He smiled. "Like Brian Randall."

"Yeah, well, like I said, that's not going to happen now. The deal has ended. Things have moved on."

"With Brian's mother, you mean?"

Sullivan's face went white and he swayed, as if struck by something. For a moment Jed thought the policeman was going to faint. Then Sullivan recovered, gave a little laugh. "What the hell are you talking about?"

"Brian told me all about it, but I didn't know who she was and what the connection was until my own dad told me what had happened.

You see, he had a fling with her too." Jed nodded, gaining courage from Sullivan's ashen face. "Yeah. The same woman. Whilst I was in Risley, Brian told me a story about you, how you'd become involved with his mum. And whilst I'm in there, listening to all of this, my own dad has a fling with the same woman. And now, here I am. Bit of a coincidence, don't you think?"

Whether coincidence or not, less than an hour later, Jed was standing in front of Mr Phillips' desk, crestfallen as his Headteacher berated him about time-keeping, responsibility, hard-work, endeavour and perseverance. He listened to it all, without saying a word. He took it on the chin because he knew he had no other choice. Then he slinked off to his next available lesson and sat at the back, unable to concentrate, just going through the motions. At break time, he got a message to return to the Head's office. He knew what it was about. The little panda car was in the school car park. As Jed went through the door, he had to step aside to allow the uniformed constable to squeeze past. He didn't say a word. But Phillips did, after he'd spent a long time looking at his fingers drumming on his desk top.

"My God, Jed, my God…"

"I didn't do it, Mr Phillips. I swear to you."

Phillips looked up. Had he even heard what Jed had said? His lips were trembling. "My God, the papers are going to have a field day."

16

He was waiting for Jed as school finished for the day. Brian Randall. He stood opposite the main gate, sitting on a garden wall, smoking a cigarette. No doubt he felt it made him look tough – school was behind him; he could do what the hell he liked. Two fingers up to authority. Jed wasn't impressed.

"Hello Brian. You waiting for me?"

Randall threw the cigarette away, half finished. "I need to talk to you."

"I'm all ears."

"Not here, dickhead. Let's walk down to the park."

The local park was just a under a hundred yards from the school, a large, uncared for space where no one ever visited. A few broken swings hung there like skeletons, dead and useless. No children played there, the broken tarmac ground waiting to cut open knees and graze hands. Jed thought it should be bulldozed over.

Brian Randall found a rickety bench and sat down, wringing his hands, staring at the ground. "I got out yesterday. Court appearance at nine, case dismissed by half past."

"That's great." Jed frowned because nothing about Randall seemed to speak of celebrations. "Isn't it?"

"I got home about eleven. Mum was out, as always. No one came to meet me at prison – I had to get the bus home. You ever been to Birkenhead Magistrates' Court?" Jed shook his head. "It's horrible.

Cold. When I came out I just wanted someone to be there, you know? Someone to say, 'well done mate!' But there was no one. Not even my bloody mother."

"Brian, I'm sorry, if I'd known…"

Randall looked up, his eyes hard, "I wouldn't have expected you to be there. This isn't what I want to talk to you about."

"Oh. Right."

"You're back at school, everything all rosy in the garden, eh?"

Frowning, Jed struggled to keep his anger under control. "What the hell are you on about?"

Randall turned away and spat onto the ground. "I got home and the house was empty. Well, at least I thought it was. I got myself something to eat, then I heard something upstairs. At first, I thought it was the floor boards creaking, the way they do. But then I heard laughing."

"Laughing?"

"Yeah. More of a *cackle*. So I went upstairs, careful like. I took the bread knife with me, for protection. There was someone up there."

"It was probably your mum."

"Let me finish." He blew out an angry breath. "So, I go upstairs, checking her bedroom first because I'm sure that whoever it is, is in there. Nothing. Then the box-room, which is next to Mum's. It was empty, filled up with all sorts of crap. My room was the same. And the bathroom." He gave Jed a measured stare. "The house was empty. I was the only one there."

Jed nodded, trying not to jump to conclusions too soon. "All right. So … Let's just take this slow. Brian, you'd been locked up in Risley, just got home from a courtroom appearance, so it's it was entirely natural that you should imagine things that weren't real. You were upset your mum hadn't been there to pick you up – she is selfish, unfeeling perhaps, or perhaps she simply didn't know. It's all perfectly understandable, mate. What I don't get is why you would think I—"

"You think I imagined it, don't you?" As Jed went to speak, Randall held up his hand, cutting him off. "Don't worry – I felt they same. At first. Anyway, I go downstairs again, thinking that it must have been outside, so I check the back garden just in case. We've got an outhouse, so I take a look in there. There isn't anyone anywhere in the whole house except me. I go back inside and sit down at the table. Then I hear it again. Laughing. I didn't hang around anymore, I just ran out. It wasn't until I got to Marlowe Road church that I realised I still had the bread knife. Anyway, there's a phone box there, so I rang my mum's friend, Joan. Mum wasn't there, but Joan said I could go round and sit with her for a while. So I did, and she gave me some cheese on toast and we talked."

Without warning, he stood up, breathing hard. He kicked a stone across the ground and went to the rusted swing a few feet away. He settled himself into the hard wooden seat, slowly swinging himself backwards and forwards. The iron chains creaked loudly. Jed watched him, waiting, knowing that there was more to come.

Bringing the swing to a halt, Randall stared into the distance, and spoke again. "She got home around six. Joan spoke to her on the phone and then I went round. Mum seemed happy enough to see me, apologising for not being home. She'd been to Birkenhead shopping, but hadn't seen me, or even thought of me. But, as I thought about it, I realised how stupid I'd been. How was she to know that I'd be getting out, that I even had the hearing? She gave me a big hug and it was all forgotten. Stupid." He fished inside his denim jacket and pulled out a crushed packet of cigarettes. He offered one to Jed, who refused. "So, we sat down for our tea and watched a bit of tele. I was so tired, didn't want to go out. Anyway, I went to bed early, crashed out straight away. But something woke me up – and you can guess what it was, yeah?"

"Laughing."

"Right first time. I sat up, rubbing my eyes, really worried now. My heart was like a hammer, banging away at my chest, trying to break out. I swung my legs out of the bed-clothes and sat still for a long time, trying to get my thoughts together, calm myself down. But I was so afraid, I couldn't think straight. Then I saw him, in the corner of my room. It was so dark he was nothing but a shadow, but I knew it was a man. And he was laughing at me, quietly, mocking me."

"A *man*? Jesus, Bri, in your room? What the hell did you do?"

"Nothing. What could I do? I just sat there and waited for something to happen. I mean, he could have just come over and cut my throat and I wouldn't have been able to do anything about it. I told you, nothing was working. My legs, they were like jelly. I couldn't even shout out to my mum." He threw his cigarette away and put his face in his hands. He was shaking. Jed wanted to put his arm around his shoulders, but resisted, unsure what Brian's reaction might be. So he sat and waited.

Randall dragged his hands down his face, pulling at his skin, exhausted and afraid. "I don't know how I did it, but I reached out and switched on my bedside lamp. Instantly, I could feel the strength coming back into my legs. Funny that, isn't it? The dark, how horrible it can be."

"And the man, Brian? What about the man?"

"That's just it. There was no man. There wasn't anybody there."

"So – so, it *was* a dream?"

Randall shrugged. "At first, I thought it was. Anyway, I went downstairs, got myself a drink. It was around three in the morning. Because I'd gone to bed so early, I didn't feel tired anymore. The house was so cold, so unfriendly at that time in the morning. I opened the back door and stood there, peering out into the backyard, holding my cup of tea, trying to think. And that's when it happened. He came up behind me and grabbed me by the shoulder. I freaked, dropping the teacup and I span round, stepping back out into the backyard. I didn't have any shoes on, but I didn't care about that. I kept walking backwards and all the while he stood there, in the kitchen doorway."

"Who, Brian? The man in your bedroom?"

Randall licked his lips. "Yeah. Except, it wasn't a man. Well, if it was, it was like no man I'd ever seen. It was the same size, and it had arms and legs, but its face, Jed…" he slapped his hands over his eyes again, shaking uncontrollably. Squatting down, Jed clutched at his arm. Randall looked at him through his fingers. "Jed – it was something from hell. A ghoul, a corpse, some sort of horrible monster! It just stood there, its face like a skull, empty eye sockets, a long, thin chin and a mouth that was *so* wide…" He took away his hands. The tears tumbled down his cheeks. "And he laughed, Jed. He stood there and laughed at me."

They walked back up to the main road in silence. It was getting late and the shops were closing. Thinking his dad would be worried, Jed stepped into a phone box and called him, to explain he would be a little late. He managed to persuade Dad all would be fine and when he came out, Randall shot him a concerned glance, one which Jed waved away, smiling. "Listen, Bri, everything is going to be okay – you've got to try and not worry about any of this."

"Not worry? That's easy for you to say – you didn't see it."

"I know, but…" What was he supposed to say that wasn't going to sound feeble? Just down the road was the *Rose and Crown* pub: although Jed wasn't a drinker, he nevertheless thought that it might help Brian in some way, settle his nerves. "Come on, the pub's just opened. I'll buy you a drink."

Randall grunted, but he followed him inside nevertheless.

There were two or three early drinkers standing around. Jed gave them a nod and Jed went to the bar. He ordered two halves and, nodding his thanks to the barmaid, took them over to a corner table. Randall sat down and took a long drink. "I would've preferred a pint," he said.

"Sorry. I'll get you another—"

"No, it doesn't matter. Thanks anyway." He drained the glass, got up and went to get himself another. Again, tipping the glass all the way back, he drained it. After the third half arrived, he joined Jed, wiping his mouth with the back of his hand, and sat down with a loud grunt. "There's something else."

"Oh?" Jed prepared himself for another tale of ghouls in the night.

"Just before I got out, I received a package of photographs."

Jed frowned, feeling uncomfortable. Randall's manner had changed, no longer afraid, more angry.

"They were of my mum, having it off with some bloke. In her bed-room." He reached inside his coat, pulled out the cigarettes, threw the pack on the table, and delved inside his pocket once more. This time he drew out a thick, manila envelope, creased and torn at the corners. Jed watched him, fascinated, as he began to reveal one photograph at a time, placing them onto the table with a deliberate snap. Jed looked down, frozen in horror at what he saw. Two adults, completely naked, making passionate love to one another. It could have been classed as pornography if it wasn't for the fact that Jed recognised both of them. When the last photograph joined the others, he looked up into Ran-dall's face and those eyes of his, wet with tears. He was struggling to keep himself under control. "I want you to tell me what's going on – and then give me one good reason why I don't go round and cut off your dad's balls."

17

There were two things nagging away at Jed as he sat on his bed, listening to *Electric Warrior* by T-Rex. Firstly, why was Brian Randall so angry about his mum and Jed's dad 'getting it together'? He knew what his mum was like, and had been through it all before with Sullivan. These things happen. Okay, it might be a little embarrassing – in all honesty, it was *really* embarrassing, but nothing to get so het-up about, surely. Jed could understand the reaction about Sullivan. A policeman, that close, especially when you had a bit of a track record, like the one Brian had, or still did. But, when it was merely a next-door neighbour. No, it just didn't feel right that Brian should be so threatening, so upset. Perhaps more worrying were the photographs. Who had taken them, and why? Whoever it was must have been in the bedroom, probably hiding in the wardrobe, waiting. To get such intimate shots, it had to be planned. That would mean that the whole affair had been pre-arranged, that there was somebody out there who wanted to manipulate the meeting, get Brian's mum to entice Dad into her bed and then make love to him. But why?

He rubbed at his face, mind going around in circles, forever ending up with the same question – why go to all those lengths to take photographs and then send them to Brian? Was it to cause a rift, to force him to threaten Dad, or perhaps something worse? Blackmail. But, blackmail for what? Dad hadn't broken any laws, he wasn't a man of influence or reputation. And, even more telling – he was not rich.

Flipping the record onto side two, Jed recalled the many conversations they had had whilst on remand. Brian's hallucinations, his paranoia. Everyone against him, plotting, threatening. Jed knew Brian smoked a lot of marijuana, cannabis, hash, or any combination – anything he could hold of in the readily available supply behind bars. His story of the sinister figure lurking in his room, wasn't that more of the same? He lived in a world of drugs. He was a small-time drug dealer, with links to major suppliers. That was Sullivan's opening gambit, when he'd first broached the subject with Jed. But the arrangement for Jed to infiltrate Brian's inner-circle no longer remained. Sullivan had ended it.

And now this. Ghouls and photographs and threats. How could anything be simple anymore, especially with Jonathan Kepowski always there, in the shadows, waiting.

Every time Jed thought of him, a glorious thrill ran right through his chest, leaving him breathless. He'd tried to fight against it, but whenever an image of Jon came into his head, he grew weak, mouth slack, the erection stirring. Christ, what the bloody hell was the matter with him? Jon possessed such power, such dominance so that even now, as Jed's mind turned to him, he grew aroused. He crashed down on his bed, blowing out his breath, and surrendered to his desires.

Whatever had gone passed between them at the lake, and later in the hospital and *The Clarion*, Jon now controlled him. Through hypnotism? Maybe. Or his supreme self-confidence, which Jed found so incredibly exhilarating. Did he actually *fancy* Jon, and would that make him gay?

Closing his eyes, he forced himself to focus on the music filling the room, Marc Bolan's gyrating rock-rhythms taking him to another place, far away. A place where there were no problems, no anxieties, only boundless light and energy and dreams galore. He drifted off to sleep.

He woke up with a start, cold and anxious. Darkness enveloped him, the silence eerie. The record having long since come to an end, Jed sat up with a jerk and fumbled for his bedside clock. It was gone 10 pm. He cursed himself for sleeping so long. Still dressed in his clothes, he felt sweaty and dirty, his eyes gritty and sore. He stood up, shaking himself. Crossing over to his window, he drew the curtains to and rubbed his arms. Shivering, he made his way downstairs.

Stumbling into the kitchen, he passed the living room, the television blaring out. He filled the kettle. A cup of tea and a piece of toast, then he would have to go back to bed again. School beckoned in the morning. Just a few more weeks, then he'd be on study-leave for 'A' levels.

A few more weeks.

Could he last that long?

The kettle boiled and Jed poured the water into the pot and gave it a good stir. He thought he'd go and ask his dad if he wanted a cup, so he padded down the hall and put his head round the door to the living room. He blinked and took a second look.

The room was empty. His dad wasn't there.

Jed waited in the living room, tea long forgotten. This wasn't like Dad, simply going off into the night without saying a word, not even leaving a note. Something must have happened, something urgent. Whatever the reason, there was nothing Jed could do except wait. He gnawed at his fingernails whilst watching the television. The minutes ticked slowly by.

At last he heard the key in the door and jumped up, almost colliding with his dad in his rush to greet him.

"Dad, where the hell—" His words died on his lips. Larry Meres was deathly white, his hands trembling, but not with the cold. "Jesus God, Dad – are you okay?"

Larry, close to tears, pushed past and fell into a chair. Jed waited in the doorway.

"I got a call. From Hannah." Slowly Jed moved across the room and sat opposite. Larry sniffed loudly. "She'd, er, had a row, with her son. Brian. Someone, nobody knows who, sent him some photographs of me and his mother...you know, shots of us both—"

"Dad, I—"

"Just a minute, Jed, please." Larry held up his hand, pulled out a handkerchief and blew his nose loudly. "He was like someone deranged, calling her every word under the sun. I could hear him in the background when she called. God knows what the neighbours must have thought. It's a wonder they didn't call the police. Anyway, by the time I ran round, he'd gone. She was sitting on the sofa, with the photos in her hand."

In the pause, Jed took the opportunity to speak, "Dad, it's all right, I know about the photographs."

Larry Meres gaped, caught off-guard. "You – you know? But how – I mean, who—?"

"Brian. He'd already told me. That's where I was at the end of school today. He was waiting for me at the gate."

"What, to show you the photographs? *You've seen them?* Christ!" He turned away, embarrassed or ashamed, a hand pressed against his mouth. "Oh God, Jed. I'm so sorry."

"It doesn't matter, Dad. I'm not shocked, or upset."

"You're not?" The relief on Larry's face was almost comical. A wide grin split his face. "Jed, I'm so—"

"Have you any idea, any clue at all as to who took them?"

"What? What do you mean?"

"The photos, Dad. Whoever took them must have been in the room with you, hiding in the wardrobe or something."

His mouth dropped again, the grin swept away. "My God – you mean, he was in there, already?"

"If it was a 'he'. But, yeah, he must have been."

"But that – no, that couldn't have happened. It's madness – Hannah would have known!"

"And what makes you think she didn't?"

Larry shook his head, eyes staring sightlessly towards the floor, deep in thought. "But – but for what purpose?"

"Blackmail?"

"Don't be absurd. *Blackmail*. No, that can't be – why would she ask me to go round there, to help her with Brian if they are all in it together? If it was some God-awful set-up? It can't be that."

"It wasn't a random act, Dad, that's for sure."

"But why would anyone do … Unless. Jesus, for a sex thing? Somebody getting their rocks-off by watching Hannah and me … Oh God. You think it might be that?"

"I don't know, but something about all of this just doesn't feel right. You know she had an affair with Sullivan, don't you?"

"Sullivan? You mean, the policeman, the one who came round here to question you?"

Jed nodded. "Brian went wild when he found out, which I can understand, Sullivan being a copper and all and Brian not being the cleanest sheet in the laundry basket." Jed stood up, needing to keep moving, help him put his mind into focus. He crossed to the mantelpiece and stared at his reflection in the large, gilded mirror above the fireplace. He looked old, older than eighteen, older every time he looked in a mirror. "She's an attractive woman, living on her own with a son who is dabbling in drugs. Using and selling them." He turned and shot his dad a quick glance. "And before you say anything – I'm not using."

"I've never suspected that. Never."

Jed grunted. "Look, she entices you back to her place and the next thing there are photos of you being splashed around. The big question is *why*. If it's not blackmail, what's it all for?"

"I think I know. I've thought about it. In fact, I've been thinking about it even before I knew about the photos. A woman like that, why did she come on so strong to me? Was it just for sex…No, that's – that's too simple. She was – God, this is so awkward…" He rubbed his face with his hands and sat there for a few moments, and Jed waited, feeling his dad's embarrassment. At last, Larry looked up again. "It was weird, Jed. Like nothing else. I mean, she was wild, out of control." Jed winced. "Sorry, I know you don't want to hear this, but …"

"It's all right. Just tell me."

"She … I thought it *meant* something, but then, to just drop me, like a hot potato. I was left reeling when she announced to me, in the street, that we shouldn't have a relationship. But, the thing is, I never said a word to her about that. This may sound crass and clichéd, but I still love your mum. Things haven't been good between us, not for ages, but that hasn't stopped me from loving her. She's still the same woman I married all those years ago. And when Hannah came on so strong, I suppose I was confused, as well as a little flattered. An attractive woman like that, fancying someone like me."

"Dad," Jed sat down next to him, "listen to me. This has been a shock, to all of us. I'm not a little boy anymore, I can handle all of this. I've known things haven't been right for a long time, but, that's just the way it is. Lots of lads at school have been through the same thing, it's not that uncommon. But, this Hannah Randall business, it's got to be linked to everything else. If, like you say, she comes onto you strong, then just drops you for no reason, that is weird. Too much is going on, Dad. Mum leaves and suddenly the world drops out of our world. Not just yours, but mine too. Less than a month ago, I was just like any other schoolboy, getting through the week, looking forward to Friday, wishing my life away. Then, *smack*, everything is torn apart. Look what has happened since Mum walked out." He ticked off each incident with his fingers, "The murders, the police, my going to Risley, meeting up with Brian Randall. You and his mum. And now the photographs. It's all more than just coincidence, dad. It's all been arranged."

"*Arranged*? What, you mean somebody planned all of this. But that – that's just nuts, Jed!"

"Is it? My becoming friendly with Brian inside, then you and his mum, the photographs. No, Dad. It's all fitting together, and I think I know who's behind it all, and who took the photos. The only person who would want to drive a wedge between us." Jed nodded as he voiced his thoughts, unravelling the whole mystery. "Yeah, it's all becoming very clear to me now. He's still in love with her, and he tried to use me to get to Brian. It's our old friend Sullivan, that's who it is."

Larry Meres licked his lips, then blew out a long, shuddering breath. "You could be right, Jed."

"I know I am. Now my only concern is was what the hell are we going to do about it?"

Later, in the darkness, Jed lay, staring. In all of his calculations and suspicions there was one piece he hadn't set before his dad. The obvious piece.

Things hadn't started falling apart after Mum left.

They had started after he'd saved Jonathan Kepowski from drowning.

18

From his dad's bookshelf, he picked out an old copy of *The Pnume* by Jack Vance, pages orange-edged. It was the cover that enthralled him. A strange, mystical looking figure, in half shadow, floating in mid air as it drifted out of a murky background. It was the perfect inspiration for the art-work he needed to prepare for his exam.

All that morning he worked on the preliminary sketches, changing the setting, the colours, going outside to sketch trees, adding them to the overall concept. By the time lunchtime came, he was feeling pleased with himself at what he had accomplished so far. Even Miss Earle, his Art teacher, cooed appreciably. Stick thin, Jed thought her mildly crazy, but she was an incredibly gifted artist and he could have spent all day, every day, in that art studio.

Later, he wandered up to Wallasey Village and went into Tate's bookshop for a quick browse along the shelves. After parting with some precious cash, Jed stepped outside with his new purchase and almost cried out in surprise as there, waiting for him, stood Jon Kepowski. Next to him, enjoying the brittle early spring sunshine were two girls, who broke into giggles the moment they saw him. Jon stepped forward, big grin on his face, hand outstretched. Jed took it as if in a trance.

"Thought I'd catch you here," said Jon, putting his arm around Jed's shoulders, steering him away from the shop. "I hear you've been having a little bit of trouble, Jed."

Jed stiffened, pulling himself away, frowning. "Trouble? How do you know about any trouble I've been having?"

Jon shrugged, giving that easy smile of his. He nodded towards the girls. "We're going off for a little drive in the country. Fancy it?"

"Drive? But, Jon, I'm at *school* – remember? This is my lunch break. I have to go back and finish off my artwork. It's for my exam."

"Ah…yeah…" he sniggered, shooting a glance towards the girls, who giggled again. "I had a word with that teacher of yours. Miss Early is it? Very nice. Very *lean…*"

Jed watched in horror as Jon licked his lips. "You mean, Miss Earle?" He held his breath.

"Yeah, that's it. She seemed fine with me taking you out for the afternoon. Said you've worked so hard this morning that she had no problems with you taking some time off."

"She said that? Honestly?"

"Jed, would I lie to you?" He gave an extravagant grin, then turned to the others, "Come on girls, we're going down to Eastham. Treat you all to a nice steak and chips at *Bernie's.*" The girls cackled with delight and Jed felt as if he were in a dream as Jon slowly took him by the arm and led him towards his parked car.

"How did you persuade her?"

Jon stopped, those eyes smouldering. "Oh, you know, I have my little ways…"

One of the girls spluttered, "Not so *little, Jon!*" Both of them rocked, their faces glowing red.

Eyes bulging, Jed looked from the girls then back to Jon, barely able to force out his words, "You – you don't mean you…Jesus."

"You just relax, Jed. Enjoy yourself. You're with your uncle Jon now."

Being with 'uncle Jon' meant sitting in the back seat of a Vauxhall FD estate, comfortably close to one of the girls, who had introduced herself as Janet. Slim, dark-haired, and very loud, Jed couldn't help but find himself drawn to her happy, smiling eyes, and dimpled cheeks. She had a spread of freckles thrown haphazardly across her cheeky face, and her skin was like alabaster, toned arms revealed through a skimpy, sleeveless dark blue top. Her jeans were tight and left nothing to the imagination. Her easy, open manner helped Jed relax, and soon joined in with Janet's laughter as Jon took the car away from the confines of the Wirral peninsula, heading along the A41 towards Eastham. By the time the car drew into the *Hooton Hotel* car park, Jed was thoroughly at ease and looking forward to whatever the day might have in store.

Jon paid for everything. Prawn cocktail starter, fillet steak and chips, ice cream. All of it washed down by red wine and a couple of brandies. The girls were in high spirits by the time they all stumbled out into the late afternoon sunshine, holding onto one another, giggling. Jon, who hadn't touched a drop of alcohol and barely eaten a mouthful of his meal, rubbed his hands with expectation. "Let's all go down to Chester. Hire a boat. What do you say, Jed?"

What could he say? Jed was floating, and had been for quite some time, growing more and more intoxicated by Janet's companionship. It would need surgery to remove her from his side she was so close. Beaming from ear to ear, he shrugged and followed Jon to the car and, as he fell into the back seat, Janet was already kissing him. He didn't resist; her lips felt warm and soft and, closing his eyes, he felt a luxurious, woozy feeling flowing over him. He was happier than he had been for a long time.

Chester was not busy that afternoon; the shops already closing and by the time they had made their way down to the river, most of the boat hirers were shut. Jon spoke to the only one still open and then gestured for the others to follow. The man showed them onto a small rowing boat and helped them get onboard. Settling themselves down, it was up to Jed to take the oars and soon they were heading up the river, in the opposite direction to the weir.

The quietness put them all into a sort of spell. Jon, with his girl Laura, lay down, eyes closed, arms and legs entwined. Janet, trailing a hand in the water, watched the ripples as the boat slipped along and Jed, who had only rowed once before, worked hard with the oars, making their journey unhurried and gentle. Strong and fit, he enjoyed the moment, the breeze in his hair, the sun shining. A beautiful, wondrous day.

Rousing himself, Jon pointed to an area, shaded by overhanging trees, where a tiny berth waited. "Pull us in over there," he said. Beside him, Laura stifled a yawn and put her head on his shoulder. "We're all a little tired. Maybe we could rest for a short while."

Securing the boat on the little beach, they clambered ashore, Jon taking Laura into the undergrowth whilst Jed and Janet lay down on the grass. It was warm, the evening still young and Jed sighed, a warm glow flowing through him. Janet snuggled into his chest and soon they were both fast asleep.

Blinking open his eyes, Jed stared towards the sky, noting the streaks of grey cloud. He sat up and checked his watch. It had stopped. Tapping the glass, it remained frozen. Next to him, Janet groaned and turned on her side. They must have been asleep for well over an hour, he estimated. Shivering, he got to his feet, rubbing his arms. They were alone, Jon and Laura presumably still deep in the surrounding undergrowth. Then he noticed Janet's wristwatch and he stooped down and tenderly turned her wrist to peer at the face. He gasped. It was almost 7 pm. They had been asleep for over two hours! Frantic, he shook the girl by the shoulders and rolled over, stretching out like a cat, yawning widely.

"We have to go," Jed whispered. He didn't understand why he whispered, but something about that place made him shiver, and not because of the cold. Peering into the impenetrable shadows of the trees, a dreadful hostility, even a malevolence, seeped out from between the branches. He took an involuntary step backwards.

"They're having fun."

He snapped his head towards Janet. "We've been gone too long. It'll be dark soon."

"So?"

"So – we have to get back." Feeling like an unwanted intruder, he faced the trees once more, took a breath and shouted out his friend's name.

The silence seemed to mock him as a reply. Nothing stirred, no birds sang, the only sound the gentle lapping of the river against the little beach. Moving over to the boat, Jed contemplated rowing back, just the two of them. As if to remind him he should first find Jon, a stiffening breeze rustled through the leaves, louder than anything else.

Janet stood and stretched, and Jed's eyes dropped to her breasts, straining against her top. As her arms came flopping down to her sides, she noticed him staring and gave a little laugh. "How old are you?"

Jed started, caught off-balance, his answer automatic, "Eighteen." He waited, holding his breath, wondering if, realising his age, she might not wish to be alone with him.

But didn't she know anyway? Hadn't he said, when they all met him outside the bookshop, he needed to be at school? He gulped as she took a step closer, his eyes hovering on her full, ample breasts.

She smiled, placing her arms on his shoulders, eyes boring into him. "You look older."

"I do?"

She traced her fingers along his arms, sucking in her bottom lip thoughtfully. "You're very muscular. Do you work out?"

His heartbeat pulsed in his throat. She was so close, chest rising and falling, brushing against him. A tiny moan escaped from between his dry lips, "We, er, we need to find the others. It's late."

"Oh, they can wait." She reached out, took his face in her hands and pulled him towards her, closing her lips over his. She forced her tongue between his teeth and explored the inside of his mouth. Lost, he groaned, responding, arms slipping around her slender waist.

She pulled back, gasping. "Mmm, God, you're nice. Are you a virgin?"

Another tiny moan, the only reply he was able to muster. He longed for this moment to last forever but now, he grew frantic, believing she might turn away, unwilling to continue with someone as inexperienced as he was. But his fears were ungrounded as she again took hold of his face, her eyes unblinking, irresistible, devouring him. "You are, aren't you?"

What was he supposed to do, lie? Of course he was a virgin; not in mind, but certainly physically. He gave a feeble shrug.

"That's okay," she said softly. "You won't be for very much longer."

She smiled, he panicked. Holding onto him, she led him over to the place where they had slept and gently pulled him to the ground. Without a pause, her hands explored his jeans, before deftly unbuckling his belt and opened his zip. "My," she said as her warm fingers reached inside, "you certainly are older than eighteen!"

With his head spinning, Jed lay back and gave himself up to the moment, her expert fingers bringing him out into the coolness of the early evening air. He groaned as he grew hard in her hand, and felt the softness of her lips as they enclosed around his blood engorged flesh.

At this point, when his world was about to enter a new stage, the other two came bursting out from the trees, laughing at the top of their voices.

Everything stopped.

And everyone looked.

Janet, laughing the loudest, drew away, allowing the others an uninterrupted view of his erection.

"Oh my God," gasped Laura.

Janet moaned, licking her lips. "Isn't he lovely?"

Hastily, Jed scrambled to his feet, stuffing himself back into his trousers, ignoring the pain and the discomfort, wanting only to hide away, to escape from their taunts and jeers.

Jon came over and clapped him on the back. "Perhaps we should give you another ten minutes?"

Janet laughed again. "We won't need that long." She leaned forward and kissed Jed lightly on the lips, winking. "Don't worry," she said in a whisper, pressing a little piece of paper into his shirt pocket, "I'm not going to let you get away."

On the drive home, Jed pretended to sleep as he sat, huddled up in the corner of the front passenger seat. Janet and Laura were in the back, chatting away incessantly. No doubt they were going to have a wonderful time recounting Jed's shame, over and over again, sharing it with everyone they knew. He squirmed at the thought of it, telling himself that from now one he would hibernate in his room and stay out of everyone's way. For a week, a month – perhaps until he was fifty!

Jon pulled the car up outside Jed's house and sat for a moment, drumming his fingers on the steering wheel. "Sorry we interrupted you back there, Jed…" he looked at his young friend. "Apart from that, you had a good time, yeah?"

Jed nodded, not wishing to prolong the conversation, his hand already folding around the door handle.

"I have a little favour to ask," said Jon, reached over to the glove compartment. He took out a small package, tightly bound in brown parcel tape. "I need you to take this down to the *The Beach*, hand it over to the manager there, a guy called Tony Laine. Do it tonight, just around ten."

"*The Beach* nightclub? Jon, I can't do this tonight – I have school tomorrow. I need to work for my—"

"This'll only take you half an hour, Jed." Jon patted him on the knee, "I know you won't let me down." Then, just as Janet had done, he took Jed's face between finger and thumb and turned him around, looking deeply into his eyes. ""You *won't* let me down, will you Jed?"

A large black hole opened up beneath him, and Jed felt as if he were floating on a warm, soothing up draft of air. Any thought of arguing simply disappeared, a wave of complete, total submissiveness overcoming all resistance. He would have gladly done anything Jon had asked him to. "No," he said softly, hardly daring to speak lest he should shatter the spell, "of course I won't. I'd do anything for you, you know that."

Jon smiled sweetly and patted his young friend's cheek. "That's my boy. Now you go and have yourself a nice shower, maybe play with yourself for a bit, yeah? Get rid of all that frustration."

"You want me to?"

Jed held his breath, waiting for the answer that he longed for. He was so hard he thought he would burst through his trousers.

Jon stroked his cheek, "Yes."

Jed almost cried he was so happy. He ran out of the car and went through his front door without stopping, bounding up the stairs and into the bathroom.

It didn't take long.

After his shower, a towelling robe wrapped tightly around him, Jed flopped down on his bed, a distinct feeling that something had happened when Jon had parked the car. He struggled to think what, but something Jon said, or arranged, niggled away inside him. Most of the day was a blur, and then the evening, after he had called a taxi to take him to the nightclub. He recalled the man called Laine, angry and shouting, pushing Jed out of the entrance, a large bouncer threatening him, telling him never to set foot in there again. The taxi driver, waiting on the other side of the street, had said something about not wanting any trouble. But Jed wasn't about to give him any trouble. The package. Had he delivered it? He couldn't remember. By the time he returned home, the fug inside his head continued, clogging up his senses. In the kitchen, he threw down four headache tablets, Dad furious with him, Jed unable to recall his words. The shower helped, but what he really needed was sleep.

But sleep didn't come. He lay with his eyes wide, trying to descramble the details of the day. He recalled the bookshop, meeting the girls and – what was her name, the one... the one who kissed him. The one thing he recalled with any clarity, that kiss. So wonderful, he could almost taste it on his lips, the taste of cherries. A stirring developed in his loins, reassuring him that his strange feelings for Jon were nothing more than hero-worship. He wasn't gay. That girl had opened up a whole new chapter for him and if he could only see her again, perhaps something ...

He sat bolt upright, elated at remembering she had put something into his pocket. He switched on his side light, got up, and almost ran to his shirt. Pulling out the paper, he scanned the words. There it was, her name. Janet. And a phone number. He closed the paper in his fist and almost swooned in relief. That kiss, those lips. Soon he would experience them again. Very soon.

19

Phillips caught up with him in the corridor the following day, scowling as usual. "Where were you yesterday afternoon, Meres?"

"I had permission, sir. From Miss Earle."

"I didn't ask you that. You weren't getting up to anything else *questionable* were you?"

"Questionable? Not at all, sir. I went home, did a bit more work on my art and then went to bed. No crime in that, sir."

Phillips sucked in his breath. "I've put my neck on the line for you, Meres. Just don't let me begin to question my decision. That's all." And with that, he stomped off.

Jed didn't give Phillips another thought throughout the rest of the day, which went, for the most part, well. Until late afternoon, when he was just putting the final changes to his artwork and Chaplain came in, grinning broadly, and grabbed Miss Earle around the waist and squeezed her. She giggled, put up a pathetic fight, then turned in his arms and looked adoringly into his eyes. "What's got into you?"

"Home time," said Chaplain, then he noticed Jed for the first time and sighed loudly. "What are you doing here, Meres?"

"Just finishing off, sir."

Chaplain was head of the art department. People said he was an ex-boxer and he certainly looked the part, but way his prime now. Although still a big man, his stomach was ample and his breathing often laboured. But Jed liked him. A character was Chaplain, and not a bad one at that.

The big man came over and looked appreciably towards Jed's painting. "Quite good, Meres. Quite good."

"Thank you very much, sir."

"All down to my excellent teaching," trilled Miss Earle, packing away her bag. "Come on, Jed. Time to go. You've still got three more days to get that done."

"Here," said Chaplain, turning to Miss Earle, "I forgot to tell you – just before I came in, I heard it on the radio. The owner of *The Beach* nightclub has been found, hanging under New Brighton pier."

Jed's hand froze above his artwork, his mouth open, listening intensely. He craned his neck, to see Miss Earle, horrified. "Oh my God," she said. "How dreadful. Did he leave a note or anything?"

"A note? Why should there be a note? Didn't you hear what I said, he was *hanging* under the pier."

"Yes, I know what you said, but they usually leave a note, don't they? Suicides?"

Chaplain rubbed his face. "Who said anything about suicide – he'd been murdered, Lucy."

Both of them turned as Jed let out a loud cry of despair.

He wanted to get home, tune into the early evening news, pick up some more information. If what Chaplain had said was true, that Tony Laine had been murdered, then it was clear the police would be calling on him again very soon. Plenty of witnesses would come forward to testify that they'd seen him. Already in the frame over Nurse Willis and Craig Watson, the police, and especially Sullivan, would circle him like a flock of vultures.

The news, as he sat in front of the television, gnawing away at his fingernails, was worse than he expected. Not only had the police found Laine's body swinging from beneath the boards of New Brighton pier, his club, *The Beach*, had been burned to the ground. Thankfully, nobody was inside at the time, but the devastation caused was dreadful.

It would take months and a huge amount of cash to rebuild the place. With Laine gone, the question was who would pick up the bill?

Wandering into the kitchen, Jed sat at the table, staring at the meal Dad had prepared. Dad, appearing distracted, didn't eat, washed some dishes, then disappeared upstairs, leaving Jed to stir through his food with a fork. He studied the congealed mass of vegetables, the shrivelled piece of charred pork and decided Dad wasn't managing. It was time for Jed to step in, cook and clean, do the shopping.

He threw down the cutlery, blew out his cheeks and thought back to Laine. Too much was going on. Murders, Hannah Randall, Dad … Jon Kepowski…

The doorbell rang. Jed moaned. He knew without a doubt who it was and when he opened the door to let Sullivan in, neither of them spoke.

He made the policeman a cup of tea without asking, then sat down opposite and waited.

"Expecting me?"

"Sort of. I had nothing to do with it."

"No. I don't suppose you did. But that's not why I'm here." He took a sip of his tea and made a face. Jed pushed over the sugar bowl and Sullivan smiled his thanks and piled in three heaped tea-spoonsful. He took another sip and smacked his lips loudly. "That's better."

"So, why are you here?"

"Don't get me wrong, Jed my lad, we're still very interested in what you were doing at *The Beach* last night, but that can wait. What can't wait is the phone call I got from Hannah Randall late last night. Where's your dad?"

"Upstairs."

Sullivan nodded, took another mouthful of tea, and leaned forward, his voice dropping to a whisper. "You know all about it, I suspect. She said you did."

"Yeah. I know all about it."

Sullivan carefully settled his cup on the table and spread out his hands. "I have a problem. Or, to be more precise, *we* have a problem. We came to an arrangement, that you would try to become close to

Brian Randall, unearth the names and the faces behind the suppliers. But now…" He shook his head and looked tired. "Why did Brian show you those photographs? What sort of game is he trying to play, and how much have you told him about you and me, Jed?"

Jed blinked, "I haven't told him anything. I could ask you exactly the same question. Why did you send Brian the photographs in the first place?"

Before Sullivan could answer, Larry Meres appeared in the kitchen doorway. Jed looked up, startled at his dad's sudden appearance. Sullivan craned his neck and gave a brief nod of greeting. Larry scowled. "I'd like you to leave, detective. Close the door on your way out."

"I only dropped in to—"

"I know what you came round for, Sullivan. Now, I've told you once, and I'm not going to repeat it. You're not welcome here."

Shrugging his shoulders, Sullivan stood up, sighing deeply. "This isn't going to go away, Mr Meres. Whatever went on between you and Hannah, it hasn't ended. And what your son is up to, that isn't going to go away either. The pair of you are in it, right up to your necks, and when I find out what exactly has been going on, I'll hunt you down and hang you out to dry – I promise you."

He pushed past Larry and slammed the door as he went out.

Jed shook his head. "That guy has serious problems."

Larry shot forward, reaching across the table, taking Jed by the collar and pulling him up close. "You have serious problems, Jed!" Larry's face was red, contorted with rage. "Whatever is going on, I don't want any more of it, do you hear? You went out last night. I don't know what you did or where you went, but from now on you don't do anything, *anything* without my say-so. Do you understand me?"

Jed could hardly breathe. He tried to free himself of his dad's grip, but it was too strong. "Dad, for God's sake."

"*Do you understand me?*"

Unable to think of anything but the pressure on his larynx, Jed blurted out, "Yes!"

Dad let him go and strode out, leaving Jed slumped in his chair, rubbing his neck, trying to hold back the tears.

20

Jed couldn't get over what had happened. His dad had never reacted like that, over anything. Always such a mild-mannered man, the stress had transformed into some sort of demon.

Over the next few days, they exchanged no words, only grunts. Jed went to school, did what he had to do, returned home, ate his tea, went to his room and that was it. The same cycle every day. By Friday, he was so sick of the situation, he made up his mind to confront his dad that same evening.

On his way home, he rehearsed his speech, but something else was playing around in his head. Janet.

Through his scrambled-up feelings over Dad, she was always there, her face filling every moment. He conjured up imagined meetings, holding her hand, stroking her hair, listening to her voice as she told him how much she loved him. In his room, back against his bed, he'd float away, leaving the real world far behind as he dreamed of being with her, holding her. Kissing her lips.

At home, he busied himself making the tea, glancing up at the wall clock every few moments. Dad would be in at any moment, and he hoped the peace-offering of grilled rump steak and fried potatoes would go some way to restoring their relationship.

But by five-forty, there was no sign of Dad.

Jed took the opportunity of doing what he'd rehearsed so many times – phone Janet. He rooted around in his pocket to find the piece of paper with her number scribbled down on it. His hand was shaking as he dialled.

"Hello?" A man's voice came down the line, gruff, unfriendly.

"Can I speak to Janet please?"

"Janet? Who is this?"

Jed took a deep breath, squeezing his eyes shut, going through his lines. "Sorry, I don't mean to disturb you, but I'm a friend. Jed. She might have mentioned me?" It was always a hope. He held his breath.

"*Mentioned* you? What did you say your name was?"

"Jed. Jed Meres."

A prolonged silence. Jed could hear the man breathing. He hadn't put the phone down, hadn't shouted out for Janet to come and answer the call. Just the breathing, getting faster. "Look, I don't know who the hell you are, but just bugger off, will you – you're sick, that's what you are. *Sick!*"

The phone went dead.

Jed stood there, for a long time, just staring at the earpiece, wondering what had just happened.

Larry Meres had made a slight detour on his way home from work. He'd been worried for the best part of the week, worried about what he'd done to Jed. Never had he raised his hand to his son, never felt it necessary, preferring to talk, calmly and patiently. The results spoke for themselves – Jed was a fine lad, despite recent events. He was bright, funny, a normal boy enjoying his youth whilst he still could. To have treated him like that, grabbing him, frightening him, that wasn't right. It wasn't something you were supposed to do, not as a father. A single parent.

He found himself wandering along the curling path leading up to the Breck, an old quarry where he used to play as a boy. A space to run around in, make dens, walk the dog. A simple, pleasant place. This evening, there was nobody about and Larry found a bench, sat down and stared at his hands. A worker's hands, gnarled and roughened through endless years of toil, and all for what? A miscreant son and a failed marriage, with a bored wife, leaving him for another bloke, a bloke who had always been there, in her memories...

Putting his face in his hands, Larry did his best to block out the images, but the one of Jed's terrified face refused to budge. To have taken it all out on him, allowing the frustration, the anger, the sense of betrayal to erupt the way it had – that was unforgiveable. Jed had suffered too, and reacted, in very different ways. A bright future, almost destroyed due to the hurt.

He sat back, the shame of it over-powering. He must apologise, mend the wounds. Jed was all he had now. Tonight. He'd take his son to a restaurant, treat him to whatever he wanted, then just talk it out. They needed to stick together, to help themselves through it all. There was no alternative.

Fired up with this new-found determination, he slapped his knees and stood, stretching, letting the day's aches fade quickly away. As he turned, he saw a figure standing some way off on top of a rocky outcrop. Tall and gangly, his face in heavy shadow, Larry nevertheless felt certain the man was looking straight at him. Bringing up his hand to shield his eyes from the low-lying sun, he tried to get a better view, but he was too far away. How long had he been standing there, Larry wondered. And what the hell was he looking at?

A dog barked behind him and Larry turned to see an elderly couple strolling along the path, laughing, a little Yorkie yapping at their heels, joining in with the fun. Larry's eyes clouded over with sadness for a brief moment. That could have been him and...

Sighing, he went to look again at the mysterious figure watching him.

But the figure had gone.

They talked, the pair of them, until it was late, both conscious of how difficult the next few months were going to be. Stress levels were going to rise, tempers at breaking point sometimes. They made allowances, Larry found the pathway towards an apology and Jed, graciously, accepted it. Although a black cloud remained, it was not longer as ominous as it had once been and slowly the atmosphere between them eased.

Jed went to bed feeling much better, his mind at rest, his sleep untroubled by dreams.

At some point in the night, he sat up in bed, woken by something. He strained to listen in the dark, but the house remained in silence, so he fell back amongst his bedclothes.

This time he did dream. He imagined being alone with Janet, her warm, yielding body next to his. Her arms around him, holding him, the smell of her heady perfume invading his nostrils. Half-asleep, he snuggled closer to her body and she lightly stroked the back of his head, her lips kissing his neck. He sighed.

Then he froze.

This was no dream.

Hardly daring to breathe, he lay there, fully awake now. He had his back to her and he could feel her legs entangled with his, the slight whisper of her breath against his back. Had she broken in, crept upstairs, and slid underneath the sheets to be with him? Was that the sound which had woken him?

She was here. Janet.

With his heartbeat pounding in his head, throat constricted, tongue too big for his mouth, he took a tremulous breath and turned to her, his erection rearing.

But it wasn't Janet who lay next to him.

Larry came through the bedroom door at a rush to find Jed in the far corner, dishevelled, face ashen, eyes wide, huddled up like a little child with knees drawn up to his chest, shaking uncontrollably. He'd stuck a thumb in his mouth, mumbling incoherently, rocking backwards and forwards. Following his stare, Larry gazed at the empty bed, the covers thrown back, the impression where bodies had laid still evident. Frowning, not understanding Jed's terror, went over to him, crouched down, and lightly touched his arm.

Jed gave a start, as if waking from a dream and the tears sprang forward and fell into his father's arms and stayed there, sobbing uncontrollably. Larry held him without speaking but, for some reason, he could not resist turning his eyes and fixing them on the empty bed.

21

"The police called me in for questioning," said Mat. "They had me in there for hours, on and on with the same damned questions. By the time they'd finished I was so wound up that when I finally got home, I couldn't get to sleep. I feel like a bag of shite."

"You look it."

"Thanks!"

Mat had met Jed after school and they were now walking home. Jed, unsteady, eyes red-rimmed, was haunted by the previous night, and now there was Mat, sporting his own haunted look.

They walked up Saint Hilary's Brow, taking the long way home. Mat's words ate away the minutes and then, he produced a crumpled and creased photograph. When Jed stared down at the face, he stopped.

"That's Ellen Willis's boyfriend." Jed frowned into Mat's face. "Sullivan showed me this, so what are you doing with it? Did Sullivan give it to you – do you know him?"

Mat pursed his lips. "There's something you need to know, Jed." With great care, he delicately plucked the photograph from his brother's fingers and stared at the black and white image. Taken some years previously, Peter Davey's smiling face showed no worries. A life to look forward to. Mat gave a brief smile. "Come on, let's walk into Liscard. I'll buy you a coffee."

It was coming up to 5 o'clock and the place buzzed with weary shoppers. Jed watched Mat waiting at the counter to be served from the window seat he had managed to find. Between his fingers was the photograph and the more he looked at it, the more he felt he knew the face, but not in person. Peter Davey. Was he famous locally, perhaps? Was that it? A footballer, cricketer, something else? Someone who had appeared in the local press? Jed sighed and sat back, hoping Mat had the answers. Strange that Mat should meet him after school, with no warning. So many years without any form of contact apart from those damned Christmas cards, then everything changing with Mum's leaving. He put down the photograph and ran his hand through his hair, feeling weary and sick of it all.

"We need to talk, Jed."

He looked up with a jerk and saw Jon Kepowski standing in front of him, his skull-face glaring. "Bloody hell, Jon – you scared the life out of me."

"That package, the one I asked you to take down to *The Beach*. It was important, and now it's gone. Burned, along with the club. You know about all that, don't you?"

"Yeah. It was on the news."

"And Sullivan? He mentioned it?"

"I – I don't remember. Jon, I hardly remember *anything* about what you asked me to do. Things are so confused and – and what the hell are you doing here?"

"I want you to go to see Brian Randall. Tell him about the package. He'll tell you what to do." Jon shot a quick look over to his right, towards the counter, then turned again to Jed. "Soon. Make it soon."

Jed saw Mat squeezing through the press of people. He held a tray with two coffees and a plate of iced-buns in his hands. Jed couldn't help but smile, turned to say something to Jon and stopped, catching his breath.

Jon Kepowski had disappeared.

"What's up, you look as though you've seen a ghost." Mat settled himself down and pushed the steaming hot cup of coffee towards his brother.

Jed, lost for words, craned his neck to look above the heads of the people the cafe's entrance. But Kepowski wasn't anywhere. He squeezed his eyes shut for a second. "I think I'm going mad."

"Yeah, well..." Mat took a sip of coffee. "Help yourself to a bun."

But Jed didn't feel much like eating. Instead, he drank from his cup. Soon he couldn't remember why he felt so troubled.

Mat was talking, very softly, forcing Jed to lean forward, straining to hear. He pressed his hand over his brother's arm. "I can't hear what you're saying, Mat."

Mat sighed and lifted his voice above the constant drone of the customers. "Sorry. I was just rambling. Jed, this photo," he picked it up, looking at it one more time, as if reminding himself of the features. "When Mum left my dad all those years ago, she went up to the Lake district. Remember I told you?"

"Yeah. She had family up there, you said."

"Nan brought me up. I didn't know much about it then, of course. How could I...Anyway, the years slipped by, as they do. I went to school, did all the usual stuff. Hardly ever saw my dad. He'd gone away too. Couldn't face up to the shame I suppose. A proud man, he couldn't stand the thought that people would be talking about him." He shrugged, finished off his coffee and sat back. "I remember he came back a different person. I'd be about ten, I think. He'd met someone else and they got married."

"*Married*? Oh my God, did Mum know?"

"I don't know if she did, or if she didn't. Even if she had found out, I doubt she would have cared. The thing is, they'd married, my dad and this woman called Diane. Diane Davey."

Jed's mouth hung open. "Davey?"

"When they married, Dad had already changed his name. It seems that he wanted a completely new beginning. I don't know whether he did it officially or what, but he'd married this girl using the name

144

Davey. And…" He sucked in his cheeks and stared at Jed for a long time, inviting him to speak.

Jed could barely force the words out. "And they had a child…a son…"

Mat nodded, a single, ominous inclination of the head. "Peter."

Hang 'em High was playing at the ABC cinema. Jed stared at the hoarding as he came out of the telephone box. He'd phoned his dad to let him know where he was. Dad appreciated the call, which, he said, stopped him from worrying. So much had happened, and now this…

"*Hang 'em High?*" Mat shook his head. "I wonder if we should do that."

"What? Hanging? Do you think it would have stopped whoever has murdered them all?"

"I don't know. Do you?"

Jed shook his head. "Whoever it is, they are on a mission, Mat. Someone, for whatever reason, is on a mission to systematically wipe out our family."

Mat pulled himself up sharply, the frown cutting deep into his skin. "That's a bit *melodramatic*, isn't it? Wiping out our family?"

"No, it's not melodramatic – it's what I think is happening."

"And how do Ellen Willis and Craig Watson fit into all of this? They're not part of our family, Jed."

"Connected though, aren't they? I knew Watson from school, and Nurse Willis…she had been in the hospital whilst I was recovering. And she just happened to be Peter Davey's girlfriend."

Mat shook his head, blowing out his cheeks. "No, Jed. They're not connected. It's just a ghastly coincidence. I don't think Craig Watson's death has anything to do with Ellen Willis, or Peter. Those two perhaps, but not Watson. That's separate."

"You think? But they were killed in exactly the same way, Mat." He could see the thought processes whirring through Mat's brain, and as his mind worked through all the permutations, his brother's features

changed. A tiny flicker ran through his eyes. The beginning of a sus-
picion that perhaps Jed could be right.

Jed, on the other hand, needed no such persuasion. He was convinced. All he had to do was prove it.

22

Phillips called Jed into his office, to talk to him about his study-leave. "Starts on Monday, Meres. When is your first exam?"

"A couple of weeks, sir. History, I think."

"You *think*? You need to check your time-table. How did the art go?"

"Not bad, I thi—" He grinned at Phillips' scowl. "Sorry – I mean it went well, sir."

"Yes, so your teacher says…Grade One, CSE, she says. Definitely. That's a GCE pass, Meres. Just like you said."

"Yes sir," returned Jed, without a hint of arrogance, "Just like I said."

"Well," Phillips stood up, stretching out his hand. Jed stared down at it in horror, then took it and shook it. "I wish you well, Meres, I really do. A-levels, they won't be as easy, but at least you're heading in the right direction. You've been through a lot; you deserve every good fortune."

Stunned into silence, all Jed could do by way of a response was to force a self-conscious smile. He stepped outside and took a huge sigh of relief, happy to be free of Phillips and his cringingly awkward words of congratulation.

She stood in the doorway and Jed, struck by how incredibly good looking she was, took a moment to gather his thoughts. She wore a white towelling robe, pulled tight at the waist, tussled hair hanging down to her shoulders. She looked as if she had just got out of bed, but that couldn't be – it was gone five o'clock in the afternoon. She yawned. Music was playing from somewhere within. *T-Rex*

Jed smiled. "Brian? Is he in?"

Without a word, she moved aside to let Jed through. He squeezed past, his chest pressing against the swell of her breasts beneath the robe. She looked at him without comment, eyes neutral, and a tiny thrill ran through his stomach. She moved slightly, readjusting the robe. A flash of bronzed flesh, the firmness of her breasts impossible to ignore. He stared for a second too long, then looked away, heat rising to his face, and rapidly moved down the hall. He walked into the living room from where the music played.

Brian sat slouched on the sofa, legs stretched out, reading a magazine called *Smash Hits*. He barely looked when Jed came in, managing a tired sounding, "Switch that off, will you?"

Jed went to the music-centre and pressed the button. The speakers gave a thump, then went dead. He stared at the record label. *Metal Guru.*

"It's from *The Slider*," said Brian, by way of explanation. "Their new L.P. You can borrow it, if you like. Or, I can copy it onto cassette, if you prefer."

"You can do that?"

Brian grunted. "That's a music-centre. See the cassette deck? It records from the turntable, and the radio. I'll record it for you, and anything you want."

"Thanks." Jed kept his eyes on the carpet. "Er – I need to talk to you about a package."

Brian nodded, without reacting. "What about it?"

That should have thrown Jed, the almost casual manner in which Brian spoke. But it didn't. All of this was the most natural thing in the world to him, so Jed decided to go along with it, keeping up his own pretence. "You know what happened to it?"

"Of course I know." Brian stood up and stretched. "It was burned in the club. Why do you ask?"

Jed shrugged, feeling a little confused. *Brian will tell you what to do,* Jon had said.

"You haven't got a clue, have you? Who sent you, Sullivan?"

"*Sullivan*? Why the hell would Sullivan—"

Brian held up his hand, "I don't care, Jed. I'm not in the least bit interested. I'm getting out of all this, you tell Sullivan that. Tell him I know what he's up to, and he'll never find anything which he can pin on me. You tell him that."

"Brian, I'm not working for Sullivan, or anyone from the police."

"Yeah, right. Like I said, I don't care. I'm going to make one more deal, then I'm finished. Me and Mum, we'll be leaving. Going down south probably. Start again, away from this shit-hole." He went over to the window. It was quiet outside. It was always quiet. "That package, it was worth – difficult to be accurate but – fifty grand?" Brian caught sight of Jed gaping at him in his reflection in the glass. He turned around, laughing. "Didn't you know? *Fifty grand.* That's a lot of money, eh?" Jed nodded, completely dumbstruck. "And it all went up in smoke. Imagine that. Bit suspicious, don't you think? Makes you wonder who would do such a thing, and why." Brian pulled out a packet of cigarettes, automatically offering one to Jed, who refused. Lighting one up, Brian pulled in the smoke as if he'd been resisting it for a long time. He gave a little cough. "I hate these things…" He continued smoking as he went back to the sofa and flopped down. "My guess is that Sullivan did it. Murdered Tony Laine, burned the place down."

Barely recovering from his shock, Jed sat down in the armchair next to the electric fire, which wasn't switched on. He leaned forward, hands on knees. "Why would he do that?"

"Take over, skim off the cream, send a message, who knows. The guy is due to retire so he wants to set himself up."

"But – burn down the place, along with that package? It doesn't make sense."

"Try not to be too stupid, eh? It was a mistake. He obviously didn't know the package had been delivered."

Jed squeezed his eyes shut, trying to recall the night, but only managing tiny fragments, snippets in a tangled up brain. There was something that wasn't adding up, something he knew wasn't right in what Brian had said, together with a distant memory of what Jon had said, about the package. He tried hard, but he couldn't remember what it was. He knew it was important, but...His fist came down hard on the arm of the chair, frustration boiling up to the surface. "Damn – I feel I've missed something, something significant."

"You've missed something? Why would you think that?" Brian stubbed out his cigarette angrily, "Sullivan needs to understand where I'm coming from, Jed. My suppliers, they're not kids. They're serious businessmen. They don't take kindly to being rushed. I'm going to make one last deal, and Sullivan will get his cut. But there will be no more. That fire was stupid – totally stupid. He could have ruined everything. You tell him that."

"Brian, for God's sake – I told you, Sullivan didn't send me."

"Don't treat me like an idiot, Jed, because I'm not. And here's some advice, yeah. You might be hard, but these guys, they're in a different league. You mess with them, you or Sullivan, and they'll crush you like a bed bug. So, tell Sullivan to be patient and wait. I'll phone you when the deal is going to go down, and then that will be the end of it. I'm out. If Sullivan wants more, he'll have to arrange it with them himself. I'm retiring."

He stood up. The conversation was over. Jed, still confused, went out into the hall again. He was surprised to see Hannah Randall standing there, leaning against the stairwell, her bathrobe not as tightly closed as it had been. Had she been listening? He gulped, trying to avert his eyes. But almost as soon as he looked away, his gaze went back again. Her skin gleamed, tanned and smooth, shimmering against the sharp contrast of the white robe.

She pushed herself off the wall, went to the door and opened it. Jed squeezed past her again, the smell of her perfume wafting into his nostrils. She hadn't been wearing perfume before. It was intoxicating.

On the step, he turned and as the door closed, was that a little smile she gave him, or was that just wishful thinking?

They ate tea in silence, Dad in another dark mood, locked in a place far, far away. Jed, his own thoughts swirling around in his brain, was grateful of the chance to think. But the more he thought, the more confused he got. He knew, if nothing else, that he had to get to the bottom of what was going on. If only he could clear the fog from his mind, release the memories. He'd gone to the club that night and seen Tony Laine. He remembered that much, and remembered how angry Laine was. What was it he had said? Something about…He pressed his lips together, exasperated. This was the point where it all became cloudy. No matter how hard he tried, Jed couldn't remember Laine's words. He remembered the bouncer pushing him out of the club. And then…

Jed opened his eyes wide. It was like looking at an old film through a misty lens slowly being wiped clean, gradually becoming clearer. The pictures were coming into focus. There had been two men. Big men, and they had taken the package from him. And that might mean that the package hadn't been left in the club to be burned along with the building after all. Who were those men, who did they work for, and how did they know that he would be there at that time?

The telephone rang, bringing Jed out of his reverie. He answered it and his heart almost stopped when her voice came floating down the earpiece. "Hi Jed. How have you been?"

It was Janet.

For a long moment, he couldn't find the strength to think, let alone talk.

"Are you there? Jed, are you all right?"

Pulling himself together, Jed's words tumbled out of him in a rush. "Yes, hi, yes, of course, hi – I didn't think you'd get in touch. I tried to talk to you, called your number, but your dad, if it was it your dad, I guess it must have been but anyway, he sounded, you know…" He was rambling. He knew it. She must have been laughing at him.

"Sorry – I didn't think, you know, I didn't think you wanted to see me again…you know…again."

He heard her, laughing, as he suspected. Laughing loud. "Jed – you're so *weird*! Why wouldn't I want to see you again? Look, do you want to meet up. I need to talk to you about something. I'll pick you up, if you like."

Pick him up? "Pick me up? How – I mean – I didn't know you could drive."

Another laugh. "Oh, Jed, you're sweet. Really sweet. Just be ready, in half-an-hour, okay?"

Half-an-hour! How could he possibly get himself ready in half-an-hour? No sooner had he put the phone down than he was racing up the stairs, taking them two at a time, ripping off his clothes and getting under the scalding water of the shower. But he didn't care, he had no time to adjust the temperature. He lathered up a sponge and rubbed his body all over, as fast as he could. It was times like this that he was grateful he kept his hair short. Thoughts of creating that Rod Stewart look would have to wait.

By the time the doorbell sounded, he was ready, having pulled on a fresh t-shirt and his best jeans. He'd also splashed on some of his dad's most expensive aftershave lotion. As he bounded down the stairs, Dad was opening the door. He caught the first whiff of the scent and Dad turned to frown at him. Then he smiled and Jed looked past his dad's shoulder to see Janet standing there. No words of explanation were required.

She drove white Viva, with red seats and twin exhausts. An SL-90. Impressed, Jed leaned back as she headed towards Belvidere Road, feeling like a movie-star. She handled the car expertly and he wondered, not for the first time, about how old she was. Twenty at least, maybe more. Something about her self-confidence made him suspect she might be older. He caught sight of her legs as she changed gear, the skirt too short, white like the car. Legs so long, the muscles rippling as she depressed the clutch, or applied the brakes. It was heaven and he hardly dared believe it was all real.

They left the car in a side street and walked through Harrison Park gates. Already the sun was sending orange streaks across the sky and as they reached the top of one of the hills, they looked out across the Irish Sea, lost in their thoughts, the evening still and pleasantly mild. She slipped her hand inside his and he looked at her awe-struck. This close, in this light, she was truly gorgeous.

She leaned over and gently kissed him on the lips. His legs almost went out from under him. "I want us to go away together," she said softly.

Gaping, he shook his head, confused. "Away? I don't understand. Go away? Go where – when?"

"You're on study leave, so you have some time."

"Time? Well, yeah, but, it's study leave – I need to, you know—"

She pressed her forefinger against his lips. "Don't worry so much. You're going to be fine, I know you will. You're so clever." She smiled, letting her finger fall away from his mouth. She took his hand in both of hers and played with his fingers. "Jon talked to you about going to Scotland, I think."

Jed frowned. Jon, Scotland? Yes, there was something, but he couldn't remember the details. "Scotland? I'm not sure…"

"Well, I'd like us to go. We can drop him off, then spend some time together – *alone*." She raised her eyes, drank him in. He went limp, thought for a moment he would faint, that look so alluring, so full of not-so-subtle innuendo. Alone. My God, to be alone with her. "What do you think?"

"Think?" He laughed. "I *think* it's the most wonderful idea I've ever heard."

She hugged him, very tightly.

It was only later, when he was alone in his room, lying in his bed, that he realized she hadn't said anything about her dad, why he had been so angry, why he had called Jed *sick*. Perhaps there was nothing in it, perhaps her dad was under pressure. Everyone seemed to be under pressure lately, and the thought of getting away, even if only for a few days, was so wonderful, and give him a chance to recharge his batteries, get things into perspective. A few days to escape from the rigours of this world, with all its pressures. Could there be anything better? He'd have to okay everything with Dad, but there wouldn't be any problems, surely. Jed had shown he was back on track, that all that nonsense with the police was nothing but a blimp.

He tore his mind away from thoughts of Brian and packages, Sullivan and deals with criminals, Craig Watson and fights in pubs. All of that was something he would have to disentangle himself from eventually. Right now, Janet made everything so much cleaner and brighter. She was worth fighting for, worth holding onto. And worth keeping out of all the dirt and danger he was embroiled in. A few days away, time to think things through, to make firm decisions, get it all sorted out. Once and for all...

Closing his eyes, one thought still burned. Why had her dad called him *sick*?

Yet one more mystery to solve.

23

The first morning of his exam leave arrived, but not the promise of lying in bed for a few glorious hours. No sooner had his dad closed the door and stomped off to work than the telephone range. It didn't stop. Relentless. Eventually, Jed dragged himself from under the covers and groped his way downstairs.

"Have you spoken to your dad yet?"

Jon, voice as dispassionate and detached as ever, nevertheless bringing with it that familiar buzz, the yearning. Jed, his weariness disappearing as if it had never existed, went light-headed, joyous, happiness brimming over in a wild upsurge of adrenalin. He pressed his palm against the wall for support, tongue thick with desire. "Jon! My God, where have you—"

"The trip to Scotland? Remember, we talked about it? Have you asked your dad whether you can go or not?"

Jed did remember, thanks to Janet, but he hadn't mentioned anything to Dad, not yet. After Dad's outburst, things were still not quite right between them, despite the awkward apologies. Dad was continuing to go through his own personal hell and Jed wasn't sure that he should burden him with the idea of being completely alone, if only for a few days. Even if it meant being alone with Janet. "I haven't really had the chance – sorry."

There was a pause, during which Jed imagined the look on Jon's face. A look of intense displeasure. "Well, my suggestion is that you mention it to him, *tonight.*"

"I will, Jon. I promise."

"Never make promises you can't keep Jed. That can be dangerous."

What was that supposed to mean? "Okay. But I will. As soon as he comes in."

The line went dead and Jed went through to the kitchen, uneasy and a little afraid.

Dad seemed disinterested as he busied himself preparing tea. Jed sat at the kitchen table, hands clasped together, staring down into nothingness. "Well, Dad? Do you think it'll be all right?"

Without turning around from the cooker, Dad shrugged his shoulders. "You can do whatever you want, Jed. As long as you're sure you can get *some* studying in."

"I will." Jed bit his lip. He recalled Jon's words. "I promise."

"Well in that case," He looked at Jed over his shoulder. "When?"

"In the next few days. It'll only be for a short while."

"Bring me back a haggis, will you?" He went back to his cooking. Jed should have felt some slight elation, it all having gone so well, but he didn't. His sense of unease grew with the thought he was about to embark on something that wasn't going to be as wonderful as he had at first believed.

Things happened quickly after the phone call. Janet called him that evening to tell him Jon had everything in hand and they would pick Jed up at six o'clock the following morning. She brushed off his complaints of barely having enough time to pack, saying, "What exactly are you going to need Jed? It's only a two day trip – you'll be back home by Thursday."

Unfortunately Dad's reaction wasn't as nonchalant as it had been earlier, deflating Jed's sense of excitement. "*Tomorrow?* What's the rush?"

"I suppose Jon has an appointment to keep. I'll be back by Thursday."

"I could have done with a bit more warning." Dad ran a hand through his sparse hair. "But, it'll be all right. I'll manage." Dad had such an annoying knack of making Jed feel so guilty over anything he wanted to do. His mother used to do that. *No, don't get up! I mean, I've only been cleaning the house all day, wouldn't want you to get your hands wet by washing a few dishes, would we?*

"I'll phone as soon as I get there."

"Jed," his dad looked at him meaningfully, "I'll be fine. You just go and enjoy yourself. You tell Jon to look after you, yeah?"

Jed suddenly realized that he hadn't mentioned anything about Janet. But it was too late now and, besides, perhaps it was for the best that Dad remained in the dark about that particular aspect of the trip. His mood wouldn't be quite so cordial if he knew.

* * *

Jed couldn't sleep. Lying there, beneath the covers, staring up at the ceiling, he tried his best to keep his thoughts neutral. He didn't want to tempt fate by conjuring up little scenarios all to do with him and Janet, alone together. He felt a surge of pure lust rush through his loins whenever he did, but he managed to keep them at bay, but not enough to aid him sleeping.

Getting up at five, he threw a few things into a holdall and then remembered his camera. It was only a little *Kodak* but it would do. He would have to get some flash-cubes from a shop on the way. A swift breakfast, thrown down, then yet another visit to the bathroom. How many times had that been since he'd got up? His stomach churned around as if it were inside a spin-dryer. Every other second, he glanced at his watch. The fingers never moved. It was painful, all this waiting. And then, as is always the case, when he flopped down on the sofa and tried to be patient, his eyelids grew heavy and sleep beckoned. Fighting against it at first, when a great wave of exhaustion hit him, he drifted off into unconsciousness.

The doorbell rang shrilly and he sat up with a jerk. It was ten minutes past six! How could that be? Rubbing his eyes, he ran to the door and tore it open. There was Jon and, behind him, parked up against the curb, Janet. She smiled and waved from the driver's seat. At last the time had come! Jed felt like a little boy at Christmas and, eagerly grabbing his holdall and coat, followed Jon out to the car.

"Aren't you going to say goodbye to your dad?"

Jed frowned, looking at Jon, then followed his friend's gaze to his father's bedroom window. Dad was there, dressed in his pyjamas, hand raised in farewell. Jed felt a shudder of guilt, forced a smile, and returned the wave before bundling himself into the back of the car and away they went.

From his vantage point, Larry Meres watched the little car speed off up the road. His heart was heavy. He was completely alone. It had been like this, when they hauled Jed off to remand. For the first time in more years than he could remember, there wasn't anyone to share moments with. An empty house, an empty life. Now, it was here again, for different reasons, but with the same outcome. Loneliness, deep and penetrating. Sighing heavily, he sat down on the edge of the bed, put his face in his hands and quietly sobbed.

Sometime later there came an insistent pounding on the door. Larry had half a mind to ignore it, but as he was about to set off for work, he decided to open it. Half expecting to see the postman standing there, he was taken aback to find, swathed in a padded jacket, Miles Foreman, Jed's closest friend.

"Hi, Mr Meres. Sorry to call so early. Is Jed in?"

Larry shook his head. "Sorry. He's gone away for a few days."

"Oh." Crestfallen, he seemed at a loss for words. He pulled in a breath. "This is a bit nosey, I know, but, do you know where he's gone?"

"Scotland. With that friend he met in the hospital. Jon is it?"

"Ah, yes – Kepowski. Yes, I know who you mean. When will he be back, did he say?"

"Two days. Was it anything important, only I've got to—"

"No, no nothing important – not really." He turned to go, then stopped, as if he had forgotten something and turned around again. "Mr Meres, would it be all right if I called round again, later on? I've got something to talk to you about. Something which I think you will find very interesting."

Intrigued, despite his mood, Larry nodded. "After tea, Miles. About sevenish?"

Sometime after nine, they pulled into a motorway service area for breakfast. Jed, after sitting crunched up in the back seat, stretched out his limbs, and glanced over to the others standing close by. He'd noticed, almost from the start, that Janet was distant, barely speaking to him, spending most of her time laughing with Jon as he leaned over to whisper in her ear every other minute. And did he press his hand on her knee more than was necessary? As he looked out of the window and watched the world racing by, Jed began to think the whole journey was a dreadful mistake. But then, as soon as Janet nosed the car into a tight parking space, she whirled around, all flashing teeth and tossing hair. "Let's go and get a coffee and a bacon butty whilst Jon goes and does some business."

Jed wanted ask what kind of business, but Jon was already heading towards the far side of the car park, his stride meaningful, his shoulders bunched. "What's happened?"

"Not much," said Janet, hooking her arm into his. "Let's go and get something to eat."

She nuzzled into his arm and suddenly the world seemed a much brighter place altogether.

It was mid-afternoon when the two policemen came. Larry was where he always was lately, at *United Molasses* painting the huge steel drums that dominated the Wallasey end of Dock Road. He'd seen their approach, but paid them little attention until he heard his name shouted across to him by Warren Taylor, the site foreman. Reaching the ground he noted how serious the two uniformed officers appeared, and a jolt of anxiety shot through him. "Is it Jed?" he asked.

"Sorry sir?"

"Is it Jed, has there been an accident?"

The two officers exchanged bemused expressions. "It's your son we want to talk to, sir. But there's been no accident."

Larry was scratching his head. "Look, if this is about that nurse, then I thought it was all cleared up. Haven't you spoken to Sullivan? To interrupt me at my work – for God's sake!"

"We have spoken to Detective Sergeant Sullivan, yes sir. He sent us. We need to talk to your son. His school said he would be at home, on exam leave. But there was no reply."

Larry was frowning. "Well what's it about?"

It was the other officer who spoke, and he began by levelling a measured stare towards Larry. "There's been a murder, sir. Another one."

24

"I don't believe this – he was here only this morning."

"And what time would that be, sir?"

"Just before I left for work. About five minutes or so before eight."

"How can you be so exact, sir?" The young officer was scribbling it all down in his notebook whilst the other, much older man, stood impassively, his eyes never leaving Larry.

"Because I always leave for work at five minutes to eight. Always."

"I see. And what time did your son set off for Scotland, did you say?"

"Six, or thereabouts."

"And he would have travelled straight there, would he?"

"I suppose so…yes."

"But you couldn't swear to it?"

Larry felt his stomach tense. "Well, not exactly, no. How could I? But…well, it had all been arranged. His friends picked him up."

"Friends? And who were they, sir?"

"Er, the guy he met in the hospital."

"*Jon Kepowski?*" It was the other policeman who spoke, his voice sounded incredulous.

Larry wasn't liking this. It felt too much like an interrogation. He wrung his hands, "Yes! He called for Jed this morning and they drove off together."

"And you actually saw him, did you, this Jon Kepowski?"

Larry stopped, frowning. "Yes…" He let his voice drift away. Thinking back, he hadn't actually seen the man's face. He just assumed it was him. There had been someone else in the car, the driver, but they hadn't got out. "Look, what is all this? My son has gone to Scotland with friends, and now you're telling me that all of this has something to do with Miles?"

"His death, yes."

Larry squeezed his eyes shut. This was becoming more and more like a living nightmare. When he opened them again it was to see the police officers still standing there, as big as life. It was no nightmare, not one you could wake from anyway. Larry sighed. "Jed had nothing to do with it, obviously. Like I said, he's gone to Scotland."

"Yes, but you also said you couldn't be certain that he had. For all you know, Mr Meres, he may never have left the Wirral."

This argument was taken up by Detective Sullivan just over an hour later. Sullivan sat across from Larry Meres at the same table, wearing the same suit, with the same tired look on his face. "This is becoming very depressing."

"Isn't it just. Can't you just make some checks, Sergeant? Get in touch with the Scottish police, ask them to find the car?"

"What car, the one you said Jed was picked up in? And what would the registration number be, exactly?" Sullivan waited. There was no reply, how could there be? Larry hadn't even thought to check the number. "You see, Mr Meres, without that sort of information, there's not a lot to go on really. All I do know, for certain, is that you didn't do it."

"Thanks!"

"You've got your alibi, at work all day. Always in the presence of someone else." Sullivan reached inside his pocket and pulled out his notebook. He flipped it open. "Miles's body was found at just after ten o'clock this morning. His head had been bashed in, just like the others. According to the pathology report, as the body was still warm, the murder had been perpetrated within a very short time before the body was discovered. Perhaps as early as nine o'clock. We know you didn't do it, you were at work on time. There is no possibility of you having murdered Miles, then trotted off to *United Molasses* to begin your day. So that only leaves Jed. And you say he has gone to Scotland."

Larry had his face in his hands, listening to the detective droning on and on. He spoke through his fingers. "Look, I saw him drive off with his friends. I told you. It had been arranged. Then, at around eight, Miles calls and tells me he wants to talk to me. We arrange for him to call round again at seven in the evening. Jed is in Scotland, just find him and sort *all of this out.*"

"Who were his friends?"

"I told the constable." Larry dragged his hands away. He felt tired and drained. He wanted his tea, then bed. It was another day tomorrow and the work was mounting up. Taylor would be furious that he'd lost an hour. Could life get any worse?

"Yes, I know what you told the constable. Let me ask you something else, Mr Meres. What father, what caring, doting father, allows his son, who is supposed to be on study leave, to go off to Scotland – if, indeed, he did – without knowing anything about who he was going with, how long he'll be away, or where he was going?"

Sullivan was right, of course he was. Larry felt ashamed at that moment, because Sullivan's words were thick with truth. He was a poor excuse of a father. It had crossed his mind to ask Jed all of those things but for some reason, some unfathomable reason, he hadn't done so. What was it, trust? Or perhaps he just didn't care. Was that the real truth? He should have felt angry at Sullivan's accusations, but he didn't. Just a deepening realisation that he didn't really care about anything or anyone. Not even Jed. It was all so bloody pointless.

"You see, if it were me, I'd want to know. Sure, he's getting older, he's a big lad. Can handle himself too, by all accounts. But, with everything that has gone on, not knowing where he's going to, that strikes me as irresponsible. Wouldn't you say?"

"I suppose…" Larry propped his head up with on hand. "He said he'd phone me later. To tell me where he is."

"And in the meantime? We just wait, is that it? Wait for him to grace us with an explanation."

"There is no need for an explanation, sergeant – he didn't do it!"

"So you say. The man who says he went off with Jon Kepowski?"

"Exactly."

"You see, that's the other really interesting thing about all of this. You didn't see his face, did you?"

"No. But Jed had told me, the night before, that..." Larry blew out his cheeks

"Ah, right. This is the same son who tells you he's going to Scotland for a couple of days, when in actual fact he didn't – he stayed here, to murder poor Miles!"

Larry looked away. He'd had enough, he could barely keep his eyes open. He was too tired to even feel angry at Sullivan's accusation. "Look, I'm getting tired now, tired of this, tired of you and your insults. Just talk to Jed, and Jon. They'll put your mind at rest, then perhaps we can all get back to living our lives."

"Oh, I'll be talking to Jed all right, don't you worry. Kepowski might be a bit trickier however. Seeing as he's dead."

They'd driven down past Glencoe, stopping briefly to take in the view, but without going to the visitors' centre. Jon seemed distant, his mind on other things. Janet was lighter, always smiling, as if she were trying, in a way, to compensate for Jon's dark mood. When Jed stepped out to stretch his legs, an elderly couple gave him a strange glance, but he soon forgot them and clambered back into the car as Janet prepared to take the car down the long, straight road, which would lead them towards Culloden.

Jon briefly came out of his bleakness to tell Janet to take a sharp right. Jed was mesmerised by the view, a single stretch of road cutting through the most desolate, beautiful and breath-taking landscape he had ever seen. For as far as the eye could see stark wilderness rolled towards the horizon, reminding him of one of those roads he'd seen in American movies, stretching on and on. He wondered what they would do if they broke down. How would they summon help? He shook himself as the car swung into a new stretch of road and looked out to see more desolation. But this time, it was different.

The mood changed, the first thing he noticed as he wound down the window and breathed in the air. It was now late afternoon and the sky was a solid, depressing grey. But it wasn't the sky that grabbed his attention, it was something more. A sinister atmosphere gripped the land and Janet, slowing down, sensed it too.

"What the hell is that?"

She stopped the car and Jed joined her, staring in disbelief at what loomed before them.

It was a wall, enormous, stretching upwards, perhaps ten feet thick and thirty feet high, possibly more and wide, wider than a terrace of ten houses. Jon was already stepping out of the car and Jed didn't hesitate in following, pushing the passenger seat forward, scrambling out into the daylight.

It was cold, a bitter wind ripping around him, and he pulled his coat closer. He stood, open-mouthed, staring at the wall. Up close, it was truly huge and, upon its surface, were strange marks, like massive splats made from what looked like eggs hurled against it. But not eggs, obviously. Splats. Splats of what?

There was no noise other than the wind, a dreadful, ghastly moan, the sound of countless lost souls, setting up their chant of despair, letting the world know of their abandonment, trapped between this world and the next. No one to help, no one to care, damned forever to wander in the twilight of existence.

Pressing his trembling hand against his mouth, Jed wondered what the hell was he thinking about, where had these ideas came from? Shaking himself, he turned to see Jon standing, a hundred yards or more so away, hands in pockets, staring at something on the ground. Jed walked over to him, looking back over his shoulder occasionally, to check that the wall was real, that it wasn't just a figment of his imagination the way the sound of the wind was.

"What is this place?"

Jon looked up, face drawn, as grey as the sky, looking more emaciated than at any other time since hospital.

"It's a target."

"A what?"

"This," Jon kicked the strange construction he stood beside. Half as tall as he was, made from metal, it looked like a symbol of some sort. Jed couldn't make it out, but from above it would be possible to read what it was. "It's a pointer, to the target – the wall."

"Seen from above?"

Jon nodded.

"A target? A target for what?"

"Typhoons." He swept his hand above him in a wide arc, "They'd fly in low and fast, firing off their missiles to hit the wall."

"Typhoons?"

"World War Two fighter-bombers. Used in droves during the Normandy offensive."

"Jon, what are we doing here? I don't like it, there's something not right about this place."

"Full of ghosts, you mean."

"Ghosts. Yes. I can … Jesus, I can *feel* them."

"We've slipped, Jed."

"Slipped? What the hell are you—"

" You've got to understand, I have no control over these things. Only control over you, and others. But not this."

Jed shook his head, "Jon, you're not making any sense. Slipped? A target?" He turned and looked over to where the car was. Except, it wasn't there anymore. He rubbed his eyes with his fists and gaped. "Jon? Where the hell is the car? Where's Janet gone with the fucking car?"

He whirled around and then he knew he was in Hell.

25

The roar of engines, far off in the distance, caused him to spin on his heels. Peering into the grey expanse of sky, he saw them, like specks of black, approaching fast. At first he thought they might be birds, but as they closed in, their shape grew more distinctive.

They were Hawker Typhoons. He recognised them, had built an *Airfix* kit some years back. Their big, powerful engines rumbled across the land, and he watched, mesmerised, as the small formation of four planes, split into two pairs. Coming in low and fast, Jed span, realising instantly what their target was.

The huge wall.

And he was mere yards away.

Head down he dived to the ground, rolling behind the massive cast-iron arrow that only moments before Jon had sat on. Now, the only person remaining on that barren landscape, was Jed. Curling himself into a ball, making himself as small as possible, he heard the great rush overhead as each plane released their RP-3 ground-attack rockets. Within seconds, the rockets struck the face of the wall, exploding with a tremendous blast, and he realised, at once, what those strange egg-splat stains were.

Chancing a look, he watched the planes peel away far above him, soaring upwards before turning once more for a second attack.

But one of them took a different course.

Crouched against the arrow, Jed saw it, the terror gripping him. For this particular Typhoon was making its second run, not towards the wall, but directly towards where he lay.

The rocket released, its vapour trail streaking out behind it, and he screamed as the world closed in all around him.

He snapped open his eyes and for a moment he didn't know where he was, but one thing was certain – he no longer sat amongst the coarse, damp grass of the open moor. He was in room, smelling of rose-water, or something similar, the kind of stuff elderly ladies dabbed on themselves to make them sweet. Sweet?

None of this was *sweet!* Anything but. Rubbing his face, he rolled over and sat up, aware of the sweat and grime clinging to his body. He was in need of a shower – even the rose-water couldn't disguise that.

"Are you all right?"

Her voice, like an angel's, soft and low, came to him from out of the corner of the room and he shook himself and turned to find Janet, smiling. It took him a second or two to reorient himself. "Where are we?"

"In a little guest house. You blacked out. I didn't realize how heavy you were until we tried to get you into the car." She came and sat down beside him on the single bed underneath a small three light window, its chintz curtains toed back by decorative red cords. Tracing the line of his bicep, she purred. "It's all muscle though…" Then she leaned across and kissed him lightly on the cheek. "Jon's next door. I'll just go and tell him you're awake."

Jed went to speak, but already she was gone, closing the door quietly behind her. He sat for a few more moments, trying to disentangle his thoughts. The last thing he could remember was seeing…He struggled. There was the wall and that huge symbol on the ground and he remembered the pot-marks on the surface… He squeezed his eyes shut and tried to conjure up the image from the depths of his memory, but everything remained fuzzy, refusing to come into focus. Made from metal, symbol and wall, and the symbol, was that an arrow, pointing towards the wall?

A muffled groan, like a prolonged sigh, came from the next room, through the paper-thin wall. He slowed his breathing, listening. There it was again, louder, more urgent this time. Jed stood up, went across the room and pressed his ear against the cold, white plaster surface.

'*Oh God…God, Jon…*'

He stepped away, his heart thumping. eyes locked on the wall, wide in disbelief.

'*Oh God…yes…YES!*'

Breath coming in short, shallow gasps, his mouth went dry as he realised what was happening. In a daze, he fumbled for the door handle and padded out into the little hallway. The door to the next bedroom was slightly ajar, the sounds from within louder, more distinct. He knew he shouldn't, but having no control over his actions, he leaned forward and peered through the crack.

Janet straddled Jon on the bed, moving up and down rhythmically, her head thrown back, her hands running through the tumbled mass of her own hair. As she moved, she cried out, her pace increasing.

Fascinated, unable to tear himself away, Jed watched, aware of his growing erection. Lost in a swirling haze of desire, all thoughts of remaining silent gone, he pushed the door open wide and stepped inside.

She turned to gaze at him and broke into a wide smile, her hands falling down over her breasts, lingering there for a moment, before travelling to Jon's chest, and she increased her movements. Jon brought his hips up to meet her, holding onto the fleshy mounds of her hips; she yelled loudly then, throwing her head back, eyes closed, and he thrust upwards in response, over and over.

Jed, every fibre of his body aching, centred all of his senses on the delicious pain spreading across his loins. He tore away at his jeans and brought himself out. Janet laughed, her tongue running across her bottom lip, "Yes Jed!"

And then he was lost to it all.

It was gone midnight when Larry Meres finally opened his front door. He felt awful, his mouth thick with the taste of the police station interview room, his clothes stinking from the fug of cigarette smoke the detectives insisted on smoking. He'd never smoked, and now his chest felt raw, stuffed with dirty cotton wool, as if he'd gone through at least a dozen cigarettes. Mounting the stairs, he was already pulling off his shirt.

The telephone rang and he turned, rushing down to answer it.

"Dad, where have you been, I've phoned you three times!"

"Sorry Jed…" He daren't tell him what had been happening, not now. His brain was too full of mush to think things through, apart from the overwhelming sense of belief he felt at the sound of his son's voice. "Is everything okay?"

"Everything's great, Dad, We went to Glencoe today and tomorrow we're going to see Culloden. You know about Culloden? Culloden Moor?"

"Er, yes, battle wasn't it?" Larry squeezed his fingers into his eyes. Jed sounded buoyant, full of joy and wonder, almost like he was a little boy again. But there was something else, something Larry couldn't quite put his finger on…

"Dad, everything is all right isn't it? Did I wake you up?"

"Jed – it's almost twenty past twelve."

"Yeah, well, like I said, I've phoned you over and over. Where have you been?"

"I, er, had to see someone. Nothing very, you know, interesting. Look, ring me tomorrow and I'll be able to talk more then. I'm really tired, Jed. But thanks for calling, yeah? I've been worried."

"No need to worry, Dad. I'm fine. I'll call you tomorrow."

The line went dead and Larry stared at the phone, twisting his mouth, trying to work out why he felt Jed wasn't telling the whole truth. It wasn't so much what he said, but the way he said it. Not like him at all – different, forced, almost as if he were reading it from a script. But that was stupid. Why would his own son… And his voice. That was different too. Perhaps he was tired, worried …

Larry yawned. It was too late for this nonsense. He'd shower in the morning, freshen himself up, gather his thoughts. If he didn't get to bed soon, he'd be falling down asleep in the hallway.

Jed lay on the bed, Janet next to him. She was sleeping. He looked at her. Her cheeks were red with a rosy glow. Completely satisfied, she had fallen asleep almost as soon as she had rolled off Jon's body. He stood, kissed her lightly on the forehead, and pulled on his shirt. Slumped in the corner, Jed watched him, ashamed, embarrassed, consumed with self-loathing, his mess all over his hand and the front of his jeans. Jon looked at him and didn't say a word before leaving the room. Jed stayed there for a few moments, then crossed to the tiny sink against the far wall, rinsing his hands and face, dabbing the front of his jeans, doing his best to wash away the stains. He hadn't brought another pair of trousers, not thinking he'd need them. Cursing, he pulled them off and lay them over the rim of the sink, then settled down next to Janet.

And that's how he was when Jon returned some time later. He gave Jed a look. "It's nearly half-past midnight, Jed. Time you were in bed."

That was all. No explanations, nothing about what had happened or why. "Jon. When we were got to the—"

"Not now Jed, there's a good lad." He pulled off his trousers and stood, as if relishing exposing himself.

"Oh my God," mumbled Jed, gaping.

"Off you go."

In a rush, Jed leaped up, grabbed his jeans and ran into his own room. Throwing himself down onto his bed and lay there, eyes open, not knowing what to do or think.

Later, he had no way of knowing how much later, he must have drifted off into sleep, roused again by the sound of the creaking bed next door. And her voice, low but urgent, *'Oh God, Jon...Oh God...'*

26

Breakfast time he sat alone at his table. The silent waitress, older than the hills, dumped the plate in front of him and shuffled off. He stared at the offering – two scrawny pieces of burnt bacon, a runny egg and a heap of slimy mushrooms. He pushed the plate away and spread hard butter on cold toast. Sitting back, he gazed out of the restaurant window towards the open grassland beyond. It was raining, in great slanting sheets, darkening his mood still further. He took a gulp of coffee, threw his half-eaten toast onto the plate and went out.

"Are you old enough to be driving that car?"

He turned towards the sound of the voice. A strange little man, glasses pushed back onto a shiny dome, stood behind the reception desk, huddled over a large ledger. Jed frowned, not sure if the man was addressing him or not. He zipped up his coat and went to move away.

"Nothing to do with me what you do, of course, but I don't want the police calling. Bad for business."

Ignoring him, Jed stepped out into the rain and was surprised to see Janet already sitting behind the wheel. She smiled at him through the misted up window. Jon was nowhere, which was a relief. Jed felt deeply embarrassed by the previous night and, as he clambered in beside her, he tried to make the first sounds of an apology, "Sorry about, you know—"

"Jon's got business," Janet said, all bubbly and full of joy, seeming to ignore Jed's awkwardness. "So, we can take the time to Culloden.

Like we planned." She smiled, put the car into gear and took it out of the car park. Soon they headed out of the little town. Jed looked at the passing buildings. He had no recollection of arriving at the guesthouse, none whatsoever. Come to think of it, he had little real recollection of anything at all. Except last night. How could he forget that…

"Why are we here?" he asked, without turning.

"Here? What do you mean?"

"In Scotland? Why have we come all this way – for what reason?"

"Well – Jon, he has business. Like I said. And he thought it would be a chance for us to be alone, you know…" She giggled. "Don't you just love him?"

"I'm not…" He peered into the grey mist, the rain obscuring the view. He said quietly, "Do you?" Then he looked at her.

She glanced over to him, frowning. "Do I what?"

"Love him? You said, *don't you just love him*. Was that literal?"

"Lit – what?"

"You seemed to 'love him' quite a lot last night."

Her cheeks reddened slightly, "Oh, that…Well – what's a girl to do, eh? He is, you know…"

"No, I don't actually. What is he?"

"God, you're in a bad mood this morning, aren't you? What's the matter with you, with all these questions?"

And why are you so angry, so defensive? Jed looked away again, finding solace in the rain. He liked the way it drained all colour from the land, making it appear so depressing. He spotted a man struggling along the road, no hat, no umbrella, stooped forward against the weather, no doubt already soaked through to the skin, and the sight made him feel better. At least someone was having a worse time of it than he was.

She turned the car into a rutted road, one that snaked through a massive Forestry Commission area. It grew dark, the great trees on either side reaching up to the sky, blocking out most of the sunlight. Fortunately, they also blocked out most of the rain. Winding down the window, Jed breathed in the fresh scent of pine, closing his eyes, imagining that this must be what Sweden or Norway smelled like. He opened his eye to watch the passing denseness of trees and wondered why everything seemed so quiet.

She swung into a quiet car park, only one other car already waiting there. She stopped and smiled at him.

"Let's take a look," she said.

He didn't fully understand her words. Take a look at what? "Where are we?" he asked.

"Culloden Moor."

Culloden Moor. Even the name sent shivers down his spine.

He stood there, a few moments later, coat zipped up against the slanting rain. The moor, a bleak, awful place, its soul ripped away, the wind moaning through the heather seeming to cry out for the fallen. Shivering, Jed sensed what it might have been like on that dreadful day, when the Highlanders met defeat. Lonely and miserable, a grey, washed-out landscape, a place full of death. He could see it, all of it, amongst the heather and the thistle, hear it in the lament of the wind. He watched English redcoats cut down the hopelessly out-gunned Scots in droves, their ancient way of life, the life of the Clan, destroyed forever. How many had they lost that day? Hundreds. And the English, a few tens. Thirty, or so. He'd have to check it up in the history books when he got home. He turned a serious, drawn face towards Janet. "Why are we here?"

"I thought you'd find it interesting."

"I do. But, why would you bring me here? Are *you* interested in any of this?"

"Sort of."

"What does that mean?"

"It means that I think you should see it. That's all. Jon thinks you should see it."

"Why? I mean, the crazy thing is, I actually *am* interested, but how could you know that? How could Jon know that?"

"Why do you always ask such strange questions?"

"Because it's not the usual thing for a girl and boy to do – travel all the way up here, to stand on this dismal piece of land and think about what it must have been like to die here. That's why."

"Well – Jon thought you'd enjoy it."

"Jon. All you ever talk about is Jon. Everything is Jon. Do you love him, Janet? Is it him you want to be with?"

Taking in a deep breath, she looked out across the vastness of that awful place, tuning in to the despair of the fallen. "You just don't understand, Jed."

"Then tell me – make me understand. Janet, I heard you having sex with him last night. And I think you wanted me to hear. I think it was all planned."

"Planned?" She laughed. "God, you really are naive."

"I suppose I am, but it's true isn't it? You brought me up here so I could witness you and him *do* what you were doing." He looked away, the memory too recent, too fresh. And too painful. "My God, I think you actually enjoyed humiliating me that way."

She reached out to stroke his cheek with the back of her hand. He flinched, but not too much. He still relished the hope that they could become something more than just friends.

"I adore him," she whispered huskily. "I can't help it, I wish I could. When I'm with him, I'm in heaven and when I'm not – all I can do is count the minutes until I'm back in his arms."

Jed heard her words, but he couldn't begin to register them. None of it made any sense; he was beyond wondering how everything fitted together. Bringing him here, stringing him a yarn, letting him believe there was a chance...

A sudden gust of wind brought him out of his reverie. He sighed loudly and turned to go, leaving her standing there, to look out across the desolate moor.

Sometime later she came up to him inside the visitors' centre. He was peering at some displays, positioned over some glass topped viewing cabinets. He didn't look at her.

"What's wrong?"

He snorted. "What the hell do you think?"

"You can't say you didn't enjoy last night... You did, didn't you?"

His stomach turned to water as the memory returned. How she'd held Jon, brought him to orgasm, so slowly, smoothly, unrushed. He closed his eyes, a lump in his throat. "Yes."

"Well then," she traced a finger along his arm, "why can't you just be content with that?"

Jed shook himself. "Content? Content with what? It's you I want, Janet, not..." he glanced at the display board again, not taking in the words or the illustrations. "If this is how it's going to be, I'd rather not. Thanks anyway."

"You don't mean that."

"Don't I? What the hell do you know what I want and don't want? You tricked me, Janet. You and Jon. You brought me up here for some... *reason*... And it's got nothing to do with what happened last night. You could have done that anywhere. So, I'm going to ask you again, what the hell are we doing here?"

"Are you all right?"

Jed's head snapped around to find a small, frail looking lady with startlingly white hair raked back from her wrinkled face, staring at him, troubled.

"No, I..." he shrugged, assuming his voice was becoming too loud. "Sorry."

"This place often makes visitors somewhat distraught. It's the ghosts."

"Ghosts?" He frowned. "What do you mean, 'ghosts'?"

"Of the men who died here, of course. Their spirits still roam the moor. Can't you feel them?"

He forced a laugh and turned to talk to Janet. But Janet wasn't there; she'd slipped outside. Jed sighed again. Was he ever going to get any answers?

"I'll make you a nice cup of tea, if you like." Then she did a surprising thing. She took him by the hand and very gently, but very determinedly, she led him over to the far side of the centre, to where there were some tables and chairs. She settled him down, patted him on the shoulder, and stepped behind the counter to prepare the tea.

Jed sat with his chin in his hand and tried to get things straight in his mind. He hated himself for falling under their spell. Both of them. Jon, with that curious hold he had over him. What was it, lust, the desire to experience the unknown? And Janet. Her charms were more obvious; she'd reeled him in like the stupid fish that he was. Eager, blind, driven by his loins, not his brain. God, it was so depressing. If only he could just sit here, in this funny little place, a million miles from every temptation, it would all be fine. Here he could think straight. Here his loins didn't burn with desire.

"There you are," the old lady settled the steaming cup of tea in front of him and sat down opposite. She smiled. "Sugar?" He nodded and she heaped in three spoonfuls. "Hope that's enough." She stirred the tea and sat back, satisfied.

It was a wonderful cup of tea, one of the best he had ever tasted. He smacked his lips. "Thank you."

"Not at all," the little old lady said, her eyes never leaving his. "I've been watching you. First out on the moor, then in here. You seem – agitated? Is that the right word?"

"Agitated? I don't know. How do you mean?"

"As if you were arguing with yourself. Have you run away, is that it?"

"Run away…" He ran a hand through his hair. "I suppose I have, in a weird sort of way."

"Nothing weird about it. Young people these days, they have all the pressures and none of the experience to cope. It's a world gone mad, everything so fast. Everything has to happen *now* – in this instant. There's no time to sit back and relax anymore. I'm glad I'm not young."

"This place, this moor, do you get many people coming here?"

"To Culloden? Goodness me, yes. The weather is no barrier to them, but today…" she shivered, "Not such a good day today. Mid-week is always quiet, but…" Her voice drifted away. The rain beat against the windows and as he turned to look, he couldn't see more than a few feet across the car-park. Janet must have got back inside the car, otherwise she'd be soaked.

"It was like this on the day, I think. On the day of the battle," he said.

"Yes. That was an awful day. The Highlanders were soaked through, starving. They hadn't eaten for days. Morale was very low. And yet, they still fought with incredibly bravery."

"But lost."

She nodded her head with great reverence. "Oh yes. They lost. But not everything; certainly not their dignity, nor their heroism. You seem like a knowledgeable young man, sensitive too. You've been here before?"

"No, never. I saw a film, on the BBC not so long ago. All about the battle. It was very moving."

"Yes. I know the one you mean. Interesting you should find it 'moving'. What's your name?"

"Jed."

"Jed. Yes, of course it is…Now," she sat upright, surprisingly sprightly for one so old. "I must get back to work. Finish your tea, it'll warm you up." She paused, reached inside her blue overall and produced a small piece of paper, neatly folded. She pressed it into his hand. "Just in case."

Puzzled, Jed watched her go back behind the counter, drank down the rest of his tea, then got up, carefully placing cup and saucer on the worktop. "Thank you," he said.

As he reached the door, the old lady's voice sounded stronger and more assured than ever as she spoke, "You take care of yourself. Remember, things aren't always as they first appear."

He waited a moment, lost in thought, then very slowly opened the door and stepped outside.

It had stopped raining, but the moor appeared as bleak and as friendless as before. He doubted if even on a brilliant summer's day it would be anything other than solemn and oppressive. Plunging his hands into his coat, he walked across the car park to where the car was. But as he got closer he could see very clearly that Janet was nowhere in sight. He tried the door. Locked.

"You forgot these!"

He turned, frowning, to find the old lady in the doorway. She was smiling, then she threw something towards him. A bunch of keys. They landed at his feet and he stooped to pick them up. When he straightened up again, she had gone. He was the only person there.

27

He didn't know how he did it, not any single part of it. Had he always known, or was it something that had come to him in his self-conscious? Whatever it was, it frightened him, yet left him strangely elated. Because if he could drive, as indeed he was now doing, then his life was going to change.

Until, that is, the police pulled him over and asked for his licence.

It was coming up to 4.30 pm. Soon his dad would be home, and he needed to talk to his dad. At the little village, he parked the car at a designated place and got out to stretch his legs. He stood there for a long time, just staring into space, not sure what to do next. In the back seat was his overnight bag and, on a sudden impulse, he opened up the boot and looked inside.

There was nothing there, except the spare wheel and car-jack. No over-night case, packed by Janet, no indication that there had been anyone else with him. He slammed the boot lid shut, suddenly angry, and leaned against the car, eyes squeezed tightly shut. He didn't feel too good, his stomach was queasy and his head banged. But most of all he felt confused. *Jed. Yes, of course it is...* That was what the old lady had said, but what did she mean by that? Why should it be *of course it is...* How could she know?

Moving across the almost empty street, he went into a telephone box and called home. Dad wouldn't be there yet, but it gave him something to do, and besides—

"Hello?"

Jed gave a start as his dad's voice came down the line. "Dad? What are you doing home?"

"Is everything all right? Jed, where are you?"

His voice sounded urgent, scared almost. Jed rubbed his face as another wave of confusion crashed over him, "What the hell – Dad, are *you* all right? What are you doing home?"

"Finished early." It was a lie; Jed knew it was a lie. His dad never finished early, it simply wasn't done. Late, yes, but never early. Not even on Christmas Eve. "I know I asked you to call, but I thought it would be later. Still, now that you're on – how is everything?"

"You asked me to call? When did you ask me to call? Dad, you're not making any sense."

"I'm not...? Jed, you phoned me yesterday. Are you on something?"

On something. My God...

Jed felt his legs go weak and suddenly he was falling, sliding down the inside of the phone-box, his senses reeling, his tongue thick in his mouth, eyes unable to focus, everything going around and around. All of it so very, very black.

He lay in a clean bed, the sheets crisp, smelling of lavender. Tucked in so tightly he was barely able to move, and he struggled to free a hand, which helped cool him down a little. It was hot, stifling. He went to sit up.

"Take it easy now." The voice calm and kindly belonged to the old lady.

Jed went to sit upright again, suddenly feeling afraid. But she pushed him back down, applying a cold, damp flannel to his forehead and her voice cooed, "There, there. Just try and relax."

"What...where am I? What's going on?"

"It's all right, you bumped your head is all. You just need to rest and, when you're a bit better, I'll explain everything. As much as I can, at least."

"But my dad, I was—"

"Your dad's fine. You're fine. Just try and rest."

He gave himself up to the voice and the cool, crisp sheets. The heat seeped out of his body and the flannel, so good on his forehead, brought such a sense of contentment he soon closed his eyes and allowed himself to drift away...

On waking the second time, the tension was gone, his body cocooned in a warm, soothing glow. Almost total darkness enveloped him, the only light coming from a pathetic oil lamp spluttering alarmingly in the far corner. Cautiously, he sat up and realized he was alone. His headache had gone and he felt human again. No less confused, but as strong as when he stepped into the phone box. When was that? Four-thirty? He squinted at his watch face, barely able to make out the time. A few minutes past ten. His heart lurched at that and he swung his legs from under the covers and went to stand up.

She came through the door in a rush, face screwed up into a scowl. "What do you think you are doing? Of all the silly nonsense – get back into bed this instant!"

Trying to fight back, his anger at having slept so long giving him a surge of strength, the old lady nevertheless pushed him back with surprising ease.

"I've got to go," he shouted, not caring for her soothing charms, all the help she had given him, "I need to explain to Dad what's going on – and I need to find Janet."

"Try and calm down," she said, tucking in the sheets.

"Who the bloody hell are you, anyway? A how the hell did I end up here, in this bed, in this bloody, bloody place?"

"I know you're anxious," she said, stroking his forehead, brushing the hair from his face, "but you have to trust me. It'll take some time for the drugs to wear off and until then, you need to rest."

"Drugs? *Drugs*? What the hell do you mean? Who are you?"

Another attempt to rise, but her hand pressed on his chest, forcing him down, so strong for someone so old and so small. "You're in shock, Jed. You just need to rest. It'll all become clear in the morning."

"Drugs you said. Who drugged me? Is that why I fainted? Drugs? You've drugged me?"

"Yes, but not that sort of drug, Jed. Antidote would be a better word for it, an antidote to all the junk they've been putting inside you."

"Anti – what? Junk *they've* put into me? What are you talking about?"

She stroked his head. calming him, tiny cooing sounds coming from her mouth. Slowly his eyes grew heavy again.

"I don't understand any of this," he said, his voice thick, head all fuzzy, clogged up with cotton wool, the fatigue, over-taking him. "I just need to talk to my dad."

"I know you do. And you will. But for the time being you concentrate on getting your strength back."

"But drugs you said. I don't…Please, just tell me."

"It was me. I gave you something, something to help. That's all. In the tea." She leaned over and kissed him lightly on the cheek. "Now sleep."

And he did.

28

Shortly after a breakfast of porridge, followed by eggs and bacon, Jed slid in behind the wheel of the little Vauxhall and turned the key. After the third attempt, the engine spluttered into life, not a promising sign. The old lady stood beside the car, drying her hands on the white apron around her waist. "You've got my number?"

Jed patted his breast pocket and smiled. Feeling awkward, he stared at the steering wheel. "I don't know what to say, where to begin."

"Don't say anything. Talk to your dad. Talk to your brother. If you need any help, you call me." She leaned in through the open window and kissed him.

"Thank you."

"God bless you, Jed."

He put the car into gear, slowly drove away from the visitors' centre, and headed for the forest road, taking him away from that mournful place.

Jed stopped only once, to fill up with petrol. He found his wallet stuffed with notes and he wondered why he had brought so much money with him. Yet one more thing of which he had no memory. He purchased a sandwich and a drink and consumed them in the car, staring into the bleak, grey unfriendly car park and thought about what the old lady had said. He'd been drugged. Hence all the confusion, the loss of memory, the idea of living two lives. Janet and Jon. Names from reading books at infant school. Names meant to be innocent.

Finishing his meagre meal, he drove down long, winding roads, never pausing, keeping the accelerator depressed all the way down to the floor.

At a large service station on the M6 motorway, when he stopped for a toilet break, a couple of police officers gave him a curious look. Their attention became diverted when someone inadvertently reversed into another parked car, and Jed was able to continue on his way unhindered. Setting a steady pace, motorways merged, the Liverpool tunnel flashing by, and soon, the time approaching early evening, he finally brought the car to a halt outside his house.

Dad was not home, which was peculiar. There was no note either, but as Jed hadn't warned him of his return, not so surprising. From now on, he would keep things to himself and not give too much away. Things might be safer that way, give him more control over his life and the direction it took. No more outside influences.

He scoured the kitchen for something to eat, finding only a few pieces of bread, which he toasted. As he prepared to make a cup of coffee, the doorbell rang. Not once, but three times, in quick succession. Jed groaned at the caller's impatience. With cup and toast in one hand, he tore open the door, a little annoyed.

"Thank God you're home – where the hell have you been?"

It took Jed a few moments to find his breath, but not before both toast and coffee fell to the floor forgotten.

Standing in the doorway, face drawn with anguish and concern, was his mother.

She'd brought some shopping with her. "I didn't think you'd have much in," she mumbled, almost to herself, as she set about filling up cupboards and the fridge with the items she had bought. Jed watched her, his head full of questions but not knowing where to begin. Trapped in confusion, he sat and gazed at her, incredulous.

When at last she'd finished, she turned to him, wiping her hands down the front of her skirt. She brushed some wayward hair from her face with the back of her hand. She looked flustered, a little annoyed, obvious that she didn't want to be there.

"You're dad's in hospital."

Jed blinked. "*What?*"

"Stupid man that he is, he was in some warehouse, getting the place ready for painting, and he moved a large cabinet. By himself. Stupid and proud." She exhaled loudly, went to the sink with the kettle and filled it up.

Jed's impatience boiled to the surface, "*And?* What happened?"

She put the kettle on the hob and sat down. "He ruptured himself."

He wanted to laugh, but the dark look on her face forced him to stop. "*Ruptured* himself? What – I don't understand. Why is he in hospital?"

She planted her elbows on the tabletop and glared at him, "Are you completely stupid? Where have you been? If you had been here, this probably would never have happened."

He gaped at her. "How do you work that one out? You said he did it in a warehouse – and you still haven't told me why he's in hospital."

"He nearly *died*. Stupid man, trying to move the damned thing on his own. What was he thinking. And you – *you!*"

And so it continued, the tirade. Blame, accusations, reproach. Jed sat in a state of shock, taking it all, making him feel numb. Dad in hospital, Mum back at home and still only Thursday. On Monday, his first exam loomed, but he couldn't for the life of him remember which one. He put his face in his hands and tried to block everything out, but without success. Mum's voice, droning on and on. He gazed up in despair.

"And whose is that car outside?"

"Janet's."

"Janet? Who is Janet?"

"A friend."

She threw back her head, having heard enough and flounced out of the kitchen, stomping her way upstairs. "We're going to the hospital," she called before slamming the bathroom door.

The telephone was ringing. Jed climbed to his feet, everything heavy, and answered it.

"You left me in Scotland."

Jon's voice sounded cold, menacing. Not knowing how to respond, Jed merely whimpered in reply, a grunt, "Uh."

"I'm not pleased. What happened?"

Jed took a breath, heartbeat banging, so loudly Jon had to have heard it. "I collapsed. Fainted. I had no way of getting in touch with you. And Janet – she disappeared."

"So where did you stay – you weren't at the guesthouse."

Jed looked up the stairs anxiously, not wanting his mother to hear. Stomping around in the bedroom, she seemed busy enough, but he kept his voice low, knowing she had hearing as acute as a bat's. "No. I stayed with a woman. An old lady."

"Old lady?" Jed sensed the change in Jon's tone. From cold, to fearful, full of urgency. "What old lady?"

"At the visitors' centre. When Janet ran off, I tried to follow, but I didn't make it. The old lady looked after me after I'd collapsed."

"Visitors' centre? What are you talking about – what visitors' centre?"

"At Culloden."

A prolonged pause followed, during which Jed could have sworn he heard Jon's own heartbeat increase alarmingly. They could start up a group, *Jon and the Heartbeats*. Jed squeezed his eyes shut. Where did that come from? A joke? He hadn't made a joke for – well, forever!

Jon's voice came again, sharp and angry. "You have no idea what you have done!" Abruptly the line went dead.

Frowning, Jed gently returned the receiver back on its cradle and turned to see his mother coming down the stairs, fresh faced and smiling. Her air of joyful abandonment left him cold and he pushed past her, determined not to catch her eye.

They came out of the hospital, both feeling depressed. Larry had barely spoken, depressed, not himself. All sorts of wires and tubes protruded from seemingly every inch of his body. He looked awful, his skin a pale yellow colour, his eyes wide, at one point rolling back into his head, as if he were brain-damaged. All of which was nonsense, of course. *He's only experienced a rupture*, Jed's mum was quick to point out. But no sooner had she left the ward than she broke down, Jed having to guide her towards the entrance as she blubbed, "He's not going to die, is he?"

The sharp, night air bit cold as they walked across the car park. Around them, people came and went as the human tide of suffering ebbed and waned. Mindful only of his mum, he helped her into the passenger seat. As he went round to the driver-s side, he looked up and caught sight of a figure standing directly beneath the glow of a nearby street lamp, as if deliberately staged purely for his benefit. He gave a muffled cry. Inspector Sullivan, laughing loudly, leaned against the post, talking to another man, the other man being the reason why Jed felt his entire world imploding. It was Matthew, his half-brother.

Neither looked up, and Jed watched them as they shook hands before going their separate ways, Matthew raising his hand in a brief, friendly 'goodbye'.

Putting his hands flat on the roof of the car, Jed's mouth went slack, his stomach lurching.

Matthew and Sullivan knew one another?

But how, and why? What was their connection, how had it come about. He rubbed his face, the confusion, the fear returning, inescapable, unrelenting.

Matthew and Sullivan.

"Come on," his mother snapped from inside the car, "I need to get home for a cup of tea."

Feeling sick, he clambered in next to her.

Not a word passed between them during the entire journey home.

The house felt cold when they got back, colder than usual. Jed made tea and she went into the living room. He heard her switching on the electric fire, a long, drawn out sigh. Coming into the room with the tea, he stopped in the doorway, saw her with her legs stretched out, head against the back of the sofa, eyes closed. It was as if time had gone backwards. His Mum, home again. Life back to normal.

He put the cups on the occasional table and sank into the armchair opposite her, knowing life could never be *normal* ever again.

"I know what you're thinking," she said, without opening her eyes or moving any part of her body.

"Oh? Do you?"

"You're thinking why I came back."

He reached forward and picked up his mug of tea. "I suppose it's because you feel guilty."

"Oh no," she said, opening her eyes. "It's not that – what have I got to feel guilty about? I fell in love. That's not something I am ashamed about." She smiled. "You probably haven't got a clue what I'm thinking. How can you. You probably hate me."

"I don't hate you." The temperature was rising, the room pressing in around him, growing uncomfortable. He didn't want to be having this conversation, not with his mum, the one who had run off and left his dad.

"But you don't understand."

He shook his head. "I'm not sure I want to." A buzz ran through his stomach. Was this what it was like to be 'grown up', to have conversations about things that matter? He'd never really talked to his mum before. She breezed along the edges of his life, the daily grind of getting up, going to work, coming home, cooking the tea. He never stopped to think of her as a person, with feelings, dreams, aspirations. How could she – she was his mum.

"I'm going to try and tell you some things, things that I think you need to know. You see, I fell in love twice – that's right, I'm in love with two men. I want to try to make you understand, to make you accept that life isn't a neatly tied up parcel. It's untidy, painful, disjointed. Let me tell you."

So he sat and listened to her story; her explanation.

29

Her words were simple, matter-of-fact, but carrying such a history of sadness, such weight of emotion that he almost believed he was listening to someone else. Never had he heard her speak so intimately, so openly. At the start, he squirmed in his chair, head down, trying not to catch her eyes, wishing he could make his excuses and leave. But as she spoke, he forgot she was his mother. She became like any other woman, one whose circumstances had torn her heart apart.

Some of the story, he had heard before, but he let her continue uninterrupted. For the most part, it differed little from the one Matthew had told, until she came to what happened after the two men in her life, her husband and her lover, had come to blows.

"Matthew's father," she said, her voice quiet, self-conscious in a way, "he was like someone possessed after I left. He would go to my mum's, pound on the front door, screaming, shouting. I had to go away, so I arranged to go up to the Lake District. We had family there, we still do. They took me in and everything was fine, at the beginning. I tried to put my life together, tried to come to terms with what had happened and what I had to do next. I waited for David to come and visit me. That was the plan, you see. We were to be together. We knew it was going to be difficult. I was a married woman, despite everything that had gone on, and it was a different world then. Very different. It was considered scandalous for a woman to leave her husband, seek a divorce. But to be with another man..." Jed looked up and he could see her pain. She brushed away a tear, shook her head, and continued. "What about Matthew? What was to become of him – it was all so horrible."

She paused and looked out of the window, and he could see her reliving how dreadful it all was, how impossible. The memories and the talking brought everything back with such immediacy, as if it had only recently happened. She dabbed at her eyes with a tissue. Jed sat, without speaking, watching her, wishing there was something he could say or do to lighten her load, but he knew there was nothing for him to do, or say. Merely listen.

Her voice continued, ragged with emotion, "In those days a single mother was looked down on. Almost as if they were a criminal. And for a married woman to have had an affair – my God, that was just too hideous to contemplate. So we had to stay apart, for the sake of Matthew, my family, and what other people would have said. Where I stayed was a close community, small, intimate. Everyone knew everyone else. It was impossible. So we decided to stay apart for a short while, until my divorce came through. We had no idea how long that would take, but we prepared ourselves for the fallout – my name would be dirt, the woman from hell they'd call me as they dragged me through the courts. And my poor child, Matthew…What was to become of him?" She shook her head, more tears coming, her tissue now a sodden mess.

Jed went out and came back with some more paper handkerchiefs. He pressed them into her hand, holding onto her for a moment. "Mum, you don't have to say anymore."

"Yes I do. I need you to understand all of this."

Jed nodded, knowing this was a form of catharsis for her, an act of cleansing, ridding herself of the guilt and shame she had stored away for so long. He sat beside her on the sofa, feeling her pain.

"We tried. David tried. But he was young, very young. I don't think either of us really realized how difficult it was all going to be. He'd come and see me, whenever he could, but my family were beginning to make concerned noises. Not for me – but for them. Always conscious of what others might think, neighbours and the like, they said that I shouldn't see him, at least not until the court case was all out of the way. So, I – I had to tell him. I can still see him now, his face, crumpling. One minute so smooth and bright and young…then I told him it was all over and he became like a little old man, all twisted up, his face…" She pressed a tissue against her nose and tried to steady herself. "We promised we'd keep in touch. Letters, that sort of thing. Then my cousin, Maggie, she got a job working for the Civil Service down in Middlesex. She said she could try and get me a job too. I didn't know what to do for a while, Matthew was so small, the divorce was always being held up because of Frank and his demands. I had to go and have a meeting with our solicitors. His and mine. We spent whole afternoons fighting, backwards and forwards, he wanted this, I wanted that…It was horrible. In the end, the solution seemed so stupidly simple that everyone wondered why we hadn't thought of it before. Frank's mum. She legally adopted Matthew in the end. So I left, went down to Middlesex with Maggie. Got a job. The Civil Service."

Jed, stunned, didn't know what to think or say. Matthew had been *adopted*? He'd never mentioned anything about that …

"…great it was, at first." She laughed, catching Jed's blank expression. "You still with me?" He nodded quickly. "I said, we got ourselves a little flat, just the two of us. It was great, at first. Freedom. Memories soon faded and we had a wonderful time, going out, meeting blokes…nothing serious. I'd had quite enough of that. Frank and I were divorced and I ended up with nothing. Not that we had very much to start with, but what we had he got. Apart from Matthew. Frank's mum had Matthew. She was very good, writing to me once a month, letting me know how it was all getting on – Matthew and his new mum…" She stood up suddenly and Jed watched her as she went over to the window and looked out towards the main road. She sniffed loudly, chose another tissue. She turned, continuing. "Then, by sheer chance, I met this bloke. Very handsome, always joking. We got on so well because, you see, he was from here. Wallasey. I couldn't believe it – there I was, working in London, trying to get away from my past, and who should I meet but some bloke from my home town!"

She laughed, looking out into the road again. "I'd got a letter, about six or nine months before. David had gone off to Korea. My God – another bloody war! It seemed things were out of my control, so what was the point in trying to resist? I started going out with this new bloke, on a regular basis, put David to the back of my mind, tried to forget. Maggie thought this bloke was 'dreamy'. She would! But, in all honesty, he *was*. Still is, I suppose." Her shoulders sagged and she looked at him, her smile full and open. "He was your dad."

Jed walked down towards the docks, alone and looked across to the enormous cranes, standing like fairytale giants against the leaden sky. Here, beside the Penny Bridge, was one of the few places he could think, no distractions, no people. The night pressed in and he allowed his mind to wander, to pick through the snippets of a life gone haywire. The murders, Sullivan, Matthew, Jon, Dad's accident. The doctors had said Dad was 'lucky'. How could pushing a cupboard result in such agony, almost cost someone their life? But they said exactly that. Massive internal bleeding

He kicked at a stone and wandered along the quayside, thinking back to what else his Mum told him when they had gone into the kitchen. As she prepared some food for them both, she spoke, quietly, almost to herself.

"The years rolled by, and we got married, your Dad and me. We moved back to Wallasey and a year later you came alone. We hardly ever saw Matthew and you grew up believing Matthew was just another distant relative, one who drifted in and out every other weekend or so when we visited your gran."

Jed prodded at his food with his fork. "I never really understood why you went to see that hard, unforgiving old lady every fortnight, why you insisted on dragging me along with you."

"Frank's mum?"

"I didn't know who she was. Not then. I do now, of course, now that it's all fallen into place. It was to see Matthew, wasn't it? Not the old lady – Frank's mum – who looked after him. Sometimes, a man was there, accompanied by a tiny sparrow of a woman by the name of Phyllis. I'll always remember her stick thin arms, used to make me feel sick."

"The man was Uncle Frank," said Jed's mum, caught his look and shrugged. "Although why he became known as 'uncle' I can't fully explain. Just seemed the easiest thing to say, I suppose."

"You mean he…" Jed shook his head, pulling back the curtain, revealing the years. "He was…that man, he was—"

She exhaled slowly. "Matthew's father – Frank. We agreed it would be for the best if you didn't know all the details. It didn't do any harm."

"No, maybe not. I remember that the atmosphere was always very tense when Frank visited. You'd tighten up, face rigid, eyes cast downwards. Not much was ever said, you'd all sit there, perched on the end of sofas and armchairs, twiddling thumbs, talking about the weather. I loathed it, all of that pretence, forced politeness and false laughter. I grew to hate Sundays with a passion and swore that, if ever I had children, I would never, ever lock them inside the ritual of Sunday visits to the grandparents."

"You should have said something."

"Oh, and you would have taken notice?"

She smiled, "No, I suppose not." Slowly her smile faded.

Jed felt the change and pushed his plate away. "This is the hard part coming up, isn't it?"

"You could say that. I'm not sure if it's something you want to hear."

"I do, trust me."

Her eyes became moist as he held his gaze. "I don't want you to hate me."

"I won't hate you, I just need to understand why."

She closed her eyes, preparing herself and Jed waited, remaining patient, knowing how difficult this all was. "The day came when, by sheer chance, David and I met each other once more. It was at Port Sunlight, at a Christmas fair. I'd only gone inside to browse around, and there he was, like he'd never been away. He looked exactly the same and for a moment I thought I'd gone back in time! He saw me and his mouth fell open. When we had both recovered from the initial shock, we went to the little cafeteria for a cup of tea and found that the feelings that we had had for one another were still as strong as ever. Both of us had built other lives, of course. I had Dad and you, but David had a wife too. A daughter *and* a son. His daughter was very ill, had been from a very early age and her condition had taken its toll, both on him and his relationship with his wife. Things weren't good, and the girl, Susan, was not going to get any better. So, we talked, and we laughed, and the years between us faded away. It was as if we had never been apart. And we both realized, there and then, that we should have toughened it out, stayed together, lived with the sidelong glances, the muttered voices of disapproval. But we chose not to and now there were two lifetimes' worth of emotional baggage to sort out." She paused, pressing her face into her hands for a moment, breathing hard.

"Mum," Jed reached out, touched the back of one of her hands with his fingers. She didn't flinch. "Mum, you don't have to talk anymore. What's done is done."

"No," she said, face still behind her hands. Then, very slowly, she pulled her fingers away, and she took his hand and squeezed it. "The thing is, we both knew, in that chance meeting, that we still wanted one another. So, amongst the cold teacups, we made a pact, that we would be together as soon as our children were old enough to look after themselves. You in particular. We would wait until you were eighteen, then we would run away – elope."

"So, is that what you've done? Eloped? I would have called it abandonment."

She looked sharply, searching his face for any signs of anger. But Jed merely leaned back, folding his arms across his chest. He met her gaze, stared her down. "You should have done it years ago, when I was younger."

"But you wouldn't have coped – your father wouldn't have coped."

"And you think he's coping now?" He gave a dismissive laugh. "Jesus, you're so fucking sanctimonious."

"*Jed!*"

"Have you any idea what this has done to him, have you?" She shook her head, face flushed. "No, I didn't think so. Me, me, *fucking* me! How could you possibly think that by waiting until I was eighteen it would make any of this okay?"

"I never said it would be okay, just easier."

"Well, it's not. Dad has fallen apart. He's not the same, and neither am I. You should have left years ago."

"You could be right, but we made our plan and that was it. But life has a habit of getting in the way of plans. Susan died. It was expected, but it still came as a terrible blow. David suffered, he argued constantly with his wife. Neither of them could share their grief with the other, and the tragedy pulled them apart, not together. Recriminations followed, words that should never have been said and David finally left." He blew out a long breath. "A few months later, I walked out on you both."

Leaning against the side rail of Penny Bridge, he stared out across the gently rippling water of the dock, recalling his mum's words. How she had sought to justify it all, finding some way to ease her conscience. He laughed, the revelations serving only to stir up more confusion in his already over-burdened mind. Life was such a shit at times.

He didn't notice the policeman until his large form loomed over him. Jed sighed and turned to offer up his explanation; he wasn't contemplating suicide, he was merely thinking. But before he could speak, the uniformed officer was placing a heavy hand on his shoulder. "Jed Meres? You're wanted for questioning."

They sat in the same sweaty room, Sullivan looking as if he hadn't slept for a week. His crumpled suit mirrored his face. Old before his time, laden down with the current case. The biggest murder investigation the Wirral had ever known, so the newspapers said. And it was getting worse. Sullivan's voice was low when he told Jed about Miles and for a long, long time, the words hung like lead in the thick, tobacco-ridden air. The walls, streaked with damp, the colour of nicotine fingers, pressed in on him from all sides.

"Miles, *dead*? Why the hell didn't anybody say anything? For Christ's sake, Miles was the only real friend I've ever had."

"No doubt your dad would have said something, if he could. It wasn't his fault that he happened to injure himself just as you returned from Scotland."

Jed's mouth stretched into a thin, taut line. "What – why do you keep *investigating* me? If you know all about my visit to Scotland then you must know I couldn't have murdered Miles."

"I never said you did, Jed. I don't believe you did."

"Then…" Jed shook his head, running his hand over his face, sniffing loudly, battling to keep the tears at bay. Miles. My God, Miles…

"It's time you knew the truth, Jed. At least, as far as we have been able to piece it all together."

"Truth? What *truth*?"

Sullivan's eyes were like beads, lifeless, unfeeling. "I think I'll leave it to my colleague to fill you in on everything we know."

"Your colleague? Sullivan, I don't—"

Jed's words died on his lips as the interview room door opened and Sullivan's colleague stepped in. He stood there, a slight, awkward smile on his face. And Jed stopped and stared, trying desperately to make some sense of everything whilst Matthew, his half-brother, pulled up a chair and sat down opposite him.

30

Wandering home through Liscard, Jed, in a sort of half-world, lost between Matthew's words and a rapidly escalating feeling he was losing, not only control, but his mind, tried to finding some meaning. The trip to Scotland, the old lady, drugs, and now Matthew, and what he had said. Was any of it true?. "We've been watching developments for quite some time," he had said. "We didn't know the extent of the operations, but when you made contact with Kepowski, we knew that we were close to cracking this case completely."

"Matthew what you're telling me, it doesn't make any sense. What case? What are you talking about?"

Then had come the words that he still couldn't fathom, words which turned Jed's world upside down and inside out "I'm a police-officer, Jed. Drugs' Squad."

He'd heard the words, but he couldn't dare to believe them.

"No," he said quietly, "no, you told me about you going down, and I saw you, up at the bowling green. You said—"

Matthew reached out to touch his arm gently. "I made up the part about me being a thief, Jed. I had to. How else was I to explain my absence? As for the rest, I was undercover, Jed. Even then. I work everywhere, trying to break into drug rings, uncover dealers, all of that. I've been doing it for years."

Jed left Manor Road police station in a whirl of mixed emotions. He'd been used, right from the beginning. And all the while, the person who had used him the most, psychologically raped him, was his own brother. Yet, how had they worked it all out? What parts were planned and scripted and which down to sheer luck? How could they have orchestrated his meeting with Jon at the park, the rescue, the time in hospital? And what about Brian, his mother and Sullivan? Scotland…

His head buzzed, so loudly he didn't hear the voice, calling him, calling him over and over. And when she tapped him frantically on the shoulder, he whirled around, hands coming up defensively and he froze like that, nothing registering. It was all just another part of his unfettered consciousness. None of it was making sense; he was spiralling out of control.

"My God, Jed – you look awful."

But so did she. Wild, hunted eyes, darting around as if she expected something, or someone, to pounce at any moment.

"Janet?" He struggled to find his voice, but now that he had, it came out in a rush and he knew he sounded angry, "What are you doing here?"

Her voice held no reaction at all, "Looking for you" She swiftly took hold of his arm and steered him away down a side street, shooting sideways glances every so often, her pace rapid. He felt like a toddler, propelled away by his mother after doing something naughty.

She took him through the rear entrance of *Woolworths*. It was late Saturday afternoon and the shop was closing. As if to underline the fact, they received a scathing stare from one of the shop assistants. Ignoring it, Janet took him over to the far side, checking down the aisles.

"Have you seen him, have you seen Jon?"

He shook his head. "I haven't spoken to him since I got back from Scotland." She closed her eyes, as if the memory of their trip was too painful. "Janet, what happened to you? Where did you go?"

"It doesn't matter. Look, everything is falling apart. It's Jon, he's…Listen, I want you to take this." She pressed a screwed up piece of paper into his hand.

"Your dad, he … Jesus, Janet, I've been thinking through how he was when I phoned him." Her face remained stoic, not even a flicker. "I wanted to talk to you, but he sounded furious, almost as if he thought you were—"

She put her finger over his mouth. "Don't say it. I have so much to be sorry for … I should have said something to him, make him try to understand but my dad, he's … Listen, nothing is as it seems, Jed. You've got to be so careful." Then she took his face between her hands, squeezing his cheeks, kissing him full on the mouth. Breathlessly, she pulled back "I wish…" She closed her eyes, took a breath, then opened them again. "Take care." Then, before Jed could say or do anything, she ran off towards the main entrance, leaving him with so much to say, so many questions to ask. So many emotions to make clear to her. But she was gone.

He fumbled for his door key as he turned into Ingleby Avenue. Entangled in the material of his jean's pocket, he stopped, cursing, and tried to free it. At that moment, he heard a voice he knew well, and he quickly darted into the alleyway running behind the houses on Mill Lane, the main road leading to Liscard centre. Pressing himself against the side wall, he tried to make himself as small as possible as, breathless, he watched Jon Kepowski saunter past. He'd been to see Mrs Randall, that much was clear, and he was whistling a tuneless melody to himself, no doubt drunk with lust. Jed stood, hardly daring to think lest it should prompt Kepowski to look in his direction.

Jed waited, counting away the seconds, then moved to the end of the alleyway and peered around the corner. Jon Kepowski had gone. Running a shaking hand across his brow, wet with sweat, he darted over the road and let himself into his house without a backward glance.

His mother was on the phone, and Jed saw that she had been crying. Deciding not to linger, he went straight down the hall to the little kitchen, where he busied himself with making a pot of tea. As he did so he could hear her, voice raised in anger. "I didn't bloody well plan it for crying out loud! What the hell do you expect me to do?" There was a pause as the other person on the line must have come back with a counter-argument, and then she slammed the phone down with all the fury that only a woman can muster. She stomped into the kitchen. "I hope your bloody father is satisfied with all of this!" She whirled around and stormed off, but Jed was behind her, catching her at the foot of the stairs before she had barely managed to begin her ascent.

"Did you know Matthew was a policeman?"

She held on to the balustrade, head down, gathering her thoughts. She hadn't flinched at Jed's words, almost as if they were long expected. "Of course I did."

"And you never thought to mention it?"

Her eyes came up, hard, unflinching. "Mention it? Why should I? Does it change anything – you hardly ever see him as it is. Would you have even given him the time of day if you'd have known?"

He struggled to keep his anger under control, his teeth clenched as he spoke. "Mum, I've been dragged into police stations, had questions fired at me, been to Risley remand centre for a murder I didn't commit – for God's sake, why the hell didn't Matthew do anything, help me through it all!"

"He did! Why do you think you got out of Risley early?"

"Early? What…you mean, you *knew* about me being in there?"

He gazed into her face and he saw that it was true. For a second he thought he was going to lose control. He came over all light-headed, a terrible buzzing building behind his eyes. He staggered backwards. "You did – you knew all about it. And him. My God – you let me stay in that place…Why?"

"Matthew needed you to make contact for some of the other inmates. It was all some massive under-cover operation. When I left your father, Matthew found me, almost straight away. He had the means to, of course. And he told me that my timing was terrible. Those were his words, '*your timing is terrible, Ma!*' Typical, unfeeling…He told me to keep away, not to come back, to make the break completely. But now, with your father so ill…Matthew is not best pleased."

"I don't give a toss about Matthew or how displeased he is! You're all the bleeding same, the lot of you! Users, each and every one! It all makes sense now."

Jed , face bright red with rage, clawed at the front door.

"Where are you going?"

"To sort this out!"

"You can't – you mustn't." She was already reaching for the telephone when he stormed out, slamming the door shut behind him.

Matthew caught up with him halfway down Victoria Road on his way towards the promenade. He pulled up in his little Mini-Cooper, blaring on the horn. Jed glared at him as Matthew reached over and pushed open the passenger side door. "Get in, for God's sake!"

Without a word, Jed did so, staring ahead as Matthew headed in the direction of Harrison Drive. Neither spoke until Matthew pulled in opposite the row of night clubs that dominated that part of New Brighton promenade. One of them was still a burned out shell, but it hadn't stopped the competition from pulling out all the stops with fancy new billboards announcing half-price drinks every night until ten o'clock. Matthew switched off the engine, wound down the window, and lit a cigarette. "Remember that night when Kepowski asked you to deliver a package?"

"That was a lifetime ago."

"Yeah, it was, but you remember it, don't you? You remember the club going up in flames, the manager being found under the pier?"

"Where is all this leading?"

"He was on our payroll. Laine, the manager. It was all a ruse, to try to lure Kepowski into the open. But, somehow, Kepowski twigged and he outflanked us – it all went arse-over-tit after that. It set us back months."

"Are you trying to say it was my fault? Because if you are—"

"Don't be so bloody stupid! It would have happened even if you had never met up with him."

"So...why bring me out here and tell me this, if I'm not so important?"

"You're a petulant little sod. Always have been."

"How would you know? Not exactly my best friend, are you?"

"Grow up, Jed! This is a heap of shit and we have to find a way through. I brought you here to try and give you some idea about just how dangerous this Kepowski guy is. Why the hell did you pull him out of that bloody lake?"

"Because he was going to drown."

"Really? You believe that do you? Did it never strike you as strange that he should be at that lake, at that precise time? And that you are the brother of one of Cheshire's top anti-drug enforcement officers?"

Jed sneered. "Is that what you are? A *top* enforcement officer? Must make you feel very proud. Pity you couldn't have told me earlier, stopped me from going into Risley."

"And how could you have met up with Brian Randall if I'd have done that?"

"You bastard!" Jed moved, his left fist shooting out in a blur. It caught Matthew before he could effectively get out of the way, moving his head slightly, the blow glancing off his cheekbone. Reacting quickly, he brought his hands around to snatch Jed's follow up and they grappled in the tight confines of the little car. Jed was strong, and big, but Matthew had lived his life in the streets and had many years' experience on his younger brother. Twisting himself, he put Jed's arm in a painful wristlock, bending the fingers backwards. Jed screamed, his other hand trying to claw away at Matthew's hair, but the pain proved too great and he screamed again in a desperate plea for mercy. Matthew released him, and jabbed his elbow hard into Jed's chest, throwing him against the passenger door. Pressing his fingers into his brother's throat, he growled, lips drawn back over his teeth, breathing hard and fast, "Bloody well pack it in, or I'll break your fucking neck!"

Jed, knowing it was useless, let the strength go out of him whilst Matthew continued to hold onto him whilst he spoke. "Of course I used you, what did you expect me to do? Being given a golden opportunity like that, my own brother saving Jon Kepowski from drowning. I might never be in that situation again, to have the chance to nail the bastard. Don't you see, don't you understand? We've been after him for years and now we had a chance. I wanted to tell you, I wanted to shield you, but if I'd have done that, Kepowski would have got wind of it and that would have been the end of it. And the end of you too." He fell back, breathing hard.

Rubbing at his throat, Jed pushed himself up into a sitting position, his mouth open, exhausted with the fight and the all-consuming rage coursing through him. "Did Sullivan know?"

"Sullivan? Do me a favour. That prat couldn't blow his own nose if he had a cold!"

"But…but he was having an affair with Brian's mother."

"Tell me something I don't know."

Stunned, Jed wondered whether Sullivan knew Matthew had manipulated him. "He must have known – he wanted to recruit me into some wild scam to do with Brian." He stopped, realisation dawning on him. This was a case of one hand not knowing what the other was doing. If it weren't so painful, it would be laughable. "So you used him too – one of your own people?"

"It's not that simple. Sullivan was bumbling around like an amateur, trying too hard to make the big arrest. He was in danger of screwing everything up. So, I had to have a little word with him, and he complied…after some persuasion. I told him that our respective superiors would be extremely interested in knowing he had been playing around with a drug dealer's mother."

"He told Dad Jon was dead."

Mathew's face grew serious. "That's what he's been led to believe."

" God, is there nothing you wouldn't do, no one you wouldn't use?"

"If it means ridding the streets of scum like Kepowski, then yes."

"Even mum?"

"Even mum."

Jed desperately wanted to hit Matthew again, but knew the time wasn't right. It would be, soon. He bit his lip. "You've got it all sewn up then. Must be quite a feather for you. Promotion beckoning?"

"Jed, you're an arse! And not as clever as you think you are, either."

"Oh really?"

"Yeah, *really!*"

"And I suppose you are, of course."

"A damn sight bloody cleverer than you, anyway."

"So that's why you know where Jon Kepowski was earlier today?"

Matthew's eyes narrowed. "What?"

"Kepowski. You must know where he was earlier this afternoon. After all, you know it all, don't you?"

Matthew's voice was very low, very serious. "Just tell me Jed."

Smiling, Jed told him and watched, with some satisfaction, as the colour drained from his brother's face.

31

He came home to find his mother crying. At first, he thought it was because of him, the way he had stormed out. Unfeeling, thoughtless, as he always was, hurting those closest to him. It had taken her a lot to unburden herself and he had done nothing to lighten the load. Sitting down beside her, he slipped his arm around her and tried his best to give her some comfort.

Her red-rimmed eyes looked up at him. Reaching to her side, she brought up a thin bundle of photographs and laid them delicately on Jed's lap. "They came through the door," she said. "Addressed to me."

Jed didn't understand. He picked up the photographs and instantly realized what they were. He had no need to look past the first one.

Her voice trembled with incredulity. "You've seen these before?"

He nodded, pushing the photographs aside. "Did you see who posted them?"

She could barely bring herself to shake her head.

"I think I do."

He stood and went into the hall to pick up the telephone. He had things to do, people to talk to. This was all becoming too close to home. Not only was Miles dead, but now they were targeting his own mother. None of this had anything to do with drugs, despite what Matthew said. These were directed attacks on his family and Jed was determined to find out why.

For days had been building up the courage to telephone Janet's number again. The last time her father had acted strangely, but he would not fob Jed off now. Jed pulled out the screwed up pieces of paper from his pocket and prepared to dial her number.

He paused and smoothed out the second piece. On it was scrawled an address, in Scotland. Jed frowned. What was that, some rendezvous point for a drugs' drop? Why give it to him, unless of course Janet knew he was in collusion with Matthew. Which was why, of course, she had come up to him in Liscard. She had been spying on him, following him. But was it of her own volition, or had Jon Kepowski directed her to do so? Believing this was the truth, he dialled the number.

The same gruff voice answered, and Jed began cautiously, not wishing to offend. "Sorry to disturb you. You might remember, but I rang before, a few days ago. I wanted to speak to Janet and I think I might have—"

"Yes, I bloody well remember you. What is your game, eh? Do you enjoy upsetting people like this? If I ever find you, I'll ring your bloody neck!"

Again, struck by the man's anger, Jed nevertheless pressed on, squeezing his eyes shut, imagining what the man looked like, twisted up face, bunched fists, seething with rage. "I'm sorry. Look, I'm just going to come right out with this, because I know all of this is difficult for you, but you have to know—"

"Difficult? *Difficult?* You bastard. I'm going to phone the police about all of this, and when they find you I'm going to take great pleasure in beating the living shit out of you!"

"*Please,* no, you've got all of this wrong. If you could just tell me where she is. It's really important. Please."

The man pulled in a long, unsteady breath. "Tell you where she is – she's *dead,* that's where she is, you evil moron! Understand? *Dead!*"

It was late by the time Jed emerged from his bedroom. He'd been sitting on the edge of his bed, staring at the carpet, at a red stain where he and Miles had dropped some theatrical stage-blood during an *Action-*

Man session. That was…he rubbed his face, trying to work it out. Five years ago? God, how he wished those days were back. Everything was so simple then and uncomplicated. He didn't have decisions to make, everything done for him. Mum and dad laughed a lot, danced in the kitchen, listened to Nat-King Cole on the record player. Not an idyllic existence, just normal. Unlike now.

Janet wasn't dead, but her dad believed it to be so. How could that be? Someone was weaving all of these elaborate stories, to confuse everyone involved. It seemed to Jed that, if he wasn't very careful, he was going to find himself slipping into some sort of alternative universe, a para-normal half-world between this life and the next?

Slipped? Wasn't that what Jon had said, when they stood beside that huge wall up in Scotland? *'We've slipped. You've got to understand, I have no control over these things. Only control over you, and others. But not this.'* What did that mean, he had control over him, *but not this.* Jed was convinced that Jon had hypnotised him, to make him do things that he wouldn't ordinarily have done. Like taking that package to the night-club, enjoying a threesome with him and Janet.

Janet. Was she also something Jon had no control over – because she had rebelled? But why. Was it simply because she had had enough of this play-acting? Or might it truly be, that she was dead? Murdered by Kepowski to keep her mouth shut? But dead when? Certainly not when she dragged Jed into Woolworth's. That was after Jed first spoke to her dad, and he recalled how distraught her dad sounded. So, was he convinced, even then, that his daughter had died?

No, something wasn't right about any of this and Jed knew instinctively that Jon Kepowski was responsible for all of it – reaping un-controlled revenge upon him, his family and anyone who attempted to get close to him?

His mother's voice cut through his thoughts. She was shouting. Feeling as if he were rooting through her most private possessions, he crept over to his door and pressed his ear close to the wood-work, listening. "I'll be back as soon as Larry is home…No, of course not! For Christ's sake, David! No!…*What*? Yes…Yes, I will. Jed's not very…Oh, well, that's just lovely! Thanks for your support! I'll talk to you tomorrow."

He quickly scampered back to his bed as his mother slammed down the receiver and came stomping up the stairs. Without ceremony, she burst through his door and stood there, eyes streaming, lips trembling. "I suppose you heard all of that?"

"Some."

"Yes, well, this visit of mine is causing all sorts of problems. David believes I'm thinking of moving in with your father again. He's begging me to go home." She put her hand over her mouth, trying to steady herself a little.

"Perhaps you should."

"What?" Her hand dropped away and she gaped at him. "You think I can just walk off, leaving you like this, with your father in hospital? Just how heartless do you think I am?"

Jed wanted to tell her, but resisted the temptation. "You could go back tonight, stay there tomorrow, come back later on. I have my first exam on Monday. I'll be spending what's left of my weekend revising."

She looked at him for a long time, then turned and went without a word, leaving Jed to consider the impact of his own words. His first exam on Monday? He couldn't remember how long it had been since he'd opened a textbook. He flopped back on his bed, closed his eyes and tried to think of something, anything that would make sense of the mess his life had become.

Mum left some time after nine. Jed didn't bother looking out of the front bedroom window, revisiting the urge to catch a glimpse of David. He heard the doors slamming, a mumbled, "Bye then," and then she left. Padding into his bedroom, Jed stared at the open textbook on his bed, unread. At least he'd made a start. He'd opened it! Crouching down, he selected an album from his collection and slipped on 'Judy Blue Eyes', the first track from the 'Crosby, Stills and Nash' recording that he'd bought the year before. As the music filled the room, he settled down to read. But the words soon blurred and without knowing how he drifted off to sleep.

From somewhere far away, a telephone rang. Or was it the front door? Reeling, he stumbled out of bed and groped for the light switch. It was late, the record on the turntable long since finished. Rubbing his eyes, he went down stairs, almost tripping on the last few steps. The telephone continued to shrill, and he snatched up the receiver, annoyed and confused.

"Jed? Where the hell have you been?" Matthew's voice sounded as brisk and as uncompromising as ever.

"Asleep."

"Asleep? Okay, listen, we need to talk. Brian Randall has come into the station and made a full confession. Splash some water over your face and switch the kettle on. I'm coming round."

The line went dead and Jed let out a long sigh, falling down on the little stool his dad had made for those longer telephone conversations which never happened. He glanced at his watch and swore. One-thirty, give or take a minute or two. He must have been asleep for around four hours. No studying done and now Matthew coming around to harass him some more. He groaned, panic welling up inside him. He had to do well on Monday, there was no argument about that. One day of study left. One day. Furiously rubbing his face with both hands, he went into the kitchen and heaped two spoonsful of coffee into mugs. By the time the kettle boiled he heard the throaty rev of the Mini-Cooper pulling up outside and he went to the door and opened it.

Matthew strode in, not even giving him the courtesy of a good morning nod of the head. Sighing, Jed gently closed the door and followed his brother into the kitchen. Matthew was already heaping sugar into his coffee. He sat down with a sigh. Jed remained standing, folded his arms across his chest and stared, waiting.

Smacking his lips loudly, Matthew leaned back and surveyed Jed with the look that Phillips, the Headteacher from school, often gave him. Distaste.

"Randall is a friend of yours?" Matthew suddenly said.

Jed sniggered. "A *friend* – you must be joking. First time I met him was at Risley."

"I know. We've been through that. It was the hope that you'd pal-up, given that you're neighbours."

"I barely knew him before then. I'd never spoken to him. He's older than me, he went to another school."

"Yeah. Wallasey Grammar. We know all about him, Jed. When we put you in there, we hoped that you would make a connection, and you did. What we didn't know was how far that connection would go."

"I…I don't understand."

It was now Matthew's turn to fold his arms, the leather sleeves of his coat creaking. "Kepowski. We had no idea that Brian and he were… *related*, shall we say. Sure, both of them were in the drug business so we assumed they must have had dealings, but we never suspected Brian was on his payroll. Not until earlier, when Randall ran into Manor Road police station demanding protection. After we'd calmed him down, he told us quite a few things we *didn't* know. What's the term they use on those old films, something about canaries? He sang like one, the whole lot. Tell me about Scotland."

Swallowing hard, Jed sat down, pressing his palms together as if in prayer. Perhaps he should pray, get some divine intervention. "Jon wanted me to go with him, me and Janet. Even now, I don't really know why. After we visited Culloden, and he disappeared. I had to make my own way back."

"On the train? Where did you get all the money?"

"No, not on a train. I drove."

"You *drove*? But you can't drive."

"That's what I thought, but apparently I can. Not that I've tried since I got back. I drove Janet's Viva, brought it all the way home."

"Viva? Where is it now?"

"In the back entry. I parked it up on the waste ground in front of the old disused garages there. You want to dust it for prints?"

Matthew scowled. "Just tell me about Scotland."

"I told you. That's it, the whole lot."

"So, you didn't go anywhere, you didn't do anything. Did you meet anyone?"

The old lady, the one at the visitors' centre. She'd helped him, done something to him...had she given him an antidote for whatever drugs Kepowski had pumped into him? He'd fallen sick, collapsing in the telephone box. Everything came back to him, a great rush of images. "No. I didn't meet anyone."

"*Him*, Jed. Kepowski. Did he meet up with anyone?"

"No, but like I said, he disappeared, so I don't know what he got up to, who he met, where he went. Nothing."

Pushing back his chair, Matthew stood up and turned to the sink, washing out his coffee cup, then slammed it face down on the drainer. "There's something not right with all this." He turned around, his face hard, appearing to struggle inside, chewing his bottom lip, thinking. "Brian told us about a house. A large manor house or castle, up in the Highlands, not far from Culloden. Apparently it's where Kepowski lives, or *holds court* as Brian explained it. Not that I know what that means. He said he'd only visited there twice so he couldn't remember anything about it. But he thinks that's where gather the drugs before they are distributed. It sits not far from a river, this castle-thing, and they get the drugs from across the North Sea, from Holland. Big business, apparently. But there's something else, something that Brian said that made me think that this isn't just about drugs. They're a big part of what Kepowski is into, but there is something more."

"What did he say?"

"He said, 'Jon promised me immortality, instead all I got was a warning that he'd kill me.' What does that mean, do you think?"

Jed shrugged. "Who knows? The whole thing is a mystery if you ask me. But..." he pulled out the piece of paper that Janet had given him. He handed it over. "I'm not sure, but I think if you check that out, you'll find that it's the address of a castle-cum-manor house in Scotland."

"Where did you get this?"

"A friend." Jed held up his hand to cut off any of Matthew's demands for more information. "I'm not telling who, but it wasn't Brian."

Matthew read the address for a second time. "I'll check this out. If it's the place, then we'll be going to Scotland, Jed. You and me."

"Er…not until after Monday I won't be. It's my first exam."

"Sod that, you'll do as you're bloody-well told."

"No I won't, Matthew! I have to take that examination on Monday, at two o'clock. My next one is on Thursday. So, we will have two and a half days. That's the deal."

Matthew ran his tongue along his top lip a few times as he considered Jed's ultimatum. "Let's hope he has the good grace to still be at home when we call."

Having 'good grace' was something Jon Kepowski would never have much of, mused Jed.

32

The sun streamed through his bedroom window when at last he rolled out of bed. Sunday, almost noon. Cursing loudly, he ran into the bathroom to swill his face and brush his teeth. Noon – how could he let himself sleep for so long? He took the stairs at a run, switching on the kettle, slicing up some bread to put under the grill. Already he had the textbook open. It was going to be a very long and a very boring day.

He was correct in his assumptions. He tried his very best but the words from the textbook refused to sink into his brain. His old notes from school were just as useless and the more he tried to concentrate, the more anxious he became. There was too much. Too much to take in. All of those months, *years* of schoolwork. History. European political history. The first of two exams, the second on Thursday. That was the British part. He was confident about the British part, had all of that nonsense about Gladstone and Disraeli neatly boxed-off into the relevant compartments of his memory. But this European stuff, it was just too complicated. Bismarck. That was the stumbling point. *Real Politick.* How was he supposed to remember all of that?

By seven o'clock he could take no more. None of it was staying in his head. He'd spent the day skimming over sections, punctuating his reading with snacks. Toast and marmalade, egg and cress, cheese and pickle. Cups of tea, drinking so much he felt like a water-balloon. It wasn't good for him, all of that sugar. All of that stress. How was he supposed to make it through these. A-levels? Then university. That was his hope. Keele. He'd always fancied Keele. He sat back on the sofa, his mouth tasting awful, teeth covered in fur. Closing his eyes, sighing loudly, he realised everything was a hopeless dream. Hopeless.

He sat up with a start, heart pounding, stress levels reaching their limits. Checking his watch, he almost cried out. It was gone eleven. *Eleven o'clock*! He should be in bed, asleep. Eight hours, give himself some sort of chance, allow his body to recover, recharge. He leaned forward, put his face in his hands. Eleven o'clock.

A sudden thought gripped him and he snapped his head up to check the clock above the fire-place. Where was his mum? She said she'd be there by nine. That was the arrangement. She hadn't rung, the telephone would have woken him. As if to reassure himself, he went over and picked up the receiver. The dialling tone purred and he settled it back down on the cradle. No disconnection. She hadn't rung. Wandering into the kitchen, he stared at the bombshell that was the table. He should clean it all up, at least stack the dirty plates by the sink. How many cups had he used, and all those breadcrumbs...He groaned and went upstairs, telling himself it would all have to wait until the morning.

It was well after four o'clock before he managed to get to sleep. And still his mother had not come home.

Jed spent the following morning preparing himself, making sure his shirt was ironed and his shoes polished. Whatever the outcome of this exam, at least he would look smart. When he sat down and went through his notes, they actually did make a kind of sense.

Keeping himself off the tea, by one o'clock he was sufficiently calm to take the slow walk towards school. He always went the same route, had done since he'd started there some four years previously. Usually he would talk to himself, trying to keep himself cheerful, dreading another day. But this time, he strolled along in silence, running through dates in his head, keeping himself focused, not allowing thoughts of Mum, Matthew, Scotland to interfere. And Dad. He should have found the time to visit him, tell him that mum had gone back to David for a short while. He promised himself he would go and see him later, after the exam and before Matthew came calling. It was only right.

It was warm and when he wandered into the hall, he took off his blazer and draped it over the back of his chair. Some of his class-mates gave him a nod. Nobody spoke, not even Mr Butler who was invigilating, already doling out the papers as Jed sat down.

He had his pens, and a pencil just in case they all failed. With the exam paper in front of him he took in a long breath, closed his eyes, waiting patiently for Butler to announce that they could begin.

Two and a half hours later, Jed walked out into the late afternoon sunshine and stood, quietly gathering his thoughts. The questions were what he had expected and he had little trouble answering all four of them. In truth, the facts poured out of him and now his hand ached with so much writing, not stopping, unaware of time until Butler announced, 'You have twenty minutes left.' Then it was suddenly over and now he was free, at least for a few days. The sun felt good as he walked home, blazer draped over his shoulder, and he hummed a few tunes to himself, feeling good.

The voice on the other end of the telephone was not one he recognised. "Is that Jed? Yes, well of course, it must be. I'm sorry, but could I speak to your mum, Jed? It's David."

Jed's mouth fell open, dry, tongue thick, the words unable to form properly. Panic gripped him. David. David, the man who had destroyed his family, the man who had caused his father to become a sobbing wreck, broken, belittled. Without a word, Jed very carefully put the receiver down. He half expected it to ring again, but it didn't.

For perhaps five minutes he stood and stared in silence, attempting to piece together his mangled thoughts. So, mum was on her way, so why had he rung, to check she'd arrived? And why hadn't he dropped her off? At work maybe? But, she should have arrived last night, and no phone call to explain anything.

Stomping into the back garden, Jed decided to drive over to the hospital and visit his dad. If the police stopped and arrested him, he didn't care. He could do with a few nights in the cells, save him from having to go up to Scotland with Matthew.

Except, the car wasn't there.

He stared into the space where he had parked it, a dark oil stain on the ground the only clue that it had ever existed.

Stolen? Could he have left it unlocked? It was more than probable – it was very likely. Tired, emotionally drained, consumed with fears over his exam, he hadn't been thinking straight.

Angry, he returned to the house and stood in the kitchen, unsure as to what to do next. He knew he should go and visit dad, but he was also aware Matthew would be calling soon. And then there was Mum. If she travelled by bus, she could arrive at any time, so he left a note, explaining everything. His meeting with Matthew, that David had phoned, that he hadn't seen dad but that the exam had gone well. She wasn't to worry, he would phone her later. He folded the note neatly and laid it against the kettle on the table. The table. It still looked like a bombsite. He should make an effort, do something to make it seem a little more presentable. But then the doorbell saved him.

It was Matthew. Without a word, Jed pushed past him, fell into the passenger seat and waited. Matthew, as stoic as his brother, started up the engine. "Are you sure you're ready for this?"

Jed stared straight ahead. "I'm ready for anything," he said quietly.

Matthew grunted, put the Mini-Cooper into gear, and set off up the road.

They stopped at a little bread and breakfast just across the border. The woman who greeted them was small and grey-haired, a little suspicious of them both until Matthew showed her his warrant card. Then it was all smiles and cheery conversation. They booked one of the two, twin-bedded rooms available and whilst Matthew took a shower, Jed went over things in his head. He gave up after about two minutes. It had been a cerebral day up to that point and thinking was beyond him for the time being. He needed to shower and go to sleep. The following morning would hopefully give him a much clearer angle on what he should do next.

Janet came to him in his dreams.

She was bloody, her dress torn and dirty, as if someone had flung her to the ground and wrestled with her in the mud. Flaxen hair was streaked with dirt, her teeth broken, eyes black coals. From something out a Nineteen Thirties' horror, she stumbled towards him, arms outstretched. 'Come to me, my love,' she moaned, 'come to me…'

He sat up with a start, pawing at his face, wiping away the images of the girl he thought he could make something of a future with. The light went on and Matthew peered at him from the other bed, face drawn, full of concern. "What is it, did you hear something?"

Jed shook his head and lay back. He looked across to his brother, who snuggled beneath the covers and put something under his pillow. Stretching out his hand, he switched off the light.

He had a gun.

The rain beat down in sheets. This was only Jed's second time in Scotland, and both times the heavens had opened. As they sat down at the breakfast table, spooning down great lumps of porridge, he thought about the night before. Not just the dream. The gun. What was Matthew planning to do? And, more to the point, what could he do, one man? Was that going to be enough for an arrest?

"Why have you got a gun?"

Matthew paused in the act of swallowing some porridge, quickly glancing around the empty breakfast room. "Keep your voice down."

"Tell me – why?"

"Why do you think?"

"British policemen don't carry guns. At least, I didn't think they did."

"Well, now you know differently. Finish your breakfast, we need to get going."

"You're expecting trouble." Matthew frowned. "Is that why you have the gun? You think Jon will resist?"

"Resist?"

"Arrest, Matthew. That's what you're going to do, isn't it? Arrest him?"

Matthew drained his coffee. "Like I said, finish your breakfast." He wiped his mouth with a napkin and got up. Jed eyed him nervously. He suddenly felt very cold and very, very afraid.

* * *

Sitting in the foyer of the hospital, waiting for the taxi to arrive, Larry Meres felt abandoned. She'd come for about five minutes, to rant and rave about the photographs. God, that was embarrassing; everyone staring, exchanging glances. He felt like squirming down under the bed-clothes, anything to escape those looks! Then she'd gone, red-faced, crying. As if *he* were the guilty one! Hadn't she left him? And Jed. Jed hadn't been to see him, not since that first time. Nothing since.

A man loomed over him, large, angry looking. "Are you the one who called a taxi?"

Grunting, Larry followed the man out into the daylight. It was a grey day, threatening rain. The taxi-driver, vexed because he had been forced to get out from behind the wheel of his car, muttered under his breath as Larry struggled into the back seat. The hospital had provided him with a single crutch to aid him with his walking. 'No strain, Mr Meres,' the doctor had said. 'You have to take it easy for a week at least. I've signed you off for a fortnight, but really, at your age, you shouldn't be climbing or stretching for at least a month.' And now, here he was, straining and climbing to get into the car without any help from a taxi-driver who resented having a fare-paying customer! What a bloody life...

It was the same at the other end. Larry paid the fare and eased himself out onto the pavement. Without giving Larry the consideration of a glance, he roared off up the road. Larry, let it go. He should have told him where to stick his bloody taxi, but with a crutch and a burning pain across the lower part of his abdomen, what could he do? He hobbled up to the door and stepped inside.

He saw the note, propped up against the kettle. 'Mum', it said. Larry opened it anyway, read it through and sank down onto a chair. So, Jed had found the time to tell his mother he was going back up to Scotland... that was nice of him. Not a single word for his dad though. Not even a 'tell dad that I hope he's okay'. Disgusted, Larry threw the note away and surveyed the table-top. The only thing Jed had time for was to make a mess.

The telephone rang. He wanted to leave it unanswered, but it wasn't stopping, so he struggled down the hallway and picked up the receiver.

"Hello," he spat, hoping he sounded sufficiently pissed off to warn the caller not to prolong the conversation needlessly.

"Hello Larry."

He knew the voice, without having to ask. Inside he raged, but managed to keep his voice calm. "What do you want?"

"I don't suppose she's there, is she?" asked David, sounding uncertain, a little nervous. There was a pause before he started again, "Only I—"

"No, she's *not* here. Now what do you want?"

A longer pause when all Larry could hear was breathing. He was about to erupt when David very quietly said, "I think we have a bit of a problem..."

She'd told him she had to go out, that she'd be back. There had been a telephone call and she seemed changed afterwards. Disturbed, pensive. striding up and down in the lounge, chewing her fingernails. David watched her with growing concern. Then the announcement and she'd rushed out. Since then, nothing. He'd telephoned the home, spoken to Jed. But she wasn't there. A whole night with no word, what was he supposed to do, what was he supposed to think?

"I've just got in from the hospital. There was a note, from Jed. He's gone to Scotland, with Matthew."

"Scotland...Why would he go there? I don't understand what's going on. Where is Mary?"

"I don't know. Listen, you have a car. I want to you to get over here, as fast as you can."

"Over there? But what's going on, Larry? You're not making any sense."

"It's very simple, David. You're going to take me up to Scotland."

"But...why?"

"Because, that is where Mary is."

33

He waited on the corner, holding onto the wall with one hand, the crutch propped up next to him. Squeezing his groin with his free hand, the agony caused him to double-up. This was stupid; no strain, the doctor had said. Why the hell couldn't he just *wait*?

But Larry was past waiting; he no longer had the patience. He'd sat around for fifteen minutes, waiting for David to come and that was fifteen minutes too long. He needed answers now, so he'd made the decision and staggered around to Hannah's house. She was the only person who could have sent Mary the photographs. Either her, or her wastrel of a son. Whoever it was, Larry needed to know why. Hannah had made it abundantly clear that she wanted nothing more to do with him and he had tried, successfully, to get her out of his mind, so what was she playing at? Causing pain and anguish for their own sake? Or was there something more, something he was missing in all of this? He had to find out and now, here he was, like a pathetic, crippled old man, clinging onto a wall for support, out of breath and feeling like shit. He should wait, wait for David.

He took a breath and moved on.

There was a white Viva parked outside Hannah's house. He didn't remember her having a car; perhaps she had visitors. Well, that wouldn't change anything. Perhaps she would be so reluctant to tell him what was going on with others there. Witnesses. Hammering on the door, not bothering with the bell, he leaned back on his crutch and waited.

A shadow loomed up behind the door's frosted glass and he held his breath, heart thumping. This was it.

The door opened.

She looked stunning.

For a moment, he was lost for words and they stood, the two of them, staring at one another. She flicked hair from her face and smiled. "Hello Larry." Then she noticed the crutch and concern crossed her features. "My God, what happened to you?"

"Accident. At work. Can I come in, or are you busy?"

A moment's hesitation. Was that a nervous look fluttering over her lovely face, her eyes darting towards the ground, or was that just his imagination? Wishful thinking.

"No," she said at last, stepping aside. "No, I'm not busy. Come on in."

She led him into the dining room. a large room, very cold. The carpet was plush and the furniture antique. Very grand, very unexpected. He always thought of her as a modern woman, with a real sense of fashion, but this room seemed trapped in turn of the century mode. He hadn't seen it on his last visit, but then he hadn't seen very much, his one concern to get between her legs as quickly as possible.

"Cup of tea, Larry?"

"No. Thanks." She smiled, he didn't. "This isn't a social call."

She nodded once, mouth becoming hard. "You'd better sit down then."

He did, wincing as he gently lowered himself into the chair and watched her as she sat down opposite. He noted she didn't cross her legs this time, not wanting him to catch a glimpse of her bronzed legs. He was pleased about that, not wanting any distractions.

"You sent photographs to my wife," he said without preamble. "I want to know why you did that."

"Photographs?" She shrugged, "Larry, I—"

"I know you sent them, you're the only that could have. I just want to know what the reason was. You have no interest in me, Hannah.

I know we had some time together, but you made it clear you didn't
want anything else. So why? Why did you do it?"

"God, you're so angry." She spread her hands, "Larry, it was just a
fling, for Christ's sake! I thought you understood that."

"Aren't you listening? I'm not *interested* in you, or any of that! The
photographs. Of us. You and me. I want to know two things – who
took them and why you sent them to Mary?"

"I didn't. And as to who took them..." she shrugged. "Isn't it obvious?"

"No, it isn't. Was it planned; it must have been planned. You lured
me in, didn't you? The whole thing – you tried to hurt me and, when
you realized that I didn't really give a damn, you decided to include
Mary in your spiteful little scheme." His breathing grew strained, the
pain in his lower abdomen like sin. He gritted his teeth. "What have
I ever done to you?"

She leaned forward, her eyes narrowing. "You? Why does everything have to revolve around *you*? What the hell are you, Larry? Just
a pathetic little man, with nothing to show for his life except for
the paint underneath your fingernails! God, it was so easy to seduce
you, you were so desperate for it! And don't kid yourself that you
haven't thought about me every night since, because you have. I know
you have. You've relived that afternoon over and over, haven't you? I
reckon you've jerked yourself silly over it. Tell me it's not true, Larry.
Tell me that you still don't want me so much it hurts?"

His eyes bulged in his head, his temples throbbing. Her words cut
like knives, severing any vestiges of self-respect he may have had.

She slid onto her knees and moved over to him. He watched her,
transfixed, her superbly manicured fingers running up his legs, reaching his crotch.

Her voice was thick with desire, "You want me so much, don't you
Larry."

Without realizing what he was doing, his hand ran through her hair
as her fingers played with the zip of his trousers.

"Say it, Larry." Her voice so low, so soft.

"Oh God, Hannah."

"Say it."

Her mouth came up towards his and his eyes closed, the anticipation of tasting her sweet lips sending him into a whirlwind of uncontrolled, mindless longing. Nothing else mattered except the touch of her, the feel of her, the need of her. "God."

"Just say it," her lips so close, brushing against his. Like cream, smooth as silk. Yielding.

"I love you."

Her lips closed on his and he was lost.

No strain, the doctor had said. Was sex included in that, he wondered. He lay on the carpet, trousers ripped away, dishevelled, abandoned, completely satiated. Hannah made tea in the kitchen, humming a song. Clawing at his hair, he groaned, dismayed. He needed more than tea, he wanted his head testing. But what was he supposed to do, with her hands and her mouth doing those things to him. She rode him so gently, so slowly, straddling him, her feet planted on the floor either side of him, sliding up and down on his hardness. Treating him with such concern, such care, she urged him to come, to give himself totally to her. Nothing else. So unselfish, so utterly irresistible.

He'd called round to have it out with her, to get to the bottom of the photographs, to find out what the hell was going on. Instead, he'd ended up having the most amazing sex of his life. He felt ashamed at his own weakness. Hadn't he put her out of his mind, hadn't he fought the demons and emerged victorious? What folly that was, what self-deceit. Wasn't it best for him to accept he was totally besotted with her? Love. That was another thing. He'd said he loved her, not once, a dozen times as she moved up and down on him, but that was in the throes of passion. Wasn't it? Surely...

Sitting up, he gingerly pulled on his trousers, stopping to examine the dressing across his stomach. There was a slight stain, like olive oil. Very carefully, he pulled the bandage away and peered at the stitches. One or two had puffed up significantly. There was blood. Nothing major, he didn't think. Nothing to be too worried about. He'd have to be careful. *No strain.* He closed his eyes, cursing himself again for being so weak.

He heard Hannah clattering tea cups, so he hurriedly patted the dressing back into place, and hitched up his trousers. He was still fumbling with his belt as she came through the door, carrying a tray with a pot of tea. She paused in the doorway, head tilted to one side, pursing her lips, looking hurt. "Ah, don't tell me you don't want seconds?"

Larry stared at her, incredulous. She smiled, put the tray down on the dining room table, and came over to him. She had pulled on her skirt and blouse, but her underwear was still lying where she had thrown it. She shook her head in mock disappointment. "Honestly, Larry, and I thought you'd missed me..." She licked her lips and squatted down next to him, already reaching for his zip. "Let's see if I can't make you change your mind."

Five minutes later, perhaps less, she poured the tea, humming to herself. Larry, in contrast, was slumped in his chair, sweat beading across his brow, totally drained. She'd brought him off with her mouth, relentlessly moving her lips over him, making him so hard he thought he would explode. He'd called out her name when he orgasmed; not so much called as shrieked, lost in the passion, the all-consuming, glorious wrongness of it all. She had conquered him, completely. She was his mistress, his controller, his entire world. Nothing else mattered. He didn't care a sot about Jed, Mary, or anyone else. All he knew was that when he was with Hannah, the whole world could fall down around him and he wouldn't care. She was everything.

She sat down next to him and gave him his tea. He pushed himself upright, wincing a little as a twinge of pain lanced across his groin. "You shouldn't exert yourself so much," she said, raising the tea cup to her lips, winking at him.

He laughed. "Does this mean...you know...us..."

Hannah put down her teacup and chewed at the inside of her lip for a moment. "I have to admit, Larry, you are quite something." She absently ran a finger along the front of his trousers. "Really, you are rather good. I think we should take it slowly, maybe you calling around once or twice a week..." She winked again, "Or perhaps three times?" Another sip of tea. "But, I want you to understand one little thing." She looked him straight in the eye. He was mesmerised. "I have quite large needs, Larry. I have... *others* who like to visit me. You understand what I'm saying?" He nodded limply. "I don't want any of that silly, petty jealousy. We'll have our evenings, and that is that. The rest of the time, we have no contact. Not unless I say so, that is. Is that clear?" She drank her tea and stood up. His eyes never left her. "You fill a need, Larry. I love to dominate, I'm sure you've noticed. My other gentlemen, well... they tend to dominate me! Variety, as they say..." She smoothed down the front of her skirt. "You can go now. I'll see you on Friday evening, seven o'clock."

A puppy dog, that's what I've become, he thought to himself. He obediently got to his feet, put the teacup down on the tray and limped out of the house without another word. She closed the door behind him and he stood, on the path, feeling like a man who had just won a million pounds. The pain in his groin was a mere memory now and he believed he could throw away the crutch and skip back to his house, everything forgotten; his anger, his decision to find out about the photographs... they were nothing now. Trivial. So what if she had sent them. She had actually been jealous, that's what it was. She must have seen Mary returning to the house and become distressed, thinking that his wife had come back permanently. So, she'd acted, in the only way a scorned woman would act. It was a natural reaction and he should have thought about it a lot more before he'd gone steaming round there. But then, if he hadn't... He grinned to himself, reliving the moment. God, she was everything. Everything.

A stab of pain and he fell against the wall, hissing through his teeth. "Larry."

He looked up suddenly at the sound of the man's voice. In that moment, the real world came flooding back in the shape of his wife's lover, David.

"I had to tie some loose ends up before I came over. I hope you haven't been waiting too long."

"I had some business. Sorry. It's all done now."

"Are you all right – you seem to be in a lot of discomfort."

Larry patted his abdomen lightly. "I'm fine."

"Well, no matter... Are you ready?"

"Ready? Ready for what?"

"Scotland! Remember, that's why you told me to come down here. Scotland, to find Mary."

Larry closed his eyes, shoulders slumping . Yes, of course, he did remember. Some of it. The Scotland bit certainly. He chuckled, "God... sorry, I completely – look, come in for a moment and..."

But then another voice made them both turn at that point. A voice of anger, shouting loudly, almost to the point of hysteria. Larry groaned inwardly as he saw the shape of Brian Randall powering towards them, fists clenched, face puffed up like a beach ball, distressed and furious. Larry leaned on his crutch, shaking his head, feeling a little self-conscious. "Brian, please don't think I—"

From nowhere, the fist exploded into the side of his face, sending him reeling backwards, floundering, grasping at the wall for support. He was more shocked than hurt, and his legs wouldn't work. He went down hard, planting his buttocks on the solid concrete with a grunt. Through a swirling mist he saw Brian moving over him, snarling, preparing to strike again. But nothing happened, and that was because of David.

"Pack it in!"

Brian span round, dashing away David's uplifted hand. He didn't know who David was, but his rage was out of control. "I'm going to kick this bastard's head all over the street, and no one is going to stop me – understand?"

"I'm warning you," said David, his voice full of menace.

"Fuck off, grease-monkey! Unless you want a kicking too."

But David was no grease monkey. Brian should have guessed, by the quiet, assured way David stood, unblinking, feet slightly apart. He should have noticed how well balanced David was, how fit, the bulges beneath the jacket a clue to his strength. But he didn't and when he tried to launch another assault, David parried the blow, turning him, pushing him away with the heel of his palm.

Brian grunted in pain, rubbing at his chest, confusion crossing his features. It should have been enough, enough to give him some insight as to the sort of man he was up against, but Brian no longer cared. He swung hard, but his punch hit fresh-air. As did the next, David bobbing and weaving. Then David hit him. Once, twice, three times and there was nothing else for Brian to worry about because Brian was on the ground, unconscious, not worrying or thinking about anything.

"How the hell…" Larry groaned as David helped him to his feet. He couldn't take his eyes from Brian's inert form, lying there, stretched out. "That was amazing."

"Who the hell is he?"

"Don't ask."

"I just have. I think you need to tell me what's going on."

Larry shook his head, trying to clear the fog. It wasn't working. But he knew one thing, very clearly; he was thankful he had never turned his anger and frustration out on David. If he had, it would be him that was lying on the ground, not Brian. "David…I don't know." And the simple truth was, he didn't know what was happening. The blow on his head had shaken him awake, in an ironic sort of way. He knew he'd been to see Hannah, but what had happened there, what they had spoken about, he didn't have a single clue. He pinched the bridge of his nose before tenderly lifting up his shirt. The patch on the dressing appeared darker now and larger. "Shit. I think I might have burst some of the stitches." He shook his head, blowing out his cheeks. "I feel like I've been drugged."

Hannah, watching from her bedroom window, cursed when she saw David felling her son. She turned and looked across to her bed and the man lying there. "I think we're going to have to move to Plan B," she said, a little sadly. "I had been quite looking forward to seducing Larry Meres again. Now, I'll have to wait a little longer for some further fun."

"You're an insatiable bitch," said Sullivan, throwing back the covers, Stepping out of bed, he ran his fingers through his hair. Hannah's encounter with Larry had excited him and the all-in wrestling he had experienced afterwards with this incredible woman left him emotionally and physically sated. He stood next to her and looked across the street. "I'll phone the station," he said. "I'll get a patrol car to come round, take them in for questioning."

"And an ambulance, perhaps."

He smirked. "For Meres, or your precious son?" He didn't give a fig about Brian. Why he ever recruited him was beyond reason. Useless and moronic. Still, he was her son. "Yes. An ambulance too."

"Larry mentioned Scotland."

"Mmm…" He rubbed his chin. "I'll give Matthew a call as well. Seems like things could come together quite nicely after all."

34

Jed stood in the hallway watching the rain. Matthew gently replaced the telephone receiver and stood next to his brother. He shivered slightly. "Horrible day."

They'd spent nearly two hours hoping the rain would relent, but it hadn't. Now Matthew had taken the decision to press on regardless. Why the rain should be a problem, Jed didn't understand. But then the proprietor had called them to say there was an urgent telephone call for Matthew. Jed was intrigued. "Who was it?"

Matthew stared at him blankly. "Sullivan."

"*Sullivan*? How did he know you were here?"

"I called in to the station. I have to. If not, they would become suspicious and then the whole bloody world would be coming down on us."

"What did he want?"

"To tell us he'd found out something about Jonathan Kepowski. Something which you're not going to like."

"There can't be much more that is going to shock me, Matthew. My brother's in the drug-squad. It doesn't get much better than that."

Matthew ignored the caustic sarcasm, turned and went into the back room to pay the old lady for their night's stay.

"It'll be blowing over soon," she said, wiping her hands on her apron as she emerged from the darkened room. Jed seemed to recall she said the same just after breakfast.

They ran out to the car and clambered in, throwing their holdalls onto the back seat. The car rapidly steamed up and Matthew opened the side window slightly. As the rain hit his face, he quickly wound it up again, turned on the engine and rubbed his hands together, putting the heater's fan on full-blast. "That'll clear it."

"Matthew. What the hell did he say?"

Staring straight ahead, gripping the steering wheel a little too tightly, Matthew closed his eyes. "Kepowski has got mum."

The wind battered the little car as they ploughed through the rain. Around them, the landscape ached with its untouched beauty. Even though the colours were smudged and indistinct, Jed had the feeling that he was travelling across the most wondrous, desolate countryside he would ever experience. But even though the beauty was breathtaking, there was a hidden menace lingering amongst the heather and across the hills. This was a land scarred by suffering, its history once steeped in violence and betrayal. Tales of Highlanders and Redcoats mingled with butchered families, raped women, torched homesteads to create a canvas of despair. The building of an empire. The deaths of the innocents.

They'd stopped for lunch not long after leaving the little bed and breakfast. Matthew was in contemplative mood and didn't speak, just gazing out of the window. It had been a leisurely lunch and Matthew didn't seem to be in any rush to continue. Afterwards they spent some time window-shopping in the little town. It was as if Matthew had an appointment to keep and was merely waiting for the right time. Jed wondered about that, thinking that perhaps it had something to do with Sullivan's phone call.

A few hours later, they finally set off again. It was still raining and Jed grew bored with the dismal weather now. He shuddered, folded his arms across his chest and sank down in his seat, trying to find refuge in sleep.

He may have slept an hour, possibly three. It felt like two minutes when Matthew struck him on the knee, rousing him. Jed sat up, rubbing his eyes. Matthew had parked the car and was already checking his gun. Not for the first time, Jed's throat became constricted. He tried to swallow, but he couldn't. "What are you doing?" he managed, in a small, frightened voice.

"We're here." Matthew pulled out the crumpled piece of paper that Janet had given Jed all those years ago in Woolworths. "This is the place." Matthew looked at his brother. "What are you going to do? Stay here, or help?"

"Matthew…don't you think we should—"

"What? Go and knock on the knocker, ring the bell? Invite ourselves in for tea and crumpets? Jed, he's got our mum in there, the bastard. Don't you know what's going on, haven't you worked it all out yet?"

Jed shook his head dumbly. How could he know what was going on, he was sixteen years of age, in the middles of his GCEs. What did he know about drug-pushers and the criminal underworld? That was Matthew's domain, his life. Why should he understand any of it?

Matthew sighed loudly. "In the boot, there's a bag. I want you to go and get it."

Jed gaped at him. He was so matter-of-fact. What was he planning on doing?

"*Go and get it!*"

Jed jumped at his brother's tone and quickly scrambled outside. It was bitterly cold, the wind raging, but at least the rain had dwindled into nothing more than a light spattering. Huddling himself into a ball, he went to the boot, pulled it open and grabbed the holdall. It was heavy. Very heavy. Moving round to the passenger door, he opened it and put the bag on the seat. "What is that?"

Matthew didn't answer, simply stuffed the pistol in his waistband and reached over to the bag. He tugged back the zipper and opened the top with a jerk. Jed gasped.

"You've got to be out of your mind!"

"Recognise them, then?"

"I've seen the films, Matthew. What the fuck are you going to do?"

"End it," he said simply and weighed the sawn-off pump-action shotgun in his hands, working the action with expert precision. "End it right here."

It was late afternoon, gone six. Although it was May, the atmosphere, so murky and drab, felt like November as they moved across the open moor, bent double, keeping themselves small, close to the ground. Matthew was an expert, weaving this way and that, hitting the ground every now and then, finding shelter behind a little hummock, or a scrap of thistle. Amongst an outcrop of jagged rocks, he stopped to check the shotgun for the umpteenth time. Jed crouched down beside him, gulping in the air, the second shotgun in his hands. He had no idea how to use it, until Matthew had shown him. "It's deadly simple," he'd said. Jed didn't doubt it. What he doubted was his capacity to use the damned thing.

"We'll wait here a while," said Matthew, leaning back against the rocks and peering up into the sky. "When it gets dark, we'll move in."

"Move 'in' where?"

Pulling open the holdall, Matthew produced a small pair of field binoculars. He handed them over to Jed, who grunted, "You've come well prepared."

"Always do." Matthew grinned. "Look out across the moor, in the direction of about one o'clock. You'll see a large house, very black, very scary looking."

Jed found the building almost immediately, appearing like something out of a gothic novel, with tall, spindly towers on either side, pointed gables, large door, steps leading to it from a winding path. The impressive gates at the front of the path appeared open, but as he strained to see, he realised they were broken. Taking the binocular away, Jed rubbed his eyes, then looked again, this time more carefully. He gasped. Everything was broken – windows smashed, tiles dislodged, the whole edifice crying out in anguish, disowned, abandoned. "It's a ruin," he said, sliding down next to his brother.

"Yes." Matthew absently stroked the smoothed down stock of the shotgun. "But only the exterior. Inside, everything else is as it always was."

Looking at his brother for a long time, he understood now why Matthew had given Janet's note a cursory glance. He already knew it. "My God, Matthew, you've been here before!"

Turning, Matthew's eyes were wet with the memory. "Oh yes, Jed. I've been here before."

35

He must have been five, perhaps a little older. Living with Gran was now normal, because she was his mum. She did everything for him and, when he'd started school that previous September, she'd gone with him, staying throughout the morning. Park Infants. It was a new building; he remembered the smell, everything so clean, bright and shiny. Mrs Butler, a formidable looking woman, was no match for Gran and they did not get on well. Despite this, everything went fine, until that first Christmas.

He remembered the man at the door, his big beaming face pressed against the glass. He came in and spoke to Miss Treacher, his class tutor. She didn't seem convinced at what he was saying and the man became a little angry. Mrs Butler appeared and silence settled as everyone in the classroom strained to listen, intrigued at what was going on. Then, without warning, Mrs Butler moved to Matthew's desk. "You're going to Liverpool," she said. "Christmas shopping. Off to see Santa in his grotto. You'll tell us all about it, won't you Matthew?"

Taking him by the hand, the man led him outside to a car waiting at the gate. A large car, white with four doors and red seats. They smelt warm and comforting, as did the woman leaning over towards him, smiling.

"We're going to have a lovely time," she said. Matthew saw that she held a baby in her arms. Not a newborn, maybe nine months. The baby stared at him, nose clogged with snot. Matthew turned away. Where was Gran?

They travelled for ages, the constant bucking and bouncing causing Matthew to throw up twice, once on the seat next to him. The woman got angry at that and hit him. It hurt and he cried. The man swore loudly and they stopped the car. He tore open the door and dragged Matthew out into the cold, miserable day, the pouring rain instantly soaking Matthew right through. The man pushed an old rag in his hand and ordered him to clean the seat. Through his tears, Matthew did as he was told. Then it was back inside and the journey continued.

He begged them to stop so he could go to the toilet.

"This was a bloody mistake Frank!"

"Shut it!" Matthew remembered how they screamed at each other and he also remembered he wet his pants.

When they stopped hitting him the second time he decided it was best just to lie down and try to sleep. Perhaps when he woke up he would be at Santa's grotto and Gran would be there. It would have been a dream.

But it wasn't.

When he woke up they were in a place he had never seen the like of before. A huge, monstrous house loomed over him like something from prehistory, an age when giants roamed the land and dragons wheeled across the skies. Matthew felt frightened and very, very small.

The man lugged suitcases from out of the boot whilst the woman strode up to the main door and opened it with a heavy looking key. The doors creaked open, as they do in all the best horror films, and she cried out when she stepped over the threshold, "It's good to be home!"

Home? Matthew span round, eyes wide with fear. Home? What did she mean, 'home'?

The man puffed past him, struggling with the two large suitcases. Even to Matthew's young eyes, he could tell these people were planning on staying for quite some time.

"I want my mum!" he screamed.

The woman emerged from the house, this time without the baby. She gave him an evil leer. "Don't we all," she said as she picked him up by the shoulder and hauled him inside.

He spent those first few hours sitting on a window seat, gazing out across the desolate moor, waiting for Gran to come down the broad path that led from the great, wrought-iron gates. Gates that shut out the world, said to it, 'Keep out!' She'd be here soon, he knew she would. Gran would never leave him with these people, whoever they were.

But Gran didn't come. He waited all day, hoping. But Gran didn't come.

By the second day he summoned up the courage to ask them who they were. Both of them laughed. "I'm your old dad," said the man and, as if these words caused even greater amusement, the two of them rolled about in fits. Matthew didn't understand. His 'old dad'? What did that mean? He looked down at the little, snotty boy who was crawling around on the floor. This must be his brother, then? "Who's that?" he asked, just to confirm it all.

The woman reached down and picked up the little boy, kissing him loudly on the cheek. "This is your little brother – Jonathan. Say 'hello', Jonathan."

But Jonathan didn't say anything and Matthew wasn't listening anyway. Matthew was crying too loudly.

He had no way of knowing how long they kept him there. It might have been weeks, even months. Perhaps years. As time moved on, the memories blurred. Snatches, little snippets would come into his mind and he replayed them over and over, trying to make sense of them, fuse them into his consciousness. He recalled people coming to the house, many people, strange people. They never spoke to him. Always they wore dark clothes, which matched their sombre faces. They would shuffle through to one of the large rooms at the rear, where the curtains were always closed. The woman, whose name he learned was Gladys, would welcome them with a slightly bowed head, hands clasped in front of her. She always wore the same dress when they arrived. He remembered that dress. Light blue ground, upon which dark blue flowers formed an interweaving pattern. He hated it.

With them all inside, the big door would close and he would hear mumbling. Jonathan would tug at his sleeve, the signal for them to go and play. Jonathan could walk by then. What would that make him, two? Eighteen months?

They locked him in the outhouse sometimes. He didn't understand why, there didn't seem to be any rhyme or reason to it. Not Jonathan, though; never him. Frank would drag him to one of the large wooden houses at the back, too big to be called sheds. Throwing him inside, Frank would stand with his fists on his heaps, growling, 'Keep your mouth shut!' He'd slam the door shut, leaving Matthew in the dark, with only the rats for company.

One day a woman came whom he had never seen before. She wasn't like the rest. She was kindly and she spoke to him. When Frank turned on her, she rebuked him, called him 'evil'. Frank didn't like that. He tried to throw her out, but she was a tough little thing and she fought back. Later, when the lady left, Frank put him in the wooden house again only this time he didn't come and let him out.

He was cold in there. Cold, hungry and afraid. When at last the door creaked open, he heard the gasps and the little lady came inside, picked him up and hugged him close.

There was no one in the house, of course. They'd all gone. The lady took him back to her house and gave him porridge. He always remembered that first taste, how salty it was. He marvelled at how the combination of sugar, milk and salt tasted so good. He had never forgotten that taste, always loved it.

The police came and shortly afterwards Gran. He didn't recognise her at first, his memories of her sketchy, uncertain. Soon, it would all come back. The love. The care.

There were never any questions. At least, he didn't think there were. Life just seemed to fall back into place. He went to Poulton School and everything became lost as time trundled by. Nothing like time, Gran would say, for healing wounds.

Except they didn't heal.

Jed sat in silence for a very long time after Matthew stopped talking. The recounting had obviously had an effect on his brother, who sat sullen, stirring through a little puddle with the barrel of the shotgun. At last, summing up the courage to speak, Jed said cautiously, "Is that what all this is about Matthew?" His brother didn't flinch. "You're here, for revenge?"

The word seemed to jump-start Matthew into life again. He looked up, and Jed could see the tear stains on his face. "Revenge. Is that what you think, Jed? Revenge?" He shook his head. "They took me away and treated me like I was dirt. I've never understood why. My father was always an abusive man, you can ask mum about that. The way he hit her, the way he treated her. What he did to me was *revenge*, Jed. Him and that wife of his, the bitch. They suited each other, those two. She was a Medium. Do you know what that is?"

"A Medium? Is that something to do with ghosts and stuff?"

"Ghosts…yeah. All those people, in their dark mourning suits and dead eyes, they came over for séances, hoping to gain an insight, some comfort, a message from beyond the grave. But she was a bloody charlatan, Jed. A cheat, a liar. She took their money and dimmed the lights and dad, he'd perform his trickery."

"Didn't anyone ever guess?"

"Oh yeah, someone did. That old lady, the one who got me away from there, she knew. She showed them up for what they were. She told me all about it, whilst she cared for me. She was the one who found Gran, got us back together. Bless her, an angel she was. A light in all that darkness. She told me all about them, how she'd suspected them for years. Because she was *real*, you see. The genuine article."

"So, she could actually speak to the dead?"

"Yeah. Weird it was. Sometimes, she'd be talking, then she'd change, her face coming over all blank and she'd start telling me stuff. Stuff that I couldn't understand. Not then."

"What happened to her?"

"She's still alive. Runs a little tea-room somewhere up in the Highlands I think."

"The Highlands?" Jed stared down at his feet for a long time, feeling strangely light-headed.

"Are you feeling all right?"

Grunting, Jed drew in a breath. "So, she'd know all about this kind of stuff. Possession, hypnotism."

"Yes. Of course."

"What about drugs. I don't mean cocaine and the like – drugs that can change your way of thinking. Hallucinatory ones?"

"I suppose so, but she must be – God, she must be all of eighty now. She still rings me, every week. We chat, but it's like she already knows everything I've got to say. It was she who first told me about Jon Kepowski. Because, Jon Kepowski was that little boy I used to play with. And now, he's up in that house and he's got mum and it's he who wants revenge, Jed. Revenge for his dad."

Jed put his face in his hands. It was dark and cold and the hunger gnawed away at the pit of his stomach. He couldn't remember the last time he'd ate. He gently propped the shotgun against the rock and hugged himself, numb with cold, barely able to feel his fingers, bones turned to ice.

The revelations, however, cut through him deeper than any cold, penetrating into his very soul. "Revenge for his dad…Matthew…" He had the thought in his head, but not the will to voice it. He was too numb, with the cold and the overload of information.

"Frank, my dad, was desperate to maintain control. Control of everyone and everything. After mum walked out on him, he went nuts. He tried to get her back, and failed. He tried to get me back, but Gran stepped in. When he remarried, for a while it all seemed fine. I'd go and visit. You would come and visit, much later. No one knew, you see. No one knew because no one believed it. Why would quiet, re-spectable Frank, who had married such a sweet young thing and had himself a little boy, why would he do resort to kidnapping me – the notion was simply ridiculous. No one said anything, not me, not dear old Edith." Jed frowned. "Edith. That was her name, the lady who'd rescued me from that damnable place. Bless her. She never told any-one because, as she said years later, it would do no good. Frank would go to prison and serve, what...six months? What was the point. So later, much, much later, after I'd joined the force, I tracked him down. I'd jot everything down, keep all the notes. He became my obsession. I knew he'd make a mistake, knew he'd slip up. Him and that wife of his. And, sure enough, they did. They'd started their little scam again. And others besides. Jon had moved away, changed his name. Perhaps he knew, perhaps he didn't care. Edith told me that he had 'the gift', that he could bend people to his will. He could hypnotise anyone into believing he was their friend. He had a real power of persuasion, she said. Something he might have got from his mother. Because, she had something, some *power*, but it wasn't all that strong. Except for the night when I called around."

"You called? You mean, you went to one of their sessions?"

"The word is séance, Jed. Séance. I found out when they were and I made the appointment. There were three others there that night, two women and a bloke. All old, all desperate for something, anything that would give them hope. Gladys gave them that all right. I don't know how they did it, but she and Frank convinced them that some-one was coming through. And it was all going well, until I started ask-ing her some questions. Real questions, things that only I could know about. And them. About the visits to Santa's grotto, the car journey to Scotland, the wooden house. I knew Gladys was scared; she sat there, rigid as a post, gawping at me. She hadn't recognised me, how could she? I was a grown man. But then..." He took a deep breath, as if he were steadying himself. "Then she changed...she started talking, but it wasn't her you see. Despite all the charade, all of the deceit, this woman actually did have something. She'd connected, she'd got through to the other side."

"Christ…" Matthew dragged his hand across his face. The tears tumbled down his face. "Who was it, who had she connected to?"

Matthew stared out into the night. "Gran," he said simply.

At first they thought it was just one car, headlights cutting through the nighttime drizzle. Jed followed their approach with the binoculars. Matthew knelt by his shoulder, breathing through his mouth, trying to keep calm. Soon, another vehicle came from the same direction, leading at least six or seven others. Saloons, all of them with full loads. "Men and women inside," said Jed, able to make them out clearly now. Lights burned from virtually every window of the old house, the headlights of the many vehicles lighting up the area as if it were a football stadium. "There's a lot of people here, Mat." He pulled down the binoculars. "What the hell is going on?"

Matthew shrugged. "You'll find out." He glanced at his watch, the first time he had done so since settling amongst the rocks. "Sullivan should be here soon."

"Him again? What has he got to do with all of this?"

"Nothing. He thinks it's a drugs' raid, nothing more. But he wants the scalp, that's his prime reason for being here. Promotion beckons. He was worried Dad might cock it all up, so he told him Jon was dead."

"But Dad saw him, didn't he."

"Yes. Another of Sullivan's little capers gone to pot. Like the one he told you."

"Told me? What do you mean?"

"Well, not *you*, to be exact – that girl's father. What was her name, the one who gave you this address?"

"Janet?"

Matthew nodded. "Sullivan never thought things through very carefully, like sending those photographs to Dad. The man is an imbecile, but he might still have his uses."

"But has he any idea the pain, the suffering he's caused? Janet's dad, he was …" Jed turned his gaze to his brother. "And you?" Matthew turned away, absently checking the shotgun again. "How many lies have you told, Matthew?"

"Only as many as I needed to."

"So how the hell can I trust you?"

"Don't worry about me, Jed. I'm here because this is personal. And that means I'm here to look after you. So – when we move, you stay close and don't say a word. It won't be long. As soon as Sullivan arrives, we start."

Another set of headlamps came bouncing across the moor, this time from a different. Snapping up the binoculars, Jed trained them on this new arrival. "Our wait is over," he said, slumping down on his backside. "Sullivan is here. And he's not alone."

The journey proved long and uncomfortable. Larry sat beside David, both of them handcuffed, right wrist to left, the other hand attached to the door handle, so there was no hope of escape. After the fight, a patrol car had come and burly police officers bundled them both into the back seat, Sullivan appearing from nowhere, grinning, telling the officers that he was taking charge. And now, they were driving across an open moor, the car jumping around like a rock in a bucket, crashing this way and that. Larry kept his eyes tight shut, not wishing to focus on anything, least of all the back of Hannah's head. He'd tried to ignore her when she got in beside Sullivan, but every time he got a whiff of her perfume, his senses clouded over and he was back in that room with her, tasting her. He fought to resurface, gasping for breath, hoping this was some horrible, ghastly nightmare? Was she in this with Sullivan? His *femme-fatale*, his Mata Hari? She'd done something to make Larry lose his sense of propriety, his knowledge of right and wrong, of intelligence, of common sense, replacing everything with utter, total stupidity.

Mercifully, the car began to slow down and Larry, craning forward, tried to make out some recognisable feature, but it proved to be too dark. With the car still jumping up and down on its rodeo drive, he sat back and tried to keep himself calm. Next to him, David sat still as a statue. He'd hardly spoken a word since the police arrived and now seemed to have fallen deep inside himself. Perhaps he was meditating; perhaps he was dead. Larry didn't care, all he wanted was for the car to stop, allow him the opportunity to empty his bladder.

And then, unbelievably, the car did stop. Larry almost cried out with thanks. Divine intervention, it worked!

Hannah reached over, unlocking Larry's handcuff around the door handle. Then, as Sullivan stepped outside, she leant over to David's side and unlocked his. Their wrists, however, remained locked to one another's. "We'll keep you together, for now," she said as she got out.

Too dark to recognise who they were, Jed brought up his hand up to shield his eyes against the glare of the headlamps. He moved cautiously forward, just as Matthew had instructed him, leaving the shotgun and binoculars propped against the rocks. Jed wondered what these orders were for – what was Matthew planning and, more importantly, where was he?

"Is that you Jed?"

He stopped as he recognised the voice. "Dad?"

"Jesus Christ! Jed!"

They emerged from the glare of the lights and Jed fell into his Dad's arms, hugging him as if he hadn't seen him for months. Groaning, Larry stepped back, and Jed caught sight of his dad's lips quivering. "Jesus, Dad, what have they done to you?"

"No, no, it's this damn bloody rupture. I'm supposed to be taking it easy."

Stepping up beside came Sullivan, breathing hard with barely controlled anger. "Where the fuck is Mat?"

Jed gave himself a moment to take in the scene before him. Dad, looking deathly, handcuffed to another man, a man he didn't know, and Hannah Randall hanging back. "Dad, what the hell is all this?"

From nowhere, Jed felt something very cold and very hard rammed up against the side of his head. He didn't need to see it to know that it was the barrel of a gun. "I'll ask you again," wheezed Sullivan, "where is Mat?"

Before Jed could answer, Matthew's voice came from out of the darkness, somewhere close. "Drop the gun Sullivan - very slowly please."

But Sullivan didn't flinch. He continued to press the barrel against Jed's head. "I'll kill him, Matthew. Don't think I won't."

"I wouldn't doubt it, Sullivan me old mate. But if you do, then I'll kill you, and your lovely piece of skirt over there. So go on, pull the trigger and then you'll both die."

"*Matthew!*" Dad's voice, sounding terrified. "Matthew, for God's sake!"

Jed heard Matthew moving, circling them in the darkness, keeping himself well out of the way of the headlamps. Jed prayed it would end soon, but not in the most obvious way. He just wanted to go home.

"I'll kill her first, if you like. So, drop your gun, Sullivan. After three...one...two..." They heard the pump action engaging pump action engaging, sounding like a cheese-grater against stone. "Okay then..." a long pause. Jed held his breath, squeezing his eyes tight shut. "*Three!*"

The shotgun boomed and in that awful moment, the whole world pitched into hell.

36

Instinctively, Jed fell to his knees, hands clamped to his head, making himself as small as he could, waiting for the terrible sound to erupt inside his brain, a sound that would herald the end of his life. The darkness wrapped around him like a protecting veil. There was no pain, no swirling cascade of images from his past life. Nothing happened. He forced himself to realize that he still lived. Chancing a glance upwards, he saw Sullivan, picked out by the headlamps, trembling, gun lowering, no longer pointing, but held limply, without desire. He's as confused as I am, thought Jed, but then stopped as a shape reared out of the blackness, and struck Sullivan across the head with something big and hard. With a guttural grunt, Sullivan collapsed to the ground, his face slapping into the dirt beside Jed.

Everything happened quickly then. Hannah's scream pierced the night. There came a crack, like a whip, Jed learning later that the sound was Matthew's fist smacking under her chin. She too crumpled, unconscious. The silence hung there, the eruption of violence stunning the others.

Jed found Matthew scrambling around, searching through Sullivan's pockets. He stood up as Jed stepped up close, and he had the policeman's keys. "You – you really would have let him kill me?"

Matthew pushed past him and snapped, "Of course." He crossed to the other two men and quickly released them.

Working the shotgun action, ejecting the one spent cartridge and feeding in another, Matthew sounded confident as he spoke. "I want you two to wait here." He reached down and picked up Sullivan's gun. He pressed it into David's hand. "You'll be good at this." He winked. "Put Sullivan and the woman in their car, handcuffed, just like you were. If they try anything," he nodded towards the gun, "use it."

"What are you going to do, Matthew?" It was Larry, his voice small, like a child's.

Matthew took in a deep breath. "Clear up this mess." He went to move away, but his dad held him by the arm.

"It doesn't have to be like this."

"Yes it does, dad. That bastard over there holds us all responsible for the deaths of his parents. I went to see them, exposed them for what they were and Edith, she wrote a scathing report for the local press. It was so good, it even made the nationals. They'd accumulated thousands, selling books, making documentaries. They were planning on creating haunted holidays here, in that house." He nodded towards the great, bleak edifice standing out against the night, blacker even than the sky. "It all came tumbling down, and a short time after the reports surfaced, they committed suicide. The two of them, in their car. Usual stuff, hose-pipe from the exhaust...They were found the following day."

Jed cleared his throat. "And Jonathan?"

Matthew gave his brother a scathing look. "That little shit took up their mantle. But he became even bigger than they could ever dream, persuading his many followers to help him in creating a cult."

"A cult?"

"Through hypnotism, drugs, blackmail, he convinced some very important people that he had the answers to many of the world's problems."

"That sounds really bizarre."

"Oh, it is. But there are plenty of people out there who are willing to swallow any old pap."

"And, this cult...Those cars, this place...Jon's summoned them?"

"They're all there, in that house. They're waiting."

"Waiting? Waiting for what?"

"They're waiting for you and me, Jed. And we're not going to disappoint them."

He might have thought that the single gunshot blast would alert those inside the house, but if he did, Matthew gave no hint. Setting his jaw hard, it was clear nothing would cause any deviation from his original plan. Jed kept close, jogging alongside as they both moved over the gently undulating moorland, zigzagging through the coarse grass, keeping low. Although he had picked up the other shotgun, Jed did not intend to use it. That would be a step too far along a pathway that he already felt had become far too dangerous. Matthew appeared to have no such qualms. He was in his element, obviously well-versed in the art of violence. Jed suddenly realized that he didn't know his brother at all, not his life, his work, his thoughts. But he was beginning to, and what he was discovering was not pleasant.

They moved through the old, dilapidated gate and, keeping close to the wall, skirted around to the back of the house. The lights blazed from the windows, illuminating large circles of ground, revealing the many cars parked in an orderly fashion. No doubt, they had met like this on many occasions; it all seemed so well rehearsed. But what were these meetings for and why now? Jed stood, steadying himself, taking in gulps of air, knowing the answers were close. He closed his eyes, wondering if he had the strength, the courage, to see this through to the end. The end, however, was something he'd rather not think about. His legs buckled underneath him. Would he – could he see this through to the end?

Matthew elbowed him in the arm. "Come on," he hissed. But Jed couldn't move. Cursing, Matthew seized him by the sleeve and hauled him along the wall.

"There's a workman's entrance somewhere on this side," he whispered as they neared the far corner. He gave a little gasp of triumph. "Here!" But he cursed again as the door remained firmly locked. He stepped back, looking up. The windows were few at this part of the house and were too high to reach. With a loud expulsion of breath, still gripping Jed's sleeve, he moved on.

They came to another door and next to it a window. Matthew tried the handle and cursed. Without hesitating, Matthew put down his shotgun and took off his leather jacket. Quickly, he wrapped it around his arm, took a breath, and smashed his elbow through the window. It shattered instantly, the noise sounding dreadful in that quiet night. Both of them stood, convinced that soon they would hear the sound of approaching footsteps. But there was nothing. Matthew very carefully put his hand through the broken window, found the latch and opened it. "Get in," he said abruptly.

"What?"

"Get through the bloody window – you're slimmer than I am. Go through and open the door."

It took Jed a good five minutes of heavy breathing as he sweated and wriggled his way through the tiny gap, but made it at last, sliding down to the floor on the other side. He waited a moment, trying to find his bearing. Beneath his feet, the shattered glass from the window crunched, and he winced with every step.

"Hurry up!"

Matthew was close to the edge, his patience gone. Jed knew he was a man on a mission, a mission to assassinate. Could that ever be justified, despite everything Kepowski had done – the brutal killings, the deceit, the treachery? Nurse Willis, her boyfriend, all those others...and Miles. *Miles.* Why the hell did he murder Miles? What had Miles ever done to him? Suddenly, everything fell into place and, with a new resolve, he stood fully upright, and took in a long breath to settle his simmering rage.

He groped along the wall for the door and pulled back the bolt. Matthew stepped inside.

"What kept you?"

"I had a little trouble, a few concerns," replied Jed, taking the proffered shotgun from Matthew's outstretched hand. He worked the action back and forth. "But that's all dealt with now."

It was pitch black, but Matthew had come fully prepared. He pulled out a torch from his holdall and shone the beam around the room. The light picked out the various pieces associated with a kitchen. Sink, worktops, fridges, pots and pans. But all of it was neglected, some of it covered in mould. No one had prepared food in that place for years. Over on the far side, the beam picked out a door and beneath it a strip of light edging under the crack. Matthew switched off his torch and dropped it back into the bag. "Quietly," he whispered. He eased open the door.

A large foyer-type space came into view, a staircase winding up to the upper storey, rooms running off in various directions. An enormous chandelier took centre stage, casting everything in a stark, unforgiving glow. The area felt very grand but, as in the kitchen, dust and grime lay thick upon everything. No one tended this place, kept it in order. It was a pitiful shadow of its former glory.

From somewhere within came the low hum of voices. A chant of some kind, coming behind the pair of closed doors on the far wall. Matthew, pressing his finger against his lip, jerked his head towards the doors, and he crept towards them, Jed close behind.

Matthew stopped and pressed his ear against the woodwork. Grinning, he signalled to Jed with an upturned thumb. Both braced themselves and Matthew went through the doors at a rush.

He ground to a halt almost instantly.

Jed, coming up close behind, froze, his mouth falling open. "Oh my God," he muttered, realising both he and his brother had made a terrible miscalculation.

David stood outside, the gun cold in his hands. He'd helped Larry drag the two unconscious bodies of Sullivan and Hannah into the back of the car. It wasn't easy, especially Sullivan, and by the time they'd finished, both men were out of breath. Larry hadn't been much help, his abdomen hurting, not daring to look at the dressing, saying, "I think these stitches need re-doing.".

Handcuffing Sullivan securely to the door handle, David watched as Larry leaned across Hannah. When her eyes flickered open, Larry cried out. She sat up. "Larry," she said, wide eyed, looking confused. "That little bastard hit me!"

Larry tried to move back, but the confines of the car prevented him. Even from outside, David could smell her perfume, the soft swell of her breasts so evident. Poor Larry was besotted, poor bloke. As if sensing this, she reached forward, her fingers falling on his arm. "Oh my, Larry, you're so excited." Larry moaned. "Where's David?"

"Outside." His throat sounded tight, his voice husky.

She stroked his cheek with the back of her hand. "Go and get the gun, Larry. Then, release me and we'll be on our way."

"On our way... What do you mean?"

"You and me, silly. We'll leave all this behind. It doesn't make any sense does it, any of it?" She stretched her neck, looking out past his shoulder into the night. "Take his gun and kill him, Larry."

"Kill him? I don't think... Christ, Hannah... *kill him?*"

"Yes." She licked her lips. She motioned towards Sullivan. "Look at him, a waste of space. Not like you," her fingers rubbed against Larry's crotch and he groaned. She smiled, her lips moist, "Not like you, Larry. Get David's gun, kill him, then come and let me free. We'll dump Sullivan and go back home." She leant forward, her lips against his, "Then we'll make love all night – every night." She smiled again and again, brushed his cheek with the back of her hand. "Go on, get it over with," she said softly.

Larry was out of the car before she said another word. He swung around and yelped in surprise to find David standing there, resolute, eyes hard, unblinking. "You cuffed them?" asked David.

"Give me the gun."

"What?"

"The gun, the one Matthew gave you. Give it to me."

"Why, Larry?" David's voice, so low, unruffled. "What are you going to do?"

Larry thrust out his hand, his voice was trembling. "Just give it to me, David."

There was a long pause as the two men stood, merely an arm's reach away from one another, staring into each other's eyes. The atmosphere between them was charged, electric almost, the tension palpable. Larry wasn't going to give way; he knew how skilled David was, he'd seen that with what had happened to Brian. But he wasn't going to back down, even if it meant he would have to wrestle the gun from David's grip.

But there was no need. David suddenly reached to his waist band and handed the gun over, holding it by the barrel. Larry looked at it for a long time, then closed his hand around the butt. "Thanks," he said through gritted teeth.

"Are you all right?"

Larry's eyes came up. He nodded, his mind made up. "I'm fine. This is just something I have to do."

Both Jed and Matthew stood, stunned by what they saw. A vast room, grandiose in its decoration, four blazing chandeliers spaced along the ceiling, each pair on either side of a large, glass skylight, which allowed natural light to pour through. Along each wall, Greek style plinths, topped with burning candles, flanked tall lancet windows. A gleaming, polished wooden floor rolled out before them, in sharp contrast to the rest of the house. This was a well looked after ballroom, fit for a fairytale prince and princess to dance the night away.

But there would be no dancing that night.

A press of people, perhaps thirty or more, stood in a semi-circle, facing the centre, and a woman, dressed in a thin cotton robe, which revealed the curves of her body beneath. Suspended from the ceiling her by taut ropes, arms stretched high above her, she stood on a tiny, wooden stool directly below the glass portal. In obvious distress, her mouth a thin line, eyes red-rimmed, the mascara stains running down her cheeks, hair a dishevelled mess, soaked in sweat, a long, gurgling moan escaped from her broken lips.

"As the first light of dawn touches her," said the voice of a man, stepping out from behind the suspended woman, face covered by a deep cowl and holding a very evil looking knife that glinted in the candle light, "it ends."

Hands quickly relieved the guns from the numbed fingers of the two gaping intruders. Roughly they were pushed towards the centre of the semi-circle, stumbling, powerless to resist. Mesmerised by the sight of the woman, Jed caught her eye and for a moment something flickered in her face, recognition, a wave of sadness and regret. Jed felt his stomach turn to mush, his bowels loosening. "Mum," he muttered in a low, terrified voice.

"Cut her down, Jonathan," said Matthew suddenly, his voice strong and loud, sounding alien in that strange, oppressive atmosphere. "Then you and I can settle this, once and for all."

The man flung back the cowl. It was Jonathan. He laughed. A maniacal cackle, without amusement. "You think this is just about you, Matthew? Always so bloody sanctimonious, always thinking that the world revolves around you and you alone." He shook his head, the smile dying on his lips. "Wrong – this is about so much more. It's about the future, everyone's future."

Jed sucked in a breath. "Please," he said. For a second, everyone in the room turned their faces to him. He noticed, for the first time, that everyone was dressed in robes, some in red, others in white. This was the cult that Matthew had spoken about, its members assembled here, but for what? Sacrifice? For what purpose? Jed looked at Jonathan pleadingly. "Let her down, Jon. She's not part of this."

"Oh but she is," spat Jonathan, stepping closer. "She's the absolute reason why this is happening now, Jed. She left my father, you see. All those years ago. Broke him, destroyed him. Then him," he jabbed his finger towards Matthew, "the Devil's spawn, caste from the same mould as her – he destroyed my father and my mother. And if that wasn't enough, she then does it all again, breaking you into pieces. You."

Someone in the circle gasped as Jonathan reached out and touched Jed's face. Jed stood rock still, unable to even breathe. A single tear rolled down Jonathan's face. "You're the innocent in this, Jed. I waited, because I knew she would leave you – you and your father. When I discovered the news, I conjured up our meeting at the lake. To draw you in. To use you."

"Use me?"

"I had no choice. What else was I supposed to do? This harridan, she broke your dreams, yours and your father's."

"So all of this was in order for you to have your revenge?"

"I've suffered, Jed. So long."

"And all of those people, the ones you murdered? Miles? My friend?"

"So sentimental."

"You're a fucking monster, Jon."

"No. Not a monster. I loved you …" His voice trailed away and for a moment it was as if he were struggling within himself, struggling to find the determination to continue. At last he sighed. "But you too must die, my sweet, innocent child. Unless…" He took a step backwards, "Unless you join us, Jed. You'd like that, wouldn't you? Tell me you would. You could be with me – with us. You would like that, wouldn't you, Jed?"

The world became a distant place, the present ethereal. Jed felt he was floating, all the fear suddenly leaving him, his heart soaring, everything light and clear and fresh. He could barely form the words, "Oh yes!" He fell to his knees and Jonathan came up to him, holding his head, pressing him close. Jed broke down, his whole body wracked in shuddering sobs. Gently, Jonathan stroked his hair and looked up, smiling in triumph. Jed turned in the direction of his gaze and saw Matthew standing there, teeth clenched, the muscle bunched along his jaw.

"You're a fiend!" screamed Matthew. He jumped back, reaching inside his coat, ripping out the automatic pistol he had concealed there.

A ripple ran through the assembly. A woman cried out, some of the men swore.

From somewhere, one man's voice rang out, dismissive, arrogant, "Your weapons can't hurt the master, you fool! This has been ordained."

Another, confident, unshakeable, shouted, "He is the chosen one, the light that will guide us. Put down that gun, surrender your will to his!"

"We need the blood of one who is blighted," said a woman, "to relieve the world of its contagion."

"Mum?" Jed looked up as Jonathan turned and walked towards the suspended figure of Mary Meres. Throughout she remained silent, teetering on the little stool, but now her mouth opened. Her lips, so dry and cracked, forced her to work hard to moisten her throat, swallowing repeatedly. "Jed," she managed at last, "Jed, try and fight it. Don't listen to him, try and—"

"It's pointless, Mary," said Jonathan, standing right beside her, "He's with me now." He looked towards her son, who still sat on his knees, staring into space. "Aren't you Jed?"

Jed smiled, "Oh yes," he gushed. "I love you."

A collective sigh oozed from the surrounding group. Time dripped by, expectation gathering. What would happen next?

Voice trembling, Matthew stepped forward, "No, Jed. No. You have to do what Mum says – you must fight it." But his voice, so weak now, held no conviction – as if he too accepted the inevitable. As if to underline the hopelessness of it all, a robed man stepped forward and gently took the pistol from him.

"It is all as it should be," said Jonathan, a slight note of regret coming into his voice. "I've waited so long for this moment, Matthew. I've dreamed about it, seen it played out in my mind a thousand times. And now that the moment has come, I find that I'm slightly saddened. Sad because with you and her gone, I will have to find a new focus. Perhaps," he rubbed the side of his mouth with a forefinger, "perhaps Jed will help me seek out others that need to be cleansed." He smiled again. "David, of course, shall be the first." Mary moaned above him and Jonathan looked to her. He brought up his hand and the knife he held played at the tail of her robe. "My only regret is that you will not see him die, Mary. But he will, trust me. In the most awful way imaginable. And Jed, my sweet, innocent Jed, he will do it for me. Won't you, Jed?"

"Oh yes. Yes, of course."

"When this is over, and you and Matthew lie eviscerated about the floor, I will bring David in and bathe him in your blood. Then Jed will dissect him, limb by limb, organ by organ. He will cut him up and burn each bit in an open fire, whilst he still lives. They used to do it in the olden days, Mary. They knew how to inflict pain, those wonderful people! We can learn so much from our forefathers, don't you think."

"You learned a lot from yours!"

Her words were like slaps across his face. Wincing, for a moment is seemed Jonathan was lost for something to say. Slowly his eyes narrowed. "Watch your mouth, your slut!"

"Your father was a bloody bastard, just like you!" She was shouting now, "A thug, a violent bully, abusing me and Matthew."

"You're talking rot, woman - *lies!*"

"Truth, Jonathan. The truth he never told you, truth you never knew. How he beat me, kept me a virtual prisoner in my own home, controlling everything I did, the people I could talk to. He was a monster, Jonathan."

"*Liar!*" Suddenly, the knife blade flashed in Jonathan's hand, slicing through her thin robe, exposing her flesh. The material fell away in long shreds and she stood there, the whiteness of her body like alabaster in the intense glare of the candlelight. The assembled group broke into, a low sort of mantra, repeated over and over. And with it, a new light grew more noticeable. The morning sun was rising, its rays coming through the glass portal above. "Corrupted, faithless harlot!" screamed Jonathan, brandishing the knife above him, preparing to kick away the stool.

"Jonathan!"

Matthew went to rush forward, but strong arms held him back and he struggled uselessly in their grip. It was all falling away, everything lost. He threw back his head and wailed.

"By the spilling of your blood, we rid the world of your malevolence as we welcome the dawn!" Jonathan tensed himself, drawing back the knife. Mary screamed as the sunlight poured down over her. "Behold, a new beginning!"

Bathed in a golden glow from the rising sun, which made her seem almost magical, Mary let her face fall back to soak up the rays. She groaned, as if she knew her life was about to end.

With a resounding crash, the great twin doors burst open. Every face turned to see Larry storm in, and stride forward.

"Jonathan!"

Kepowski's mouth quivered. "How...?" he managed in a stunned voice.

Larry merely smiled, brought up the gun and shot Jonathan right between the eyes.

For a moment, a ripple of disbelief ran through the assembled crowd. As Jonathan crumpled to the ground, the knife clattering beside him, all hell broke loose, the assembly screaming as one, scattering in all directions, their reason for remaining now gone, lying grotesquely on the highly polished floor, the blood ballooning around his shattered head.

Breathing hard, Larry stared down at Jonathan Kepowski's dead body, as the stampede of people buffeted past him, escaping, not a thought for anything or anyone anymore.

Matthew pushed his way over to his mother and very gingerly, using the knife Jonathan planned to use in a much deadlier way, cut through the rope that suspended her from the ceiling. Her body fell limp into his arms and he gently eased her to the floor. He brushed the hair from her brow and held her, glancing towards Larry. "She's okay."

Nodding his head, a distant look on his face, Larry stuffed the pistol into his waistband. He went over to Jed, standing as if in a sort of trance and gently laid his hand on his son's shoulder. "Are you all right?"

Jed's lips moved, but no sound escaped and his eyes, as he looked up, seemed glazed, unable to focus.

"He will be," said Matthew, voice echoing around that vast, now empty space. They were alone, the sound of motor cars outside starting up and roaring off into the distance indicating that the assembly was making good its escape.

Larry put his arm around Jed and held him close. "I hope so. Dear God in heaven, I hope so."

37

The wind blew unbelievably strong, almost knocking him over as he stood, hands deep in the pockets of his padded coat, staring out across the bleak, unforgiving moor. It was said that there had been no cover for the men as they stood, in clumps, bombarded by the Hanoverian guns, shattered from a distance, frustrated that they could not get to grips with the enemy. But in this weather, how could anyone move, let alone fight? He marvelled, not for the first time, at their heroism but also felt depressed that they had not retired and sought a better place to fight and die.

"Come inside."

Jed turned, her voice bringing him out of his thoughts. He smiled. The rain lashed across her face, but it didn't seem to bother her. No doubt she was used to it, living and working here daily. It was a place where the sun rarely shined.

Edith took his hand in hers and led him back inside the visitors' centre. It was warm and dry in there, but the atmosphere remained gloomy. There was no one else. Was there ever anyone else? She seemed to sense his thoughts and her face looked sad. "This can be a soul-destroying place at times. Culloden... synonymous with our lives, don't you think?"

"Edith, you know too much."

They both laughed at that, even though, quite possibly, he had spoken the truth.

She brought him a cup of tea and studied him. "What will you do now?"

Jed shook his head, stirring the spoon around and around, "Go back home. Mum will probably move back in, look after me for a while. I've got my place in University, so it'll only be for a few months."

"University…" her voice faded away, her face taking on a dreamy, faraway look. "Your father won't be away for long."

"Won't he? I don't know – he killed someone, Edith. I think they'll lock him away for a long time."

"But it was all due to such extraordinary circumstances. I think the court will be lenient, especially when all the facts come out."

"You think they will, *all* of them?"

A little laugh. "Well – perhaps not 'all', but your father was acting out of self-defence, or preservation. He saved your mother's life, yours and Matthew's too I shouldn't wonder."

Jed pushed the tea away, not having taken a single sip. "Jon said I was to become one of his own. I don't think he would have killed me."

"And that makes it better? Could you have stood there and watched him kill your mother?"

"I can't remember a thing about any of it… only his voice. That was all that mattered at the time."

"You were under his spell, as they all were. He had enormous influence over everyone he met. He melded everyone to his will. Sometimes that influence could lead them to commit the most dreadful acts. I think, as the investigation continues, we'll discover that some of the others in that room were responsible for the deaths of those poor innocents who had crossed his path."

"I think Brian Randall was responsible for most of them. Nurse Willis, her boyfriend. My friend, Miles … He was Jon's instrument."

"His acolyte."

Jed rubbed his face with both hands, suddenly feeling very tired. "I hope they find him."

"That might have to be up to you, Jed."

He stared at her and although he felt like arguing, it soon dawned on him that she spoke the truth. His life would never be the same again or, most certainly would never be safe until Brian Randall was behind bars.

"And that girl, the one who brought you here?"

"Janet?" He shook his head, the memory of her consisting only of a few, fleeting images. "I don't know. Why she ever gave me that note, I'll never know."

"Perhaps she had woken up from her dream, the dream he had conjured up for her. Jonathan's persuasive powers knew no bounds. Will you look for her?"

"Where do I begin?" He thought about it all. Brian and Janet, one an enemy, one a friend. A friend. Was that what she was? Could she ever be possibly more than that, or was that all just part of the fantasy. But to seek them out, to find the answers, he would have to delve once more into the darkness that Jonathan Kepowski had created. It would be best to leave it all up to Matthew. He could pick up the pieces, tidy everything up. And not just Brian and Janet. Hannah Randall and Inspector Sullivan, they would pay for what they had done. And Dad. Poor Dad. How long would he have to languish inside a prison cell? Mum and David, could they rekindle their flame? Perhaps. Perhaps not. So much had happened, so many things ripping away the vestiges of self-respect. Could anything be salvaged, he wondered.

"Time," said Edith, patting his hand lightly. "Time will solve it all, heal all your wounds."

"You think so?"

She nodded, just once. "But if ever you need any help, Jed, any words of comfort or guidance, you know where to find me."

"Yes." And his other hand fell over hers and squeezed it tightly. They sat like that for a long time, lost in their own thoughts of what was to come, of what might be.

The television blared from the living room when he came through the door. His mum, perched on the edge of the sofa, swung around and he gasped when he saw her eyes, so red. His stomach lurched. "What the hell has happened now?"

Sniffing, she gave a tiny shrug. "They were driving. The reports are sketchy, but the police don't believe he was drinking. Apparently, the steering column came away. It snapped, all of it rotten with rust and they—"

"Mum, who are you talking about?"

"Brian Randall. He was in a car-crash with that girl, Janet." Jed groped for the back of the sofa, his legs losing all strength. "He's dead, but she ... Thank God – she's all right."

Swallowing hard, he managed to form some strangulated words. "When did it happen?"

"This afternoon."

Without another word, Jed tore out of the house and made his way to the local hospital. He didn't know what he would find, but he needed to be with her, to let her know he didn't blame for anything.

They met outside the ward, Jed not realising who he was until, about to move up to Janet's bedside, the man threw out his arm to bar the way. "And who the bloody hell are you?"

Taking a step back, Jed looked over the man's shoulder to where Janet lay, her face swollen, arms bandaged, tubes and drips sprouting from her body. Breathing hard, having run all the way from the hospital car park, Jed turned his head to the man. "I'm Jed."

For a moment, the man appeared at a loss for words. His mouth fell open slightly, lips trembling. "You ... You're the one who called me."

"I knew she wasn't dead."

"How could you know that?"

"Because she is as much a victim as I am."

"You mean ... the one who was driving?"

"No. I mean Jon Kepowski. He drugged her, or hypnotised her. Maybe both. He did the same to Brian, forced him to do his bidding. The truth has died with him." He dragged in a deep breath, setting his jaw hard. "I need to talk to her."

"You can't – she needs rest. She barely made it out of that crash alive. Damn that bloody stupid car, they said it could have gone out of control at any moment."

Something hard and heavy lodged in Jed's throat. Closing his eyes, he gave up a small prayer of thanks, remembering the many times he sat behind the wheel of the little Viva, before he continued. "I'll only be a moment."

The impasse remained, her dad not willing to budge, Jed desperate.

And then her voice. As sweet as he remembered, but so weak sounding, so small. "Jed, is that you?"

The two men exchanged a look and Jed saw her dad surrendering, his shoulders slumping. "Go on then," he said, "but try not to cause her too much stress."

"We've both had enough of that to last a life time," said Jed, giving a short nod. Stepping up to the bed, he saw her bruised and battered face and felt that all-too familiar lurch in his stomach. But then she smiled and he knew, with total certainty, that everything was going to be so much better from now on.

The End

Dear reader,

We hope you enjoyed reading *Splintered Ice*. Please take a moment to leave a review, even if it's a short one. Your opinion is important to us.

Discover more books by Stuart G. Yates at https://www.nextchapter.pub/authors/stuart-g-yates

Want to know when one of our books is free or discounted? Join the newsletter at http://eepurl.com/bqqB3H

Best regards,
Stuart G. Yates and the Next Chapter Team

About the Author

Stuart G Yates is the author of a eclectic mix of books, ranging from historical fiction through to contemporary thrillers. Hailing from Merseyside, he now lives in southern Spain, where he teaches history, but dreams of living on a narrowboat in Shropshire.

Splintered Ice
ISBN: 978-4-86751-546-4

Published by
Next Chapter
1-60-20 Minami-Otsuka
170-0005 Toshima-Ku, Tokyo
+818035793528
3rd July 2021